BLADE OF MERCY

A BOOK OF THE VIRAGO

S.E. BABIN

OLIVERHEBERBOOKS

LANDS OF LUNAMOOR

KINGDOM OF
ROSES

KINGDOM OF
THORNEWOOD

KINGDOM OF
LIGHT

KINGDOM OF
CRYSTAL

LAKE
OF
SORROW

KINGDOM OF
WOLVES

KINGDOM OF
BEASTS

KINGDOM OF
WITCHES

LAKE OF MYSTICS

KINGDOM OF
SHADOW

PROLOGUE
DELUSION

Corruption gleamed against the pale iridescence of the Luna stones. Lucien leaned against the door to the secret chamber, a thunderous frown on his usually smooth brow, as he realized what he was looking at. His sister watched him, an annoyed twist to her lips.

"Oh relax," Celestine snapped. "It's nothing to worry about." Her blood rushed through her veins in a whooshing roar, as she uttered the words even knowing in her heart they were a lie.

"If you can't feel the rot pouring off those stones, you have much less magic than I assumed," Lucien said wryly. He pushed off the wall and came closer, never as close as he used to before all this happened, but close enough to study the darkness pulsing against the stone's former vibrance.

The stones were the key to magic. They only needed to be unlocked. And that was the crux of the problem. Many years ago, Magnus Stonehand, a legendary long-dead mage had spelled the Luna stones under orders from the

Thornewood queen. Magic had trickled away, slowly at first, then all at once, cutting everyone's power off at the knees.

Celestine had long suspected some people still had some semblance of their power. Why, she still hadn't figured out. Thornewood was the first to lose its magic, then the spell had spread to other kingdoms. Hers—the Kingdom of Roses, then to the Kingdom of Light. Rumor told her the others farther away had put up a magic barrier to prevent the spell from creeping across their borders. Whether it was true, Celestine didn't know.

She didn't want to admit he might be right. Otherwise, everything she'd done might be for naught. The Virago were a shadow of what they once were; a few who'd led her charge disappearing after the death of the queen. There were still some Virago left, though she didn't see what good they were to her anymore. Still, she kept them on and forced the girl... Celestine couldn't remember her name, to continue their training. The others had slipped away or been killed in the takeover, never to be seen again. Good riddance to them. The weak warriors always weeded themselves out. Celestine couldn't afford them if she were to hold on to this coveted place while she searched for how to restore her power to its full capacity.

Her takeover was necessary. If she hadn't done it, their power would still be in a chokehold from the Thornewood queen. But it wasn't as successful as it could have been. Magic was still in a chokehold, Celestine no closer to breaking the spell today than she had been the day she'd murdered the queen.

Lucien rarely spoke against her. They'd always been on

each other's side. Until she'd overtaken the Thornewood castle. Now he barely spoke to her. She wasn't sure if it was because of her actions or because his betrothed, the beautiful but irritating Desminda, had escaped, leaving him once again an unattached prince.

If Celestine had anything to say about it, he wouldn't be that way for long. There were many other kingdoms they could ally with. Though she'd long shunned marriage, even Celestine wasn't above selling herself if it meant achieving her goals.

Lucien reached a hand toward the stones.

Celestine sucked in a breath, slapping it away. "Don't touch it!"

Her brother barked a laugh. "If it weren't anything to fret about, you wouldn't be worried about me touching it, would you, *sister*?"

The word was a disgusted sneer. Celestine's lips turned into a frown as she straightened. "I won't dignify that with a response," she sniffed, adjusting her skirts as she turned toward the door. "We'll call in a magician from a neighboring kingdom to help."

Lucien followed behind her, his snort barely audible. "No one will come," he said matter-of-factly. "I'm surprised we don't have a host of troops on our doorstep waiting to crucify you for what you've done."

She whirled to face him. "What I've *done*," she snarled, "is free this place of a tyrant queen who tried to take a piece of everyone."

Lucien's eyes flashed. He couldn't disagree. The tyrant queen had taken their magic, and now they all knew it.

Everyone wanted it back. He disagreed with how she'd gone about it, and now, since she had yet to free the power, Celestine knew he wondered if this had all been for nothing.

But Celestine wouldn't entertain the notion. She here, and while she might be the queen of a stolen crown, if she figured out how to free magic, the people would reward her with the power that should rightfully be hers anyway.

Lucien exhaled a deep breath. "I know you think you've done the right thing, but the people are restless. The other kingdoms are restless. They will not wait forever for you to come to your senses."

Celestine didn't respond. Lucien would see.

They would all see.

And when they did, she wouldn't stop with Thornewood. The lands of Lunamoor would bow.

CHAPTER ONE

THE SPIRITS WHISPER

I n this land of shadow, Bloom felt more at home than she'd ever felt anywhere else. She sat at the top of a hill, surrounded by tiny white wildflowers, the wind a whisper of sound in her ears. Magic flowed through her veins, pictures of thousands of futures flicking through her mind—an unfinished story where choice and courage would make the difference between victory or crushing defeat.

She'd become used to the sensation by now, after spending her time in Nova's kingdom learning her magic once again. Now she could focus on what she wanted to see and tune everything else out.

But what she wanted to see wasn't what she'd hoped.

Darkness lay ahead for them all, hope a distant light in a winding, treacherous tunnel. Bloom exhaled, her fingers running through the carpet of velvet wildflowers. The wind sang against her skin, teasing her hair out of her long braid. She lay back, eyes to the starry sky, and wondered how long they'd have to fight to secure a future.

And if it was worth it at all.

Harlow and Desminda had splintered, the former queen's betrayal a knife in the young mage's heart. Harlow had not fully accepted her part in this upcoming war, but Bloom knew Harlow was critical to their success, and getting her on board might be one of the most difficult roles Bloom had to play.

She held empathy for the girl, but destiny overrode Bloom's sometimes tender heart. Harlow was the daughter of Magnus Stonehand, a legendary mage responsible for magic's fall and long thought dead. She'd been hidden her entire life, having no idea of the power blossoming through her veins, and if it hadn't been for the intervention of Nova, the Shadow Queen, Harlow would have died years ago.

At the risk of her own safety, Nova had stepped in to save the toddler, with no thought of her own kingdom or responsibilities. She'd seen the danger Harlow had been in and offered to sacrifice herself instead, revealing a dangerous secret about herself before whisking Harlow to safety.

Bloom had long dreamed of serving a queen like Nova.

She wanted to stay here after everything was over. Bloom had no home to go back to, and this place sang to the loneliness inside her heart. Survival had to come first—the future too uncertain to make plans.

Exhaustion leached through her bones, and her eyes were fluttering shut, rocked to rest by the gentle wind, when the first whispers crossed the wind.

"*Corruption*," came the first.

"*Rot*," came another.

"*Darkness*," whispered yet another spirit.

"The heart of magic is corrupted," a much closer spirit said.

Bloom sat up, gasping at the apparition floating in front of her. It had been female at one time, clad in a gauzy, modest nightdress. Her silvery hair flowed like a tattered ribbon behind her.

"Where?" Bloom demanded.

"Everywhere," it whispered, the spirit's hand floating out in a sweeping gesture.

Bloom's heartbeat sped up, a sense of dread unfurling in her stomach.

"Can we stop it?"

The spirit didn't answer her question. *"Hurry,"* it whispered. *"Hurry. The Magic Breaker must be warned."*

Bloom's brow furrowed. "Who?"

"Magic Breaker. Tell the Magic Breaker..." The spirit drifted away with the wind, its power expended once she delivered her warning.

The Magic Breaker. She'd only heard one person described that way.

Harlow Stonehand.

Bloom scrambled to her feet. The castle was a full day's ride away, and there were no other Seers there she could mentally relay the message to. After a double check of her bag to check her provisions, Bloom swung into the saddle and pushed the horse as fast as it could go.

CHAPTER TWO

NO MERCY

Mercy had no place in Harlow's heart. Not anymore. Thornewood had no right to ask it of her. The golden-eyed throneless queen had no right to ask it of her. *Desminda* had no right to ask anything of her any longer.

The princess sat beside her, knees tucked under her chin, those bright eyes watching, cataloging everything in Nova's palace. Plotting, scheming. Harlow put nothing past her anymore. *This is what royals do,* she told herself. *They scheme, they lie, they plot, all to keep their own power base secured.*

But Desminda no longer had any power to speak of. She was merely a girl with royal blood, a queen with no throne, a pawn in a game that had gone far beyond the abilities of what she was now—a lost and destitute teenage girl.

If Harlow had even a hint more of a callous heart, she'd gloat over Desminda's fate, but as it was, Harlow sidled closer to the deposed queen, sympathy filling her heart at the sadness in Desminda's eyes. Those golden eyes slid over to her, cataloging Harlow's shining hair, cornflower blue eyes, and pale skin before sliding away, but not before Harlow caught the flash of guilt inside of them.

Even if the princess apologized, Harlow probably wouldn't accept it. What she'd done wasn't so terrible if you looked at it in the way a politician would—the way a rival would. But Harlow was neither. She'd been a fool—a foolish young girl with stars in her eyes and a wide open heart. Nova had tried to warn her after all, hadn't she?

Harlow's eyes followed the other queen, her *sister*, as she practically glided along the cold, stone floor, murmuring instructions to the gaggle of servants who followed her. Nova was just as beautiful and kind as Harlow remembered, but this secret...the information she'd kept from her stood between them like a thick, glass wall. It could be shattered, but Harlow didn't have the strength to do it.

She just wanted to...wallow.

Just for a little while. To bemoan her fate and sink into the pit of awfulness that had befallen her.

And she knew if Nova caught her, the queen would pull her up by the ear and give her the tongue lashing she would no doubt deserve.

But Nova's attention was fixed elsewhere now, so Harlow sat there, watching the sister she loved more than the moon, yearning to bridge the gap between them, that awful black space between her head and her heart, and knowing she couldn't do it.

Not right now.

"She deserves your love," came a voice above and to the

side of her. Harlow squeezed her eyes shut for a brief moment before peering up. Shade watched Nova like a hawk watched a field mouse. Quiet and alert. Hunting her. But Harlow knew Nova was not prey and Shade was no predator. She didn't know what had happened between the two so long ago, but since the thought of it made her want to curl into the fetal position and scream, Harlow instead chose to ignore it.

She was getting really good at ignoring a lot of things these days.

Though from the look Shade gave her when his attention wavered from Nova, she expected she was close to the end of that behavior.

Why couldn't anyone in this godsforsaken place just let her *wallow*?

If not for a little while.

Harlow groaned and flopped her head onto the arms resting on top of her knees. "Go away, Shade," she grumbled. A few weeks ago, she wouldn't have dared speaking to him like that, but things were different now.

The dark man above her snorted. "Today," he said quietly. "Today is the last day of this, Harlow. Your kingdom awaits you. Your sister needs you. But you are still young, and for that reason alone, I'll allow this small mercy."

Harlow felt the weight of his heated stare, though she sensed no anger there. Perhaps even a touch of empathy. His stare glided from her over to Desminda. The girl next to her stiffened and scooted a few inches away from Harlow, as if she could get away from the cutting edge of Shade's knowing gaze.

A smile curled Harlow's lips as she reburied her head

into her arms. Desminda might be royalty, but no one was immune to the full effect of a Shade Montello stare.

Not even a future queen.

CHAPTER THREE

A BLUR OF BLADES

This kingdom was not his. Its queen was not his. Not yet. Shade never cared to rule, rarely bothered with the offers of power in trade for subterfuge or the machinations that came with court schemers, but this place differed from Thornewood. He watched Nova, unable to tear his eyes away, as she glided through the court, stopping now and then to speak to someone. It wasn't always about business. Sometimes Nova stopped just to chat. Not because she wanted or needed something. Because she cared.

No ruler Shade had ever served lowered themselves to speaking with the citizenry. In dropping her formality, she became even more of a queen in Shade's eyes. From the way her subjects stared up at Nova with adoration, he believed they felt the same.

He shouldn't get his hopes up with her, but he knew how Nova felt about him. It burned within her eyes every time she looked at him, filling his heart with gladness. Even if, when she turned away, the feeling turned to ash in his chest.

He had no royal blood. No title or lands. Not even much money. All his life he'd served, beholden to rulers who only cared for the bite of his sword at an enemy's neck, not the sharp edges of his mind. Until now, he supposed. Rulerless, jobless as well, though Nova had sought his expertise in training the youth interested in serving their queen as soldiers in the future, and he'd gladly accepted. He had nothing to offer her other than his ragged heart.

He tore his eyes away from Nova and turned his attention to the queen at his feet. Desminda sat on the floor, her knees to her chest, golden eyes dim with grief and sorrow. She watched Nova, curiosity and something else in her eyes, as she walked. Her mouth trembled and Shade watched her shoulders bow and her head droop. Harlow had left her a few minutes ago, no doubt to find a safe space where she could let her grief and anger out. Much of it directed at the queen who sat at his feet.

He'd tried to warn Harlow about the games royalty played. They rarely cared about the destruction they left in their wake, even if someone's heart was at stake. Desminda had played Harlow like a skilled bard played a lute, making the girl believe she might have gained the heart of a future queen. Instead, Desminda had led Harlow to believe she would become a future queen's most trusted guard, and perhaps something more, when Desminda had no intention of ever following through.

But that betrayal wasn't the only Harlow had suffered. When her magic revealed itself, the Virago had splintered, most running straight into the machinations of Celestine, a princess from the Kingdom of Roses. Thornewood's downfall came only a short time later.

Shade inhaled a deep breath as his mind spun with possibility. His lands were held hostage by a cruel ruler, and he was in what had always been known as an enemy kingdom with a throneless queen and a girl who might very well save their world.

If she didn't break it first.

How the gods must have laughed when they dropped Harlow into his life, knowing how twisted her path would be to embrace both herself and the unholy power lurking inside her she still didn't fully grasp.

Nova turned, her gaze catching and snagging Shade's. She turned him inside out, his heart laid bare for her to catch. The silver eyes that captured his soul the very first time he'd laid eyes on her sparkled, even as a small smile lurked on her generous lips.

Her beauty and ferocity struck him dumb every time he saw her, and Shade had to suppress the urge to fall to his knees. He returned her smile with a promise in his eyes, one that made Nova's eyes turn molten.

Later, her gaze promised him.

Shade was the first to look away. Like a schoolboy caught in the throes of a first crush, his cheeks colored.

A queen.

And yet, he still hoped she would one day have another title.

His.

CHAPTER FOUR

A QUEEN NO MORE

She had nothing, not even a copper in her pocket, and yet it didn't feel much different from before. How could that be? Had she been so blind to everything happening around her that she'd failed to see the truth? The schemes, the lies, the plotting, the betrayal, much of it done by her, had gotten her nowhere. A lost queen, a lost queendom, friendless and adrift.

Desminda huffed and put her knees down, crossing her legs at the ankle and adjusting her skirts around her. She might not have a castle, but she was still royalty. For how little that meant to anyone around her. Harlow's condemning stare and the pity in Shade's eyes made her want to rail and scream and throw things. She inhaled and exhaled, shoving down the futile rage and grief, and focused on the woman gliding along the stone floor like a dancer.

Anyone with half a brain wouldn't miss the heated looks the queen threw Shade when she thought no one else was looking. How had they met? Why had she never heard of this...Nova, Queen of Shadows, if she'd been in her queendom and Shade had never traveled to hers. Thornewood was the only place Shade could have met her. There was more to this story than she had been told.

Her eyes narrowed as Nova stopped to speak to almost everyone, reaching out to touch the hands of the merchants, the children racing around squealing with delight, their parents who looked at her with such fervor.

"You are jealous," observed Shade.

Desminda's lips thinned. For all that her mother thought Shade was a guard, he was so much more. Power came in observance. Lying in wait, listening, and learning. He'd mastered them all so well. She couldn't help but love him as a father despite the secrets he'd kept from her. His noble heart would get him killed one day, of that she had no doubt, but he would always keep her safe. "No," Desminda murmured. "I am...thinking."

"Oh?" Shade sat beside her, curling his long legs underneath him. She blinked at him in surprise. She'd never seen him so at ease. So casual. Desminda wasn't sure she liked it.

"Jealousy is for the weak." The words sounded snappish even to her. She sighed and tried again. "I'm wondering how she came into play here. Why are we in the Shadow Kingdom, and what do we have to gain by it?"

From the way his eyes tightened at the edges, she knew he was displeased by her words. "Sometimes things happen the way they are meant to be. Sometimes there is no foresight, no cunning, no planning. Not everything is done for gain." He shook his head. "Your parents taught you to think of power as a game."

Her breath caught at the casual mention of her parents. She hadn't had time to process everything that had happened over these last few weeks. Their deaths, her defection, her queendom in the hands of her enemy.

"They were wrong." Shade watched Nova for a moment before he flicked his gaze to her. "Power is not a game. It is life and death and horrible choices and grief. If it were a game, it would be a chess match played by such skilled players that no one ever wins. There is so much more to being a queen than ruling."

She snorted. "And you would know?"

The words, meant to cut, only amused him. "I would. And if you were any smarter, you would learn." The barb stung, Desminda's cheeks reddening with embarrassment. He shook his head. "A true queen never rules by herself or for herself. She surrounds herself with people skilled in areas she is deficient and makes judgment on what is best for her entire kingdom, not the good of a single group. Your parents—"

She cut him off. "Are *dead*," she snapped. "They are dead, and I am alone. I do not want to hear you speak of what I should or could be because I might as well be dead, too. I am nothing. Adrift. Unwelcome in a kingdom I should never be in." Desminda turned to look at him, his stony expression giving nothing away. A harsh laugh cracked from her. "I know I am a fool, Shade. I haven't quite realized the extent of it yet, and when I do, I am sure that I will break." She looked away. "I do not need you to speed it along for me."

A soft sigh escaped him, and he rose, his movements like liquid—sleek and quiet. "Sometimes a broken thing becomes beautiful. Sometimes our cracks and sharp edges are what keep us alive." He bowed his head. "I am needed elsewhere."

Desminda stayed silent. Just a little while ago, his bow would have been deeper, his words more measured.

Discomfort rose in her as she watched him walk away, his spine straighter and his bearing prouder walking toward Nova than it ever had been with her. Another crack formed at the edge of her heart, spider-webbing to the center. She couldn't count all the cracks anymore. Her heart was so damaged it felt like it would shatter into a million pieces. And yet, every time she spoke, venom spewed from her, pouring out like a cask of ale.

She couldn't seem to stop it.

She was a queen of nothing.

And maybe she'd always been that way.

CHAPTER FIVE

THE UNKNOWING KING

S hade belonged here in this land of silver and shadow. His darkness complemented the constant twilight of her kingdom, and his kindness brought light where she had gone dark. Nova walked among her people, offering words of comfort or a soft greeting to those who milled around her. She tried to meet with her people as much as possible. Holding the title of queen meant little if she kept herself locked in a tower.

Nova tried not to watch as he stalked toward her, his attention a balm to her wounded soul. Shade moved gracefully, like a panther stalking prey, but she'd long grown used to his silent ways. He never said more than he had to, but he always said enough. His few words taught her more over these last years than any of her advisors had.

And Harlow. Here at last. There would never be enough ways to thank him for what he'd done for her and her sister. She tried every single day to thank him again, but Shade would jerk his head once in the negative and tell her no thanks were needed. Her family was his, and he would always put his life on the line if it meant ensuring their safety.

How had she gotten so lucky?

His dark eyes burned as they watched her. A soft smile curved her lips as she turned away to greet someone else. She yearned to touch him all the time, but they had to be oh-so careful right now. Shade had no royal blood, but Nova would one day make him her king. He had no such compunctions and thought he was merely a page in her long book, and Nova felt the heaviness of his gaze against her skin when he thought she wasn't looking. Even though he never said the words, she knew Shade thought it was only a matter of time before she took someone else as her king and fulfilled the duties passed down to her by the crown.

But this was the Shadow Kingdom, and they rarely did anything like the others. Their laws were harsher and crueler than others, but most of their rulers married for only two reasons: to strengthen their rule or love. Some might view it as fickle, but Nova had never felt more like a queen than when Shade was at her side.

She'd tell him soon. He wasn't ready yet. Her kingdom wasn't ready yet. A pall lay over them, and most could sense something lay on the horizon. Something dark. A sigh escaped her as she greeted the last person milling around.

"Your Highness," Shade said as he stopped before her and dipped his head to acknowledge her position.

Her lips curved. "Shade. How nice to see you."

This game they played heated her blood. "Will you walk with me?" she asked.

"Of course." He held his arm out, and Nova curled her fingers around the corded muscle. With a last nod, she allowed him to lead her away from the noisy crowd. Harlow and Desminda sat apart from each other, the bond between them broken. Shade had said little about them, but Nova could always tell when Harlow was troubled. From her glimpses over to the throneless queen, she knew who behind it.

Perhaps in time, they would mend it, but Nova knew her sister. Harlow was slow to forgive. Whatever trespasses Desminda might have committed would be difficult to overcome if Harlow were this angry and hurt about it. Her sister had the right to be hurt by the many betrayals she'd experienced over these last years—Nova's being the worst of all.

Harlow had avoided her since she'd arrived, and Nova had allowed it. For now. Soon, though, she'd corner her sister and explain the reasons behind her actions. Even if Harlow didn't understand them now, she would soon.

War had come to their lands, and they'd need to stand with each other to survive it.

Shade led her around a corner, and Nova chanced a glance at him. He stood straight and tall, his back stiff as he walked, though his eyes caught everything going on around them. Nova tugged him to the left. Shade's brow furrowed, but he allowed her to lead them to a dark alcove, where she spun him and pressed against his chest as his back hit the cool stone.

Shade inhaled sharply, though his arms gathered around her. Nova tucked her head under his chin and wrapped her arms around his waist. "You suffer," she murmured, inhaling the fresh, clean scent of him. She always felt safe and cherished when she was in his arms.

A soft chuckle broke from him. "Harlow and Desminda. They couldn't be more different, but right now, they're so maudlin I can barely stand to be around them."

Nova huffed a quiet laugh. "They've both lost much."

Shade sighed, and Nova shifted, burying her face against him. It was as if she could never get close enough, even when they lay skin to skin. Shade held something back from her, and Nova couldn't help but wonder if it was the last piece of him. Of his heart. As if giving it to her would break him.

He didn't know the things she did. Nova would never let him go, and if someone tried to take him from her, she would decimate their kingdom with her darkness without a single regret.

"They've lost much, but they stand to gain so much more. Harlow will come around sooner than Desminda. She's suffered much loss in her life. Desminda..." his voice trailed off.

"She's royalty. Parents often use kid gloves and kind words when raising princesses," Nova filled in. "Some lessons cannot be taught with a buffer. She's never known true hardship or failure. This is something she must work through. How she does it will reveal whether she's meant to be a queen..."

"Or an exile." Shade exhaled and pressed a kiss to the top of her head.

"Yes. Either way, it is not for you to decide. Guide and mentor her, but ultimately Desminda will have to decide what kind of person she wants to be."

"You are wise," Shade said. "And beautiful."

Her grip tightened around him. Lifting her head, she peered into those dark, fathomless eyes. "Oh?" A smile toyed with her lips.

Shade rarely smiled with his entire heart. When he did, it cracked her wide open. The thing in her chest she thought was broken unfurled like a rose. Her breath caught as she stood up on her tiptoes and brushed her lips against his.

"I have two hours until my next engagement," she whispered.

His teeth flashed white. Nova pressed her fingers against one of the gray stones next to Shade's shoulder. It opened with a slight click. Shade's eyes widened even as amusement simmered in their depths.

"Is this a seduction?" he murmured. "Am I being stolen and dragged back to your lair?"

She chuckled as she led him into the dark corridor, holding his hand and tugging him forward. Her bedroom wasn't far. She wanted to whisper everything she felt against his skin.

He sucked in a breath as she clicked another stone, and the door swung open, revealing the interior of her bedroom. "Wicked girl," he growled.

"You have no idea how wicked I can be, Shade," she murmured as she pulled him in, urgently tugging at his vest. His eyes fluttered shut as she undid the laces and tugged them down.

"Nova." His teeth clenched as he whispered her name.

She pressed a finger against his lips. "You must be quiet," she urged, her lips twitching at his leashed restraint. "We don't want the maids to hear. They gossip like old church wives."

Shade unhooked her fingers from his shirt and walked her back toward the bed. Her knees hit, forcing her to sit. He stared at her for a moment before he kneeled between her legs.

Nova sucked in a breath. His dark hair lay disheveled against his face, and his eyes burned with desire.

"Shade." She licked her lips, now unsure. He'd been restrained with her. Cautious, she realized. From the look on his face now, those days might be over.

A wicked grin curved his lips as he took in her sudden nervousness. "You must be quiet," he echoed as he took her ankle in his hand and lifted it to sit on top of his shoulder. His hands slid up her thighs, burning a trail where his fingers caressed. Her head dropped back at the urgent sweep of his touch.

"The maids mustn't hear," he continued. "Whatever will they think of us?" A wicked chuckle slithered against her skin, erotic and deep.

When his dark head dipped between her skirts, Nova lost all coherent thought.

This. Him.

All of him would be hers. She would make it so.

No matter what it cost her.

CHAPTER SIX

THE TALK

F ew people paid Harlow any attention as she roamed
through the castle halls. They'd been here a few weeks
now, and while Shade's dark grace made him a natural in
Nova's halls, Harlow walked them like a sullen ghost.
Desminda hardly bothered to venture out at all, preferring to
stay within the cool comfort of her quarters.

The castle itself resembled something out of a fairy tale,
one with fantastical stories about princesses in high towers
and handsome knights to rescue them. Cool white stone rose
high above her, carved with ornate scenes. Several places had
no roof, exposing its inhabitants to cool winds and foggy
skies.

She had yet to see rain or inclement weather, almost like
Nova or someone else controlled the climate. Harlow
wouldn't doubt her sister commanded that kind of power.
She'd avoided Nova and Shade, becoming something of an
expert on their whereabouts and slipping away if she even

felt a hint of their presence. It worked for a while, but Harlow suspected they'd allowed it to happen, rather than believing her stealth skills were better than they actually were.

What her antics led to, however, was a stale sense of boredom and extreme hunger. The kitchen staff didn't look kindly on Harlow's late-night forays into the kitchens, and after the third time, leftovers became either scarce or hidden even from her hunting skills. Even they were trying to force her to become a productive member of Nova's court.

Which led her to now, standing outside the massive dining hall, the scent of roasted venison and potatoes tickling her nose. Harlow's stomach growled, and just as she stepped forward, a flicker of silver teased the corner of her eye, and the familiar star-kissed scent of her sister came through the air.

Almost. She'd almost made it.

"Harlow," Nova said, her skirts swishing as she moved to block her entrance, "I'll have dinner served in my room."

"I'll eat in the dining hall if it's all the same."

One of Nova's dark eyebrows lifted. "It's not." She took Harlow by the arm and turned her toward the stairs.

Harlow could have fought, but Nova was the queen.

Either way, she'd lose.

With a put-upon sigh that made her sister laugh, Harlow allowed herself to be led up the stairs and into Nova's private quarters.

Two guards stood outside the entrance, dressed in night-black armor. One male, one female. The male towered over the female, his face a mask of blankness. The female stood only an inch or two taller than Harlow's slight frame, but her eyes burned with life.

Harlow blinked at the woman and the intensity in her stare.

"Evara and Tristan," Nova said, nodding to both. They stepped forward as one, opening the doors, each step and push matched in perfect unison.

"Thank you." Nova gestured Harlow inside, stopping to speak to her guards. Whatever she said, Harlow couldn't hear, but a moment later, Nova glided inside, sighing as the door shut behind them.

To Harlow's surprise, her sister kicked her slippers off and groaned before flopping onto the elegant couch closest to the door. Nova stared up at her, flicking her fingers at the other couch. "You know you want to," she said with a smirk. "Make yourself comfortable. Dinner will be up in a few minutes."

Harlow didn't return her smile. Instead, Nova's familiar expression chipped the cavern in her heart a few inches deeper. She turned and sat on the edge of the couch, crossing her hands in her lap, and waited.

"Harlow." Nova sat up, her tiara askew on her head. Relaxed like this, she possessed none of the queenly grace Harlow had seen over the past weeks. Her gown tugged above her ankles, exposing lightly muscled calves and tan legs, at odds with the almost eternal dusk of her kingdom. "I know I have a lot to explain, and you must have a thousand questions, but I am still your sister."

"Are you?" The coldness in her voice made Nova pale.

Guilt flooded her, but she couldn't bring herself to apologize for it. Nova *left* her. There one day, gone the next, a stone and a note the only things left of the sister she'd seen almost every day for years of her life. Nova's absence had left her cold and empty, her sheer will to survive the only thing that kept her going after her parents' deaths.

Harlow watched as a myriad of expressions crossed Nova's face. Hurt, anger, grief, before they morphed into careful blankness, an expression Harlow had only seen a time or two before when Nova's emotions would get the better of her.

"I deserved that," her sister said quietly. "You get one blow. One opportunity to take all your anger and grief out on me. It's just you and me. Harlow and Nova. Say or do whatever you need to, but after that, you *will* listen to what I have to say."

Harlow's face crumpled, hot tears spilling down her cheeks. Grief and hurt spilled through her veins, the feeling of abandonment roaring up her throat and turning into a hoarse wail.

Nova's inhaled breath and crinkling fabric were all she heard before her face was buried in Nova's collarbone, her sister stroking a hand down Harlow's riot of curls. "I am sorry for it all, Harlow. If I could have done it any other way, I would have. I swear to you."

"You *lied*," Harlow screamed. "And you left me. Alone. I was only fifteen! Mom and Dad—" she hiccupped.

"I know. I know." Nova kissed the top of her head. "I heard. I—I didn't know when it happened. There was no way for me to know." Her inhale sounded ragged to Harlow's ears. "My parents in the Shadow Kingdom had pushed for two years for me to return home. I wouldn't go."

Hot tears flowed from Harlow's eyes, and she couldn't stop them even if she wanted to. Everything she'd felt and experienced since Nova had left her spilled forth in a torrent of grief, her words an almost incoherent babble.

Nova let her cry for a while until Harlow wiped her face and nose with her sleeve. Her sister laughed and pushed a handkerchief into her hand. "Mother would be appalled. Here."

A quiet knock sounded on the door. Harlow stiffened, but Nova shook her head. "They are my most trusted," she whispered, standing in a fluff of skirts as she hurried to the door. A servant came in with a rolling table but set it right inside the door at Nova's quiet command.

She left without a word, Evara closing the door behind her.

Nova rolled the table over, setting it right in front of Harlow before she settled next to her. Harlow's stomach let out an inopportune growl, making Nova laugh. "You always were a sucker for dinner," Nova said, her lips curling into a smile. "Like a little bloodhound waiting at the table at the exact minute dinner would start."

If only Nova knew the story of her hunched over, eating berries in the woods during her training. She pushed a covered plate over to Harlow, buttered two rolls and pushed them over as well before she uncovered her own plate.

The scent of roasted venison made Harlow's mouth

water. As soon as Nova picked up her fork, Harlow followed, uncovering the plate to dig in with wild abandon. They ate in silence for a few moments before Nova began to speak, her words slow and hesitant, telling Harlow the reasons why everything fell apart.

"When a member of the royal family in the Kingdom of Shadows turns fourteen, they are sent to a family in a neighboring kingdom in a blind fosterage. It has always been our way."

Harlow paused, the fork halfway to her mouth. "Do the other kingdoms know?"

Nova shook her head. "Never. It is too dangerous."

"The families don't either?"

"No. We carefully choose the families and pursue the fosterage through a third party."

Harlow thought about it. "It sounds dangerous even without the royal family in the other kingdom knowing about it."

Nova chuckled. "I suppose it can be."

"It is," Harlow said quietly, the implications of Nova's behavior all those years ago finally penetrating. "You saved me during the raids." The memory of Nova's trauma surfaced, and Harlow saw the moment she thought about it too. Her sister fell quiet for a long moment before she smiled, locking those memories away as she'd done the entire time they were together.

"I did. But my fosterage was chosen because our allies suggested it. They knew where you were and wanted a member of our house there. Just in case."

Harlow stared at her. "But you could have died."

Nova's smile turned bitter. Something perhaps much worse had happened to her. "I didn't. And I found you." Her sister gripped her hand tight and squeezed. "And you were worth it all."

Tears shimmered in Harlow's eyes, a piece of her fractured heart slowly clicking back into place.

CHAPTER SEVEN

A FAMILIAL SURPRISE

They'd just finished dinner and had moved on to dessert when a slight knock sounded on the door.

"Enter," Nova said.

A mountain of a man stepped inside.

Harlow knew who he was before her sister even opened her mouth. The fork she held clattered onto the plate as Harlow gawked.

Magnus Stonehand stood in the entrance, his bright blue gaze sweeping the room, searching for threats, before it landed on her.

He sucked in a breath and stopped. Hesitated.

Nova got to her feet. "Magnus!" She rushed over and threw herself into his arms. He wrapped her into a bear hug and lifted her off her feet before dropping a kiss atop her head.

Harlow blinked at the scene. Magnus set Nova aside but didn't venture further into the room. Instead, he waited. The guards closed the door, shutting them in together. Her chest felt tight. Harlow opened her mouth to say something, anything, but the power of speech had abandoned her.

Magnus loomed above Nova, one of his arms the size of her sister's waist. His chest spanned several hand lengths, tapering into a narrow waist encircled by a belt full of tools and weapons. An ornate axe hung at his hip, one that made her green with envy.

"Hello, Harlow," he said. It was the same voice she heard that night with Astrid in the forest when her magic had gotten away from her. Deep, commanding, and rumbling with authority.

Harlow wiped her hands down her pants and stood on shaky legs. She didn't even reach her father's chest.

"Hello," she said, her voice wobbly.

Nova stepped away from him. "Harlow, I know you've met Magnus already." She licked her lips. "He is a guest in our kingdom and performs Nightmage duties for us."

Harlow stared at her sister. She sounded uncomfortable. Nova wasn't prone to babbling, but that's what she was doing.

Magnus' lips twitched.

"He came to us several months ago and asked for a place to stay. Perhaps he saw something no one else did." Nova wrung her fingers together.

"You're my father," Harlow said. She had never been one to soften a verbal blow. First, she never thought of it. If words had to be said, why did everyone tiptoe around them? They might hurt either way, so wasn't it best to just get it over with?

Nova cleared her throat and touched Magnus on the arm

before turning to leave the room. "I'll fetch some tea. I'll be back in a moment."

When the door closed, Magnus chuckled. "She's the queen. Nova never gets her own tea."

She couldn't muster the strength to smile. Her entire body felt wrecked, and she'd locked her knees so tight she couldn't move if she wanted to.

His smile faded. "I'm sure you have many questions."

A million. More than he'd ever be able to answer. "You left me," she croaked.

His face fell, grief shining in his eyes. A long moment stretched between them. "I did," he finally said.

"Why?" Her voice was barely a whisper.

His answer came almost instantly. "To keep you safe."

A tear slipped down her cheek. "Nova said the same thing."

She didn't mean for it to be a blow, but Magnus flinched. "I know." His voice cracked. "And thank the gods she was there."

"She suffered."

Magnus took a step forward. "I know that, too. I'd do anything to take the pain away from her, but you are here. In the flesh. I haven't held you since you were a child and—"

Harlow took a step back. That vast pit of power roiled and turned in her stomach, awake and aware. She held a hand up. "Don't. I'm not ready. I may never be ready."

He stopped, his eyes flickering with grief. "Of course. I'm sorry. It's just—" Magnus scrubbed a hand over his face. "You look so much like her." His voice broke, and he squeezed his eyes shut for a moment. When he opened them, a suspicious brightness lingered there.

Her mother. He spoke of Marion, his wife, and a woman she'd never met. Harlow tilted her head. "It seems I look like you." His golden hair and blue eyes were similar to her own.

"No." A fond smile turned his lips up. "One day I will show you what she looked like. In the flesh. If you allow it." He touched his hand to his heart. "She lives forever here, but I have the ability to project a memory to another."

She blinked tears away. "Yes," Harlow said, too quickly. She wanted that more than anything. What happened to her, and why had they let her go?

The door opened again, and Nova pushed another rolling tray in, this one filled with a teapot, three cups, and an assortment of cookies.

She rolled it past and stopped by the couches, carefully pouring each of them a cup.

"Come," she said. "Let us chat while we enjoy this new tea blend."

Magnus shook his head and gestured for Harlow to go first. She took the chair opposite the couch. A disapproving look flashed on Nova's face, but she schooled it into a bland smile as she pushed over a tray of chocolate cookies.

Traitor. Nova knew those were her favorites.

Magnus reached for the lemon, taking a couple while he waited for the tea to brew.

"So," Nova drawled, "as family reunions go, this one is a little rough."

Magnus blew out an annoyed breath. "Nova." The word was a growl.

She waved a hand at him. "Relax. You have plenty of time to catch up."

"Time being the key," he said.

Her gaze darted back and forth as they bickered. "You two seem friendly."

"The Witch Kingdom sent him here," Nova said, her eyes flickering as she mentioned him. Harlow still couldn't wrap her head around them.

It took a second for her words to register. "The witches?"

Magnus nodded.

"My mother and their queen were good friends." Nova blew on her tea as she picked up her cup. "They gave Magnus a letter of recommendation." She grinned at him. "Though they didn't allow him to stay while he awaited our decision."

"Glad I came so highly recommended," Magnus said dryly.

"I didn't say that." Nova's eyes twinkled, but she sobered when she saw Harlow's expression. "Enough levity. I'm sorry. I know this has been difficult."

Difficult wasn't the right word. Traumatic, awful, frightening, those were all things she'd describe this as. Both of her parents abandoned her when she was newly born. Her first foster family died in the raids. Her second from a fever that ravaged the village. And now this man sitting in front of her thought to be a father to her?

The power inside of her roiled in her gut, churning and sloshing inside like an angry sea. She forced it down, searching for the right words to say—a safer topic of conversation. Harlow couldn't talk about him now. He sat right in front of her and all she felt was burning rage.

"My mother. She was a witch?"

Magnus nodded. "A powerful one. I'd never seen a nature mage with more magic than she had."

"Nature?" Harlow questioned. "Like animals?" Luci appeared in her mind, preening in the starlit night. She visited the vain horse every day, and most times she found her running wild in the pastures behind the castle. Hundreds of acres for the horse to expend all her energy, but Luci never seemed to tire. Harlow hadn't ridden her again. She had no reason to, but perhaps soon, she'd go exploring again with the massive mare.

Luci had been her only friend when she came to Thornewood, and it started with Harlow being afraid to sleep alone and seeking out an animal in the stables for comfort. Though to look at Luci, one did not see comfort. She was a terrifying sight to behold, but Harlow had been drawn to the keen intellect in her eyes and a need for comfort.

Freeing her had never been part of Harlow's plans until they grew closer, and she realized Luci's spirit would break if Thornewood caged her any longer. But instead of running away forever, Luci reappeared when Harlow had most needed her, saving her life, and getting her out of the kingdom with the help of Shade and the others.

Magnus' eyes lit. "Animals. Plants. Wind. Sky. The ground beneath us." He shrugged. "She had a way with it all." His expression sobered, his mouth turned down with grief. "When Marion was outside, the land responded."

"So I—" Harlow choked off the words, but Magnus knew what she was asking.

"I can only assume. We can practice whenever you like. I'm here to stay, to help you in whatever way I can. Marion's power runs through the female bloodline, but sometimes the witch's power doesn't manifest the same way in their children."

"And you?" she inquired.

He held his hands out and shrugged. "I am more of a mix."

One of Nova's dark eyebrows lifted.

"I have no main power," he admitted. "My power heeds my will, but I am very good at breaking things."

"Breaking things?" Harlow repeated, confused about what he meant, but it came to her a second later. "You mean magic."

"Magic. Land. Kingdoms." The weight of his choices flashed on his face. "I never make those decisions lightly."

"Why make those decisions at all?" Harlow blurted.

Magnus' laugh sounded bitter. "When you have a power like I possess, you rarely get free will."

Nova poured him another cup of tea as Harlow studied her father. "So you broke magic because of the Thornewood queen's will, but you broke it in such a way no one else can control it."

"I did," Magnus admitted. "No one but me or my blood-line will be able to repair it." His gaze fell heavily on Harlow's skin. "Which is why I'd like to assess your abilities and help you with your magic."

The magic she could barely suppress.

"And if I don't want to?" Harlow asked.

Nova sucked in a breath. "Harlow!"

Magnus held a hand up. "Much has been thrown at you. I understand. Even if you do not want a relationship with me, you'd be wise to accept my offer. Power like yours will not stay docile. The sooner you learn to control it, the safer everyone will be."

How could he presume to know who she was or what she needed? What Harlow needed was a break. Then safety, honesty, freedom.

"Magnus," Nova murmured.

Her father watched as Harlow set her tea mug down. She stood, her pulse fluttering against her throat, clenching her fists by her side. Magic licked up her throat, and she tried to swallow it down.

"Harlow," Magnus said, a note of urgency in his voice. He set his cup down and rose, one hand held out in front of him.

"You've lied to me my entire life," Harlow said. "And you as well." She pointed to Nova. "I don't want to be involved in any of this. I never wanted to be a guard to the queen, a Virago. All it brought me was pain."

Her entire body shimmered with golden light, the magic spilling from inside to outside.

Magnus' eyes narrowed. "You have to calm down."

"Calm down?" Harlow seethed. "When does telling someone to calm down actually result in them *calming down*?"

Power burst from her skin, cascading over the walls and furniture.

A shocked scream from outside the doors penetrated her anger, but she couldn't control the power as it seeped into the very bones of Nova's kingdom.

Magnus took a step forward, magic spilling from his palms. His power covered hers, a deeper, burnished gold than her vivid one.

"Breathe," he instructed. "Breathe through your emotions. Our power responds to our state of mind, especially in an untrained mage. You must bring your emotions under control before your magic will respond to your commands."

He twisted his wrist, pulling Harlow's power back into the room, off the walls, and furniture, away from the tea set, and held it there, a vibrant, swirling wash of color.

Her chest heaved, tears running down her face. She was —she was being awful. "I'm so-so-sorry," she stuttered.

"No," Magnus rumbled. "No. Not a single part of this is your fault. Just breathe. There's plenty of time to talk later. No one was there to teach you any of this. How could they?" His jaw tightened. "The only thing I need you to do now is imagine the magic soaking back into you. It needs to go somewhere, and the amount you've expended today is too dangerous to let out into the kingdom."

"How do I do that?"

Her father smiled, a soft, tentative thing. "Close your eyes."

She allowed her eyes to flutter shut, the feeling of the magic crawling over her skin like a thousand fire ants.

"Imagine pulling the power, a strand at a time, back

inside you. Put it back into the pool and let it settle. That's all."

Harlow took a few deep breaths and did as he asked. Nothing happened at first, but soon the weight grew lighter and lighter until she could see no more of her power, only her father's.

"Good," Magnus said, releasing his magic. "Open your eyes."

Magnus was awash in light, glimmers of magic glinting on his hair and skin. His eyes had turned an odd hazel color, blue mixed with green and burnished gold. "You need to train."

"I train all the time," Harlow murmured, fascinated by the magic flowing around him. It looked soft, even friendly, like it had bonded to her father and enjoyed serving him.

"Not with Shade," Magnus said. "With me. Nova's kingdom possesses numerous mages. While none will have our exact powers, they know enough of magic theory to help you. When the bard returns, she will assist as well."

Astrid was hard to pin down. The bard was a nomad, never staying in one place for long, and when Harlow asked, everyone shrugged and smiled, as if Astrid's resistance to rest and stability was a funny, normal thing. And perhaps it was for her, but to Harlow, who only longed for a family and a home, it seemed strange indeed.

Bloom was similar, though she'd become more of a daytime wanderer, usually returning to the kingdom once the weak sun had set. As the tall Virago had her powers restored, her visage became a little more ethereal, her eyes taking on an unfocused look, as if she could sense all the threads of fate around her and hadn't yet chosen which to pluck.

If Harlow had this gift, the least she could do was hone it to keep others safe. With a short nod, she agreed.

Relief flashed over Magnus' face there and gone so quickly she thought she'd imagined it. "Come to the training grounds at nine tomorrow morning, then."

Harlow nodded. Magnus stood there for a moment longer. His mouth opened, but he shook his head once, and dipped his head before turning and hurrying out the door.

Nova had stayed silent, but as soon as the door clicked shut, she spoke. "He's trying, you know."

Harlow sighed. "It's hard to see him as my father. I don't know who he is."

"Easily remedied," Nova mused. She snagged another cookie off the plate and handed it to Harlow.

"Says you," Harlow muttered, but she took the delicious peace offering anyway.

Cookies always made everything a little better.

CHAPTER EIGHT

A BLOOM OF SURPRISE

Harlow ate so much she groaned when she shifted in her seat. She sat alone, away from Nova's people. Mostly by choice, but a little by circumstance. She'd made it to the dining hall an hour and a half after breakfast already started and most of the tables were filled.

She'd never seen so much food in her life. Bacon, eggs, little cylindrical sausages, some kind of grain she saw everyone filling their bowls with and adding sugar and a heady spice. There was freshly squeezed juice, fresh fruit and vegetables. Thornewood had a decent dining hall, but it was nothing like this. Everyone chattered happily, lounging around after their breakfast was done. They all seemed content, satisfied with their lives here.

It made her happy, but a small thread of jealousy strung her along. Nova had this the entire time and Harlow... She exhaled a breath. They'd all made their decisions, and Nova had suffered for them. If Harlow were a better person, she'd feel happy that her sister had such a strong family to come home too. And she did. But she also wondered why she didn't have the same.

Thornewood was home, but she'd never felt completely comfortable there. There was always something holding her back. Even with her foster parents, Harlow felt an itching need under her skin to be more. It didn't mean she wanted this. Not at all. She only wanted a place to belong.

Maybe after this, whatever this was, ended, she could find that place here. The thought settled in her, warming her insides, and a small smile played on her lips.

The dining hall doors burst open, a bloodied, harried woman stumbling inside. Her pretty face was scratched in several places, her riding leathers covered with dirt and blood. The woman's blonde braid had partially come loose, wild strands of pale hair floating around her head.

"Harlow!"

Harlow scraped back her chair and gawked at the girl's harried appearance. "Bloom?"

"I need to see the queen. Come!" Before she even finished barking the command, Bloom spun on her heel and hurried away from the hall.

Murmurs and whispers rose, all eyes turning to Harlow. Heat crept up her cheeks as she scraped up the remains of her breakfast, discarding them on the way out. A flash of messy blonde braid turned the corner several feet away, and Harlow hurried after her, blood rushing in her veins. Bloom never looked anything but perfectly put together, so to see her like this, something grave must have happened.

As Harlow rounded the corner, she skidded to a stop at Shade's presence. He loomed over the other Virago, his face a blank mask. She wasn't close enough to overhear them, but Bloom's worried face sent Harlow's stomach plummeting to her feet. Shade took her by the elbow and jerked his head toward Nova's quarters when he noticed Harlow.

Without a word, she followed. Evara stood at the entrance, her weapons sheathed. Her posture tensed when she noticed them, straightening as they grew closer to Nova's rooms.

"We are here to see the queen," Shade said.

Evara looked them all over, her eyes lingering on Harlow. "For what purposes?"

Shade's eyes narrowed. "Purposes that are none of your concern, guard," he snapped.

Harlow glanced at Shade. Anger beat from his skin as he stared down Evara, but Nova's guard didn't quail in fright. Instead, she tilted her head, her cat-like eyes narrowing. "I am Nova's Queensguard. No one passes through here without my knowledge or approval. It is our way. If you don't like it, you are welcome to try to pass." A savage smile curled her lips. "It would be my pleasure to show you how strongly the Shadow Kingdom enforces our rules."

The door creaked open, Nova's dark head peering out. She rolled her eyes. "Evara. Enough. I told you to let Shade pass whenever he needed to."

Evara winked at Harlow and stepped aside.

Shade gave her a long, dark look and brushed past, escorting Bloom inside the chambers. When Harlow tried to follow, Evara stepped in front of her, forcing Harlow to an abrupt stop. The guard was slightly taller than Harlow, leanly muscled and clad in all black leather armor. She wore a sword strapped to one side of her hip and two daggers at the other. A silver shield peeked above her back. Her curly dark hair was loosely tied with a black ribbon, unusual for someone in her position. Harlow usually only saw braids or hairstyles where every inch of hair was secured. It was one of Shade's first rules. *Never give your enemy a convenient weapon to subdue you.*

Evara's eyes were an odd shade of hazel, green and gold, reminding her of Magnus' eyes when they were full of magic. Her skin was pale, and her features finely made—straight, small nose, pink rosebud lips, and high cheekbones. Evara might be deadly, but she was beautiful, too—a deadly combination if someone underestimated her. If Harlow had seen her in passing, she might think her at home in a duke's manor, having tea with other nobles.

"She didn't say you, Sunshine." Evara's smile sharpened at Harlow's discomfort. Her direct gaze catalogued Harlow's features, eyes lingering on Harlow's hair. "Pray tell me, what business does a ray of light have lingering where the shadows live?"

"Evara!" Nova barked, exasperation in her voice. "Let my sister pass!"

The guard's brows lifted, amusement sparkling in the hazel depths of her eyes. "As my queen requests," she murmured, stepping away from Harlow to allow her to pass.

Just as Harlow stepped forward, the guard whispered, "Remember, little ray of light, don't let the shadows consume you."

A shiver passed down Harlow's spine. Refusing to acknowledge the guard's words, Harlow stepped into Nova's chambers, the doors thumping behind her with a booming finality.

Bloom had already sunk into one of Nova's plush couches, a cup of tea trembling in her hand. Her eyes met Harlow's as she walked in, matching purple shadows of exhaustion under Bloom's lower lashes.

"Ah good, Harlow," Nova said, rolling her eyes. "Sorry about Evara. She's a bit of a loose cannon sometimes."

And also a little frightening, Harlow thought, but refrained from saying.

Nova poured her a cup of tea, tipping in a small spoonful of sugar before handing it to Harlow on a pretty little blue and white saucer. Shade stood on the other side of the room, dark and watchful. He greeted Harlow with a nod, but otherwise stayed silent.

Her sister wore unusual clothing today. Clad in dark breeches, high lace-up boots, and a royal blue flowing blouse, the queen looked decidedly causal. Her dark hair was unbound, curling loosely around her back and shoulders, and her face was free of cosmetics. She looked far younger and less serious than usual, and Harlow relaxed, familiar with this version of Nova, her shoulders falling as she settled in a chair opposite them.

But the feeling didn't last for long. As soon as Bloom spoke, her words soft and hesitant, voice trembling as she told them of what the spirits had whispered on the wind, Harlow's tension crept back in full force, tightening her neck and shoulders.

"Magic is corrupted," Bloom finished. "Not all, not yet,

but if we don't do something soon, and Celestine figures out how to use the Luna stones, all hope may be lost."

The doors cracked open then. Magnus stood at the entrance, a thunderous look on his brow.

"You're late for our training session," he said to Harlow, striding into the room like he belonged there. Perhaps he did. Perhaps Harlow was the only one out of place.

Nova's lips thinned. "This is more important, Magnus," she said, her voice sharp.

His brows drew together at her tone. Magnus nodded to Shade, but when his gaze fell on Bloom, his demeanor changed. "News?"

Shade straightened. "Trouble in Thornewood. Something is wrong with the Luna stones."

"Corruption," Bloom clarified. "A rot in the stones spreading farther every day."

Magnus sank down in a seat next to Harlow, and rubbed his jaw. A thoughtful look stole over his face. "Hmm. The stones have never been corrupted before. They should be incorruptible."

He and Shade locked gazes. "Unless something or someone has corrupted them. But how?"

To Harlow, it sounded like they were speaking in a foreign language. Even though she was familiar with the Luna stones and had unknowingly possessed one for years, Harlow wasn't sure how to help or what to say.

"Foreign magic?" Shade supplied. "Perhaps Celestine's activities in Thornewood are...unpopular and someone has taken it upon themselves to prevent her from accessing her magic. People want magic back, but they don't want it at the cost of installing a despot on the throne."

"She's implied before she wants to control it all," Nova mused. "It's a theory we can consider, I think."

"What if it's something different?"

Every head turned to Harlow. Uncomfortable, she shrugged. "We aren't sure what it is. What if something else is corrupting the stones? Something we don't have control over."

Magnus' brow furrowed. "It's not out of the realm of possibility. I'm too far away to sense anything happening in Thornewood."

Harlow stared. "You can sense other magic?"

"You can too," he said. "Once we explore your powers, you'll be amazed with how your senses will open."

Bloom handed her teacup back. Without asking, Nova poured her another cup and pressed it back into her hands. "The spirits are active here, more than they were in Thornewood. If I hear anything, I'll let everyone know." She grimaced. "They don't speak in full sentences usually. Depends on how old their spirit is."

Magnus studied her. "You're a Seer then."

Bloom nodded, a wan smile on her face. "Guilty as charged."

His eyes met Nova's. "Have you introduced her to Maggie?"

"Not yet," Nova murmured. "Everyone needed time to adjust to regaining their magic. I'll see if Maggie is available tomorrow."

"Maggie?" Bloom asked. She brushed a stray strand of hair out of her face.

"The Castle Seer. She's the most powerful one I've ever seen," Nova admitted. "It will pain me to lose her."

"Lose her?" Harlow asked.

"She's ancient," Shade said with a huff of laughter. "Far older than she should be," he said with a wry glance at Nova.

She smiled serenely. "People are long-lived in my kingdom. But it is time for Maggie to retire. She's having trouble going up and down the stairs, and she's spoken about going to live at her daughter's house in the Light Kingdom. Their kingdoms host fantastic gardens rivaling even the Rose Kingdom." Her eyes twinkled. "Wouldn't Celestine love that?"

Shade's grin was dark.

Magnus chuckled. "Against my better judgment, I happen to like Lucien, but he has much to learn. He is still young, but he's far too smart to allow Celestine such sway over him."

Harlow didn't know how to feel about Lucien. He'd helped her a few times, saving her life when they were trying to escape the castle, but there was more to him than met the eye, and Harlow didn't like the unknown. The thought almost made her laugh out loud. She'd been living in the unknown since her foster parents died and now, she was in a brand-new kingdom and had no idea of her place in the world anymore. Everything about her life was unknown.

"Astrid should return from Thornewood soon," Shade interjected. "She will know more." His gaze went to Magnus. "Until then, we should move Harlow's timeline up to ensure she is in control of her magic as soon as possible."

Magnus nodded. "Agreed. We planned to start today." He held his hand out to Harlow. "We can still get some training in before lunch."

Harlow hesitated, not because of the thought of training. Touching her father seemed unreal to her. She'd always thought him dead and now here he was, this larger-than-life infamous mage.

Magnus' eyes softened. He didn't withdraw his hand, only waited as Harlow made up her mind. When she finally slipped her tiny hand in his, relief flashed over his face—there and gone in an instant.

Her father's power crackled against her palm, a warm, tingling feeling her magic responded to as if it recognized Magnus' blood. She allowed him to pull her to her feet and held on a moment longer than necessary before dropping her hand.

"Come," he said, his voice gruff. "I'll escort you to the training grounds." Magnus glanced at the others. "As long as that is all?"

Nova smiled. "We're finished. I'll send messages out and see if we can get a bigger picture of what's happening in Thornewood. Containing this corruption should be the first priority."

Magnus bowed his head and held the door open for Harlow. She trailed after him, glancing back at Bloom. The Seer normally looked pristine, the picture of health. Today, her tall frame slumped, and her mouth held tight lines of stress. Her eyes crinkled at the edges in a small smile, but Harlow knew it took an effort.

When the doors closed behind them, Harlow exhaled and shoved her hands in her pockets.

Magnus held an arm out. "Do not worry. Everything has a solution."

Harlow slid her hand over the crook in his arm and allowed him to lead her toward the training ring. Their conversation died, Harlow too tired to make an effort, and Magnus lost in his thoughts.

She had yet to explore the grounds, after keeping to her rooms in a state of pique. A feeling of shame stole over her, cheeks coloring with embarrassment at her behavior. All she could do now was move forward and try to be better. Harlow scrubbed a hand over her face and followed her father inside the dusty grounds, halting to gawk at the massive circular compound. Several people milled around in various states of practice, all sweaty and covered in dirt. No one paid them a lick of attention as they ventured further inside. The grounds were covered in a strange, pale-colored dirt. It looked familiar, but Harlow couldn't place where she'd seen it before. A large rack of weapons stood to her right. Swords, daggers, spears, shields, and other things she'd never seen before hung neatly on hooks. Her gaze dragged over them all, snagging on something at the bottom—a dull, dark-colored axe with an ebony wood handle. She took an involuntary step toward it.

Magnus spotted what she was looking at. "Shade trained you with an axe?" he inquired, a note of surprise in his voice.

She shook her head. "He insisted on daggers and swords, but Nova taught me a little."

His eyebrows lifted. Magnus jerked his head over to the rack. "Grab it if you like. I'm skilled with an axe, though I use it only when I'm desperate. Magicians should rely most on their power. Mundane weapons always come second. There's too much to go wrong in physical combat. If you can escape danger with magic, you should."

Harlow took a hesitant step toward the rack, her fingers outstretched. She missed her axe, but picking another one up felt like it might be a betrayal. Ridiculous, she knew, but still, Harlow couldn't bring herself to take it up.

Magnus reached over, snagged the axe from the hook, and wrapped her palm around the handle. "You're only borrowing it. That's all," he said quietly.

The heft of it was different. Her old axe weighed the perfect amount, the handle molded to her hand, worn dents where her fingers rested over and over again. This one was made for a man, her fingers unable to touch together as she held it. The blade was sharpened but pocked from age and use, perhaps a little rust, too, finely polished away.

Harlow nodded, her throat tight. Magnus unhooked his axe from his belt and jerked his head at her to follow. Several practice dummies littered the field, gouged and worn but still upright. She followed her father as he strode through the grounds, totally at ease in this kingdom, his posture loose and relaxed. How he did it, Harlow couldn't guess. Even in Thornewood, she kept her head down as best she could. Trouble sometimes found her, but she couldn't say she ever felt completely comfortable with her place in the world even when she was home. Only when she'd been with Nova— before the world had stepped in to complicate everything and uproot her life.

"I thought we were supposed to work on magic during

training." The axe brought back memories she didn't want to think about—of happier times and a place Harlow might never see again.

"We will," Magnus assured her. "Shade has told me about some of your Virago training, but he never had the opportunity to show you all that he can do." His eyes darkened. "The former queen would not allow it."

Her head jerked in surprise. "She wouldn't?"

A rueful smiled curved his lips. "No, Harlow. You'll find those in power do not like the people under them to have their own."

He stopped at a space toward the back of the grounds, mostly empty, but with two practice dummies on either side. "Here is a good enough spot as any," he murmured mostly to himself. Magnus scuffed a place in the earth with his worn boot and unhooked his belt from his hips. It fell to the ground with a thunk, and he nudged it away with his foot. He still held his axe. If Harlow saw him in the woods, she'd assume he was a carpenter, not the all-powerful being her father had become.

Magnus looked relaxed here—at peace, something Harlow had yet to feel or experience since she'd left her home. Perhaps it was never her home at all. Maybe this was where she was always meant to be, but the thought didn't sit right with her. If home was where your family was, why did she feel an itch between her shoulder blades and a whisper in her mind telling her this was not where she would end up when it was all over?

The thought of it sent a shiver down her spine. If she didn't belong with Nova, did she belong anywhere at all?

CHAPTER NINE

THE MAGIC OF AN AXE

Magnus motioned for her to come closer. Harlow dragged her feet, reluctantly following her father to face one of the practice dummies.

"Take your axe in hand," he commanded. "Since you have some skill, we'll begin with a one-handed throw." Magnus glanced down, his brows lifting as he waited for confirmation.

Harlow nodded.

"Good."

She took the axe in hand, grimacing at the foreign feel of it. Magnus put his hands over her hand and wrist, gently situating her position for the best strike. Muscle memory locked into place. "Show me," he said.

Harlow inhaled, squinting as she peered at the target. It wasn't too far away, but her skills were rusty. An uncomfortable feeling squirmed in her stomach. She wanted to impress him, show Magnus she had not idled her years away while he'd been doing...whatever he'd been doing. She squashed the feeling down, gripped the axe and held it above her ear. Magnus stepped away, watching keenly.

As soon as she threw it, she realized it was a poor throw. Harlow hit the target, but it was toward the bottom. Easily a miss for a nimble target.

Magnus nodded as he walked over to retrieve it. When he came back, he situated her again, his hands surprisingly gentle. This time, he lifted her arm a little higher.

"Don't tilt left or right." A smile hesitated over his lips. "You don't want to lose a precious ear on the throw."

Harlow didn't smile.

Magnus cleared his throat. "Initially, settle in by lifting your elbow a little higher than normal and loosen your grip. When you get ready to throw, ensure it's close to your shoulder, and only release when the grip is straight up and down. Clear?"

Harlow nodded, loosening her grip. She sank into her posture as Magnus stepped away, marking the area she wanted to hit in her mind. At her next inhale, she released on the exhale, flinging the axe in a steady motion.

It struck true, but not quite to the center of the target.

Magnus' eyes narrowed, but he didn't study the target. His attention was on Harlow, a thoughtful expression on his stoic face. She shifted, and Magnus dropped his gaze, turning on his heel to retrieve the axe.

"Again," he commanded, handing it back to her.

Her brows lifted. "Same way?"

"However you're comfortable," he said this time.

Confused, Harlow shrugged, but lifted the axe again and

assumed the same position. She threw on the exhale. This time the axe struck true center. A smile played over her lips.

Again, Magnus wasn't looking at the target.

"Is something wrong?" she asked.

Magnus said nothing, again retrieving the axe and handing it back to her. "Again."

Harlow blinked. He didn't sound angry. More perplexed. Which, of course, was making Harlow feel perplexed.

Again she threw. Again, the axe struck true.

A few people had gathered around after her last throw. Harlow glanced at them, an uneasy feeling growing in her stomach.

This time, Magnus moved the target several feet back from where it was. He handed the axe back and jerked his head at it.

Harlow said nothing, only adjusted a hair and threw the axe again.

True center.

Magnus snorted. He moved the target back again, this time so far back, Harlow's squint was true. A larger crowd gathered around them. Sweat trickled down her back, pooling at the waistband of her pants.

When he handed the axe back to her this time, she tilted her head and studied him. "What's this about?"

He ignored her, flicking his hand at the target. "Again."

"Magnus."

"A theory," he allowed, but would say nothing more.

Sighing, she shook her head, lined up her shot and threw it again.

Dead center.

And so it went, half a dozen more times until even Harlow began to understand the significance of what was occurring.

When the target was almost clear to the other side of the grounds, Harlow planted her feet and refused to do it again. "What is happening?" she whispered.

Magnus' eyes sparkled. "Your magic is responding to your desires. I've never seen it respond like this, but your power has long been crippled due to Thornewood."

Shock widened her eyes. "But I'm not using any!"

His chuckle angered her. Magnus waved a hand at the target. "Do you think anyone could do what you've done?"

Her arm felt like pudding, wiggly and gooey. "Yes," she said sullenly.

"No," someone from the audience called. A woman stepped forward, dressed all in black, her eyes flashing with curiosity. Evara.

Harlow sighed. "You," she growled.

Evara had the nerve to laugh. "Me." She bowed to Magnus. "Reflex, if I had to guess."

Her father nodded. "You've never done this with a sword?"

Harlow blinked. "I've never been in the habit of throwing my sword," she said slowly.

Magnus laughed. "Fair enough. Daggers?"

She shrugged. "I've always preferred the axe."

Evara and Magnus exchanged a look. "Perhaps we can remedy that," the warrior said.

Harlow shook her head. "No. I don't want this one. They feel...off in my hands."

Evara tilted her head. "And you still hit the target every time?"

Crimson colored Harlow's cheeks. "I wasn't aware I was doing anything."

Magnus reached for the axe. "I'll put it back. We are done for today, Harlow. Feel free to use the rest of the day to explore the grounds."

Without another look at Evara or her father, Harlow turned and walked away, the crowd parting before her. The feeling of stares made her skin feel itchy. She picked up speed, not daring to take a full breath until she'd gone into the tunnels back into the dressing areas.

Never one to feel comfortable with attention, Harlow found a quiet corner and sagged against the wall.

The magic hummed inside of her, content and stretching like a cat. Harlow harrumphed. "Happy with yourself, are you? Thanks a lot."

Her power didn't respond, but peace settled over her, the pressure she'd felt for weeks now easing just a little.

Perhaps this was what her father had meant when he encouraged her to release the magic before it overpowered her. A smile stole over her face. She'd used an axe. Even though the weapon she held wasn't comfortable, the heft and feel of the blade had felt like coming home.

She had no real money to speak of, but maybe her sister would consider commissioning one for her. It would take a while to pay her back, but Harlow would find a way. She always had.

Satisfied with the first real goal she'd had in a while,

Harlow pushed away from the wall and headed out into the cool afternoon air.

Going back to the castle sounded awful. Now that she'd stretched her muscles and ventured away, Harlow longed for a bit of exploring. She'd long lost track of the current day, but when she stepped into the square, it bustled with people. Men, women, and children dressed in a dazzling variety of colors and styles milled around. Some carried baskets, some held small velvet bags. Others pulled wheeled carts behind them, fruits, vegetables and perishables filling the attached wooden boxes. Most people wore smiles, expressions of peace Harlow hadn't seen much of in Thornewood.

Despite the anger she still held toward Nova, even Harlow had to admit she was a good ruler. Her people were prosperous and happy. There was no indication of poverty or hunger in the clean streets of the Shadow Kingdom. Vendors wore smiles as they hawked their wares, and Harlow didn't catch a single dealer price gouging.

She wished she had a little coin. The smell of baked goods in the air made her stomach growl. As she walked, she noticed a booth filled with golden brown pastries. Harlow walked closer, peering at the plethora of goodies. Multicolored fruit fillings marked one section. Raspberry, blueberry, something golden she couldn't identify, but all smelled of real butter and gleamed with toppings of shiny crystalline sugar.

"Would the princess like to sample something?" a sly voice said.

Harlow's head jerked up. She looked around, but Harlow was the only customer around. Princess?

"Oh no," Harlow said slowly. "I'm afraid I've brought no coin."

The dealer, a small woman with rosy cheeks snorted. "The queen's sister never pays at market, child. If you'd like to sample something, you'll take it with my pleasure."

Harlow blinked in surprise.

The woman's brow furrowed before a bright smile came over her face. "Och. You're a sweet, innocent one, aren't you?" She laughed and reached down, snagging one with a purple filling, and putting it into a small paper bag. "Besides, child," the woman said, "if someone sees the princess eating from my stall, I'll be smothered in customers before you're ten feet away." The vendor winked and pushed the pastry into her hand.

Harlow took it, unable to help herself from smiling back. The woman shooed her away. "Now go on with yourself and don't hide that bag! I have to prepare for the masses." She softened her words with a wink, and Harlow did as she asked, holding the bag up to where everyone could see it, not because she was heeding the woman's words, but because she couldn't resist biting into the pastry.

Flavor exploded in her mouth, the fruit both sweet and tart, caramelized sugar and flaky golden crust melding into something Harlow had never experienced. She swallowed down her groan and took another bite before she'd fully chewed the first one. When she looked back, three new customers had swarmed the dealer.

A happy smile broke over her face. She lifted her hand in a wave that the dealer saw but ignored and went on her way.

But Harlow didn't miss the dimple peeking out from the woman's cheek as their eyes met.

Happiness and contentment bubbled up inside Harlow, the surprise of it bringing tears to her eyes. Maybe the Shadow Kingdom wasn't so bad.

Finding a place here wouldn't be the worst thing, she supposed.

CHAPTER TEN

A MYSTERIOUS VENDOR

The pastry didn't last long, but it put a damper on the gnawing hunger she'd experienced since her training. She was tired, but in a different way than normal. Magic use, even if she didn't realize that's what she was doing until Magnus had told her, apparently used way more energy than normal physical exertion. Harlow made a mental note to remember that the next time she practiced with Magnus.

The kitchen normally kept extra oat and fruit bars on hands for warriors on practice day. She'd take some with her next time. Harlow still held the pastry bag in her hand. Or she'd explore more of the food vendors and experience more of their wares if they were all as good as this one had been.

Overhead, the sky still held the normal grayish of Nova's kingdom, a slight chill in the air that made Harlow glad she still wore her leather armor. Her hair held a fine, dewy mist, and curls escaped her braid, clinging to her forehead and temples. If she had to guess, she'd put the time at around two or three p.m. There was still plenty of time to explore, so

Harlow meandered through the marketplace, pausing to study things she'd never seen before and asking questions when she had the courage to.

Everyone was welcoming, perhaps overly so. They all recognized who she was, and all called her some form of princess. Harlow tried to correct them, but they all had given her a funny look and brushed her words away like she'd never spoken them. She'd have to ask Nova what was going on and ask her to correct them next time.

She was no princess and never would be. The thought of it made her chuckle, amusement filling her as a picture of her in a too heavy dress and a jewel encrusted crown formed in her mind, followed by her promptly tripping down the stairs and breaking her neck.

Morbid, but amusing, because Harlow in heels would never happen. Not if she had anything to say about it.

She passed by a cart manned by a lovely young woman with mysterious green eyes and dark hair covered by a stunning teal scarf, the occasional strand escaping as a soft wind blew. They locked eyes, and the woman motioned for Harlow over.

Unable to resist, Harlow moved toward her, eyes drawn to the offerings in the woman's cart. Stones of all shapes and sizes, some glittering, some dark, some round, and others oddly shaped. Her gaze swept past those, snagging on a display with a variety of wire wrapped necklaces, one catching her attention.

An iridescent white stone glimmered toward the back. Harlow's breath caught. Her fingers reached for it, gently flicking through the selection until she reached it. Magic pulsed against her palm as the stone brushed against her skin.

"Ah," the woman said. "You have discerning taste." A mysterious smile curved her lips, there and gone in a heartbeat. "Allow me," she said, brushing Harlow's hand away. With deft fingers, the woman unhooked the necklace and handed it to Harlow.

"How much?" she asked, knowing this would not be offered for free.

The woman studied Harlow, avarice and intellect warring within the depths of her emerald gaze. "The necklace is costly," she began. Harlow took a tiny step back.

"But not in coin," the woman rushed to say.

Harlow's brows narrowed with suspicion. The vendor held it out to Harlow, but she hesitated before taking it back. "If not in coin, then what?" Harlow asked, her tone mulish.

The woman laughed. "I am at this market once a month," she said. "Take the necklace for now. Come and see me in a turn of the moon and offer me something in exchange."

Harlow studied the woman. "Anything?"

She shrugged. "Anything you think would equal the value."

It seemed far too good to be true which made Harlow instantly wary. "I have nothing."

Not a lie. She might live in the castle, but nothing there belonged to her.

Something flashed in the woman's eyes. Sympathy, perhaps something deeper. "Ah," she said. "I do not mean monetary value."

Harlow glanced down at the wrapped stone, her stomach twisting. "I'm afraid I do not understand."

The woman reached over and squeezed Harlow's hand. "You will." A smile flashed over her mouth. "Take it. Come see me again. If you are not here in a month, I will come find you."

Harlow's mouth opened to protest, but the woman waved her away. With a thudding heart and an odd emotion unfurling in her belly, Harlow nodded and turned to walk away, tucking the necklace deep inside her pocket.

Not just any necklace.

One with a Luna stone nestled inside the silver wire cage.

Its magic thrummed against her hip the entire way back to the castle.

CHAPTER ELEVEN

A MEETING OF TWO QUEENS

S he'd taken to wandering the castle aimlessly, but as the days passed with no news and no change, Desminda began exploring, searching for any information she could use in an effort to win a better position than the one she had.

Today she'd ended up in the west wing, a place with winding halls and so many doors it made her head spin. Nothing was labeled, and every door she opened felt like walking into a new world. Only a quarter of them had been bedrooms, and fortunately she hadn't disturbed anyone's slumber...or other activities. She'd taken to knocking after one encounter with a shirtless, disgruntled man she'd never seen before.

Her cheeks still burned crimson over the encounter more than twenty minutes later.

The sounds of glass and silver tinkling and the low drone of conversation led her to explore further down the hall, turning a corner to stumble into an expansive kitchen. No one noticed her at first, allowing Desminda to drink her fill of the internal workings of some of Nova's staff.

Just when she was about to turn and leave, the sound of a delicate throat clearing snapped her spine straight. There was only one person with a voice like silver bells who could sound that imperious without saying a word.

Desminda stifled her sigh and ducked her head in a slight bow. She might not be the current queen, but she was still of royal blood. She'd bow to no one.

Nova glided toward her, dark hair spilling over her shoulders. A dusting of flour sprayed across her nose gave her a decidedly unqueenly, mischievous look. Her mother would never be in the kitchens, not to mention helping one of the staff roll out what looked to be sweet buns. The current queen wiped her hands on the apron tied over her blue grey dress. "Desminda," Nova said, "I'm surprised to see you here."

Desminda bristled at Nova's casual use of her first name. "Merely exploring. I grow weary of staying in my chambers."

Nova's eyes flashed at the intended slight. "You are a guest in my kingdom, welcome to go wherever your heart desires." A slight smile played over her lips. "And free to leave whenever you'd like."

The noise in the kitchen died abruptly at Nova's words, a blip in the activity that lasted only for a moment, as if everyone there was stunned to hear the queen say such a thing. Desminda bristled, color heating her cheeks once more.

Nova was well aware Desminda had not a single copper

to line her pockets. She'd taken some jewels from Thornewood, yes, but she wouldn't dream of exchanging them until her situation was so dire she had no choice.

"How could I leave such a hospitable place?" Desminda said, recovering quickly. This, too, was a game, like all politics. She'd never been thrust into a situation quite like this, but her mother, for all her flaws, had taught her how to play this game well. "Although I didn't expect such..." Desminda paused and rubbed her hands over her arms, "a dark, humid place."

One of the kitchen staff gasped at their polite verbal sparring.

"Ah yes," Nova said, not missing a beat. "Our climate can be trying for those of more...delicate constitutions."

Desminda's lips parted. Of all the—

"Excuse me," a man's dulcet tones interrupted. "How nice to see both of you together."

Shade came into view, amusement sparkling in his fathomless eyes. "Desminda," he said with a nod, "it's nice to see you out and about."

Even her loyal Commander had taken to the casual use of her given name. She blinked up at him, her feelings hurt, the sense of falling far from her once gloried station still foreign but painful.

"Are you interested in a pastry and some tea?" Nova offered Desminda. She'd taken an unconscious step toward Shade, seeming to bloom in his presence. Her cheeks flushed prettily, and Desminda wondered, not for the first time, if their interactions continued nocturnally.

She shoved down the feeling of wanting to shrivel up and die and smiled at Nova. "I would love that, yes."

Shade's eyes narrowed. Desminda didn't dare look at him. He knew her far too well, but was he still loyal to Thornewood or had he thrown his allegiance to this woman of darkness?

"Wonderful," Nova said. She turned and murmured something to a round woman with curly hair tied in a high bun. The woman's gaze slid to Desminda, a hostility brimming in their topaz depths reserved solely for the Thornewood queen.

Desminda never expected to make friends with these people, but even she hadn't been prepared for the depth of their dislike.

When the woman adjusted her skirts and walked away, Nova turned and smiled. "Shall we take this to the parlor?" she asked, motioning with a delicate hand.

Shade dipped his head. "After you," he said to Desminda.

With no option but to fall behind, Desminda turned and headed down the hall.

The tea, like everything else Nova served, was excellent. Black tea, with a hint of lemon and bergamot. Desminda inhaled the brew before having a sip. Delicate, painstakingly decorated lace cookies lay on the tray before her, neatly organized in piles of three—enough for everyone to have a few.

Desminda knew those would be delicious too.

Shade had taken a seat between them, one ankle crossed over his knee, his fingers steepled together. He'd changed since he'd left her kingdom. As much as Desminda hated to admit it, he looked better. The dark circles almost always present in Thornewood had disappeared. His complexion had filled out, and his hair was darker and shinier than before, even in the absence of continuous sunshine.

His smile was quicker and more sincere, and he had gained even more lean muscle, something Desminda wouldn't have thought possible before. Shade's skin was a dark gold, gleaming like burnished copper, even in the lower light.

The dusting of flour still graced Nova's face. Shade had noticed it, an amused smile curling his lips every time he looked at it.

Desminda never felt out of place. She was a queen. There was a place for her wherever she went, and everyone knew it.

Except...there wasn't. Not in this place of darkness and shadow.

She was a stranger here, a foreigner with no friends and no allies.

She'd never felt more out of place in her entire life.

They chattered for a while, inane small talk that served to do nothing more than to fill the silence. Shade was content to sit back and listen, his gaze occasionally straying to Nova, eyes softening every time he glanced at her.

Desminda's staunchest supporter had fallen in love. She'd stake her kingdom on it.

Her mother had always warned her against the foreign emotion. It will weaken your conviction, she'd said. Make you feel like you were going crazy. It could make you do things you never thought you would, throw everything away if only to feel the heat of someone's gaze for a moment more.

She always thought her mother seemed melodramatic but sitting here now with Shade's rapt attention on the young queen, she realized her mother had been right all along. Her thoughts strayed to the golden-haired Virago who'd all but refused to speak to her since they arrived. Desminda's heart twinged even as she knew it was for the best.

Harlow's infatuation had to die, the sooner the better. Desminda didn't need a lover or a friend. She needed a warrior, an army. She needed someone to walk alongside of her and take her kingdom back.

Love wouldn't save her life.

Fury wouldn't save her kingdom.

Cold hard steel would win the day, and if it didn't, then Desminda would win it back the same way women had won power for centuries.

She'd sell herself and her hand to get it, but she'd do it on her terms.

Nova said something Desminda missed. The saucer in her hand jerked, tea sloshing over the edges of the delicate teacup.

"I'm sorry," Desminda said, a sheepish smile on her face. "Sleep was long coming last night, and I'm afraid I'm my wits are less sharp than I mean to be." It was a lie. She'd slept like a baby since she'd arrived, which made her angry every time she woke up well rested and refreshed.

Nova smiled, but it didn't reach her eyes as if she could smell the untruth. "I was only asking what your plans are now that you've arrived."

Plans? Gain her kingdom back. Drive a dagger into that coward Lucien's heart. String his bitch sister up in the town square and show her kingdom who their true ruler was. An apologetic smile crossed her lips, also insincere. "Everything has been such a surprise since...Thornewood." Desminda allowed her fingers to tremble. Just a little. No need to seem overdramatic. "I'm afraid I haven't thought much of the future. Existing each day has been enough for now."

Nova studied her for a moment. "And your kingdom?"

"Queendom," Desminda snapped.

Nova's eyebrows lifted, her lips curving. Desminda wanted to curse at how cleverly she'd been caught. "I sense your passion," Nova continued. "Have you any thoughts about how to regain your throne?"

None she would share with an enemy, Desminda thought. "I'm afraid that's why I have Shade." The laugh she gave sounded false even to her ears. "He's always been our Chief Strategist, though we haven't had a true conflict for a long time."

Shade studied her, his face masked with careful blankness.

"I see," Nova said. "Peace is always hard earned, is it not?"

"It is," Desminda agreed. "I hope to bring it back to Thornewood as soon as Shade and I have some time to sit down and come up with a plan."

The queen's lips tightened at her words. Delight curled within Desminda at the tell. Nova did not like how possessive of Shade Desminda sounded. Love is weakness, she reminded herself. Nova herself had shown it in the short time they'd spent sipping tea.

"Is this something you truly desire?" Shade interjected.

Desminda started in surprise. "Securing Thornewood?" she asked in disbelief.

"Yes." Shade's dark gaze was unreadable.

The laugh bubbled from her before she could stop it. "What else would I desire?" Desminda breathed. "Thornewood is my home. It is mine by blood and right."

Nova stiffened. Desminda brushed the reaction off, anger fueling her words. "My family bled for our queendom, Shade. Why are you asking me such questions?"

Anger flashed in his dark eyes. "Your family bled?"

Desminda's brow furrowed. "You question this?"

"Your soldiers and your people bled for your lands," Shade said, fury lacing every clipped word. "*I* bled for Thornewood. Harlow and Bloom bled for Virago. You were led out like a sheltered wallflower, protected and coddled."

Nova's face darkened. Her recriminating look seared against Desminda's skin.

Desminda reared back, eyes wide at his words. "Shade, you cannot—"

Her once most loyal servant raised his hand, cutting her words off.

"You *dare*?" she seethed.

"You are no one's queen," Shade snapped. "Thornewood is out of our reach for now. If you wish to be queen of those lands again, there are several things you must do. First," he emphasized, "is to ensure you really want it."

Desminda gaped at him. "Of course I want it. How could you doubt—"

He interrupted again. "Second, you must gather allies to your side. My intelligence forces are splintered since the invasion. Celestine has brought her kingdom's armies in and combined them with ours. While Thornewood's numbers are lower than they were, do not expect any loyalty from them."

Desminda blinked.

Shade snorted. "They are paid servants, Desminda. The loyal ones have long fled the kingdom. Whether they search for us or for another to back, I do not yet know."

When he paused, Desminda opened her mouth to speak, but Shade barreled on. "And last, you must become a queen."

Desminda's brows drew together.

"A true queen," he emphasized. "I do not see one sitting before me today."

Tense silence fell in the room for a long moment. Shade had always been truthful, but Desminda finally realized he'd always tempered his words, coating them in a veneer of politeness and compliments.

He'd feared her in Thornewood. What she might do if he spoke his true heart. The thought sent something sharp twisting in her chest. Instead of lashing out like she wanted to, Desminda set her cup down, the saucer clicking against the glass table, and stood, smoothing her skirts around her hips. "Well." She cleared her throat. "If you will excuse me, I must see to a personal need." Desminda dipped her head to Nova. "Thank you for the tea, Your Majesty."

Nova's silver eyes were unreadable. "Would you like an escort back or do you prefer to continue *exploring*?" The emphasis Nova put on the word sent heat searing into Desminda's cheeks.

"I will escort myself," Desminda said stiffly, turning on her heel and exiting the room, the doors opening as if by magic. The two guards at each door carefully looked away as she swept past.

Desminda flinched when the doors boomed shut behind her.

CHAPTER TWELVE

THROWING DOWN THE GAUNTLET

Nova studied the one she loved, sensing the fine tension trembling through his lean frame.

"You were quite harsh with her," she mused, careful to keep any judgment out of her tone. She had no judgment for him. Shade had uttered nothing but truth, but had left any polish back in Thornewood, it seemed. "She is still young and untried." Even with the way her kingdom had fallen, Desminda was still treated with kid gloves.

Unlike Nova's own upbringing. She squashed those memories down, focusing on the man in front of her.

Shade reached forward and snatched a handful of cookies from the tray. "She is spoiled."

Nova snorted. "I do not disagree, though I must tell you most royals are." She tempered her words with a soft smile.

"You are not." His dark eyes held hers.

"We do things differently in the Shadow Kingdom," Nova said quietly.

"No." The light caught Shade's ebony hair when he

shook his head. "There were mitigating factors in your upbringing that have molded you in fire, Nova. You are not like other royals. I suspect you never have been."

"I am not flawless," she murmured.

"I did not say you were. You are a polished stone, honed against the crashing surf." Nova watched him bite into the cookie, desire thrumming through her at the simple motion and his words. He always knew the right words and the right combination to use them in.

"And you are an oak tree. Strong and mighty," she said quietly.

He held out a cookie. Nova leaned forward, biting into it. The crunch of caramelized sugar hit her tongue, and her eyes fluttered shut.

"Things are changing," Shade mused.

"That's the way of the world," Nova said with a smile, her eyes opening as she chewed. Shade's eyes on her, watching her throat work, felt like a brand.

"She has to become a tempered blade to make it through this," he mused.

Nova tilted her head. "Desminda or Harlow?"

"Both." He ran a hand through his hair. "Celestine is a snake, manipulative and cunning. Lucien..." He paused. "I can't figure out if he is a coward, or if something more resides inside him."

"He saved Harlow, did he not?" Nova took another cookie and dipped it into her tea.

Shade nodded. "At the risk of his own skin, but Celestine is unaware."

"Perhaps only brave when attention is directed elsewhere," Nova observed.

"Time will tell." Shade swallowed. He dropped his gaze and cleared his throat. "Nova."

Nova snorted and rose, her skirts falling to the floor with a heavy thud. "You keep trying to bring this up, and I refuse to listen to your self-recriminations," she said quietly.

"Another missive came," he said quietly. "Other kingdoms step up their efforts to gain your hand."

Nova stiffened, her hand stilling as she set the cookie on the edge of the tray. "Let them come," she said after a moment, her words light. "Let them come from all the foreign and domestic lands. They do not matter."

"Nova," Shade chided, "you are a powerful queen in a mighty kingdom brimming with magic. You can't possibly think to refuse—"

She didn't want to hear it. Not from the man she loved more than life itself. "I will refuse until my dying breath, Shade Montello." Nova straightened to her full height, even then still barely taller than Shade sitting down. "My hand is not for sale."

Shade's eyes softened. "You would punish your kingdom with your refusal?"

Nova gasped. "How dare you?" she seethed. "I belong to no man. And I thought you of all people would understand that."

"I possess no magic," Shade said, his voice trembling.

"Magic is not only supernatural power," Nova said, her words low and hard. "Magic is driving men to listen. Magic is strategy, cunning, bravery. There are many types of magic, and I will not settle for anything less than someone who accepts this." She bent over him, her hair brushing against his shoulders.

He reached up and brushed his fingers over her nose, the tips coming away white. "Nova," he whispered.

"Do not try to convince me to give my hand away again, Shade," she warned, pulling away from him and walking toward the door, her heart beating against her chest, the ever-present ache pulling against her ribcage.

This would all be for naught if he could not accept her choice. The thought of marrying someone else always sent her into a near panic. Now that Shade had come into her life, Nova would rather dive off a cliff than marry someone else.

She only had to make him see her sincerity.

And his worth.

CHAPTER THIRTEEN

THE ROT OF THORNEWOOD

Astrid swept the glamour across her shoulders, grunting with effort as the magic slipped through her fingers twice before it worked. Her brows knitted together at how difficult it was, but she shook her head and stepped into the crowd pushing toward the marketplace. A few odd things had happened since she'd returned to this place at Shade's behest.

Bards made great spies, and Astrid found herself enjoying it more than she thought she would. He'd sent her back with a fat coin purse and little instruction other than to watch and report back.

Nothing much had changed as far as its appearance, but there was a tension in Thornewood's citizens, a shift in the way everyone behaved. Astrid had never seen much happiness or laughter in its people, but there were always sporadic incidents. Even in an oppressed people, joy could be found. And she couldn't say its citizens were oppressed, not in the way other kingdoms suffered, but it was well known the former queen of Thornewood did not take kindly to criticism of her rule and would come down hard on anyone who dared test her.

This felt different. A frisson of nervousness ran through the marketplace. People held their children tighter, and their coin purses were tucked away into deep skirts or trousers.

Even if she wanted to, she wouldn't be able to filch a purse with the way everyone was acting. Or maybe she could, but it wasn't worth the risk these days. The back of her neck prickled as she walked, her boots silent on the cobblestones. The glamour disguised her lute and the blood red color of her hair, marking her as a traveler rather than a bard.

Even if Celestine's goal seemed to be the recovery of magic, Astrid wasn't comfortable revealing her true nature to a despot. She had yet to gain access to the castle. Celestine was even more paranoid than Desminda's mother, and that was saying something. Lucien was rarely seen, and Astrid had to get clever to catch him out, stepping up her surveillance until she finally figured out he came to the markets only on Tuesdays and only for an hour before he swept back into the castle unseen again until seven full days later.

Annoying is what it was, and it made her job four times as difficult.

Fortunately, today was Tuesday. She'd missed him last week, expecting him to shop and mill for more than an hour, but as soon as the clock struck, guards had surrounded the prince and swept him back to the castle.

Almost like he was a...prisoner.

Astrid frowned at the thought. Was that what he had

become? Imprisoned by his sister's false rule? Perhaps gaining his trust would come easier than she thought.

A flash of wine-red hair caught her eye. Astrid stepped quicker, navigating easily through the crowd until she came up behind Lucien's guards. It was the top of the hour. She had fifty minutes to find a way through his detail and whisper a meeting place to him.

And then she had to hope he was curious enough to show up.

A host of things could go wrong.

Astrid settled the glamour tighter around her shoulders, the magic pulling against her will like taffy. Odd. Lucien's steps were sure but slow. He meandered through the stalls, smiling at the citizens and vendors. The prince seemed better liked than his sister, though Astrid noticed conversation shriveled and died when he passed by.

The guard's gazes swept the crowds, their hands resting on the pommels of their swords. Thornewood's citizens had never turned violent, so why all the sudden caution? What had she missed?

Her steps faltered as magic pulsed and stuttered. The glamour shimmered around her, stretching and pulling against her will. She struggled to contain it, gasping with effort as she brought it under control. What in the world? Even when magic fell in this and some of the surrounding kingdoms, it still came easier to the bards. They'd lost some of their power, but it had never been so difficult to maintain a simple glamour.

A thread of concern strummed through her body. She tucked it away and focused her concentration on the prince, waiting for the moment the guards' focus slipped. Thornewood castle loomed in the distance, a stunning testament to the once powerful queen who ruled it. With her death and Desminda's absence, the castle's shine had dulled, the upkeep lessened now that Celestine held it.

Lucien finally stopped at a booth where a painfully stunning, dark-haired and green-eyed woman wearing a colorful headscarf called out and held up her wares—jewelry, colorful stones, and other knick-knacks. Nothing different from anything else she'd seen around the market. Lucien's guards split and took their places on either side of her booth. The woman's gaze flicked toward them for a brief moment before dismissing them and returning her attention to Lucien.

She smiled at him. "It's been some time since I've seen you, Prince."

Lucien dipped his head. "Many things require my attention inside the castle, Velmina."

Astrid's attention jerked to the woman. Her name...

She took a few steps closer, tugging her hood further to disguise her face from Lucien. Whether he'd seen her during the raids or with Harlow remained to be seen, but she wouldn't risk it now.

With a quick smile at the guards, who dismissed her as innocent almost immediately, Astrid rolled her eyes and stepped up beside Lucien. She didn't acknowledge him, merely bent to study the stones.

The two kept up their dialogue, though Velmina's tone carried more than a hint of flirtation. She dipped her head closer to Lucien. "Same place?" she whispered.

Lucien's gaze flicked to Astrid, but the bard pretended a

bright purple stone held her attention. He murmured an assent, so low the guards suspected nothing.

Velmina nodded, and Lucien swept away, his guards stepping up behind him. Moments later, he was lost in the crowd.

Astrid should have gone after him, but something about Velmina encouraged her to stay.

A thin, tanned hand reached out and slapped the stone out of her hand. "It's about time you got here," Velmina hissed.

Astrid blinked at the woman, eyes narrowed. She concentrated a thread of magic on the vendor until her vision peeled away the glamour clinging to Velmina. Still beautiful, green-eyed, and dark-haired, her beauty had blunted into something easier to look at.

"Velma," Astrid said bluntly. "Why am I not surprised?"

Velmina rolled her eyes at the nickname and tugged Astrid to the back of the booth. "Come. There are things you must see."

Astrid allowed herself to be pulled inside, enjoying the brief warmth of Velma's hand around her wrist before the other woman dropped it like it was diseased. Astrid snorted, settling into one of the soft chairs Velma had set up when she took a break from selling her cheap stones and accouterments. All a sham. Almost like the woman herself.

They had personal history. None of it good.

Velma had the personality of a thousand people. Great for a spying bard. Terrible for interpersonal relationships. Astrid had known her for years and still didn't feel like she knew anything about Velma at all. The woman in question kicked off her slippers and pulled a bottle of wine over, pouring them each a glass.

The wine would be excellent, Astrid knew. Velma did nothing by halves. The only thing cheap about her was the fake storefront she'd set up outside.

"What's your business with the prince?" Astrid asked after the first sip of wine.

White teeth flashed against Velma's tan skin. "Always so forward, Astrid." Velma clicked her tongue. "Can't two old friends enjoy a glass of wine together and catch up?"

"We aren't friends," Astrid drawled. "You insisted on that four years ago."

Velma rolled her eyes, tucking her feet underneath her as she curled onto one of the plush chairs.

Astrid's eyes strayed to the front of the cart. "Aren't you worried about thieves?"

Velma waved her hand. "Nothing out there is worth a copper to me. All gathered wild or stolen. I had one thing of value but gave it away to a girl in another kingdom." Her dimple flashed. "She's to meet me in a moon's time for a trade."

Astrid sighed. Nothing good ever came from Velma's trades. At least for the other person. She drained the wine glass and set it on the ornate glass table with a click. "Why am I here?"

Velma's expression grew serious. "We may have history, Astrid, but we both want the same thing for our people."

She didn't dispute it. The bards all wanted magic returned, and all were currently working to achieve that goal, including Velma. Every bard had a unique skill set. Astrid possessed a remarkable sensitivity to magic, which is why she'd traveled to Thornewood in the first place. She had a sense something powerful and potentially world shattering resided in this kingdom and ended up finding Harlow.

How it would all turn out was up to the fates, but that was why she'd ensured Bloom stuck around, too. Astrid had a feeling about her as well.

She offered a short nod to Velma. With magic stifled, the land suffered. Humans and most partial to magic wouldn't notice, but bards were attuned to the earth and all its creatures. Thornewood was slowly dying and had been from the moment magic blinked out.

Velma reached beneath her feet and pulled out a box. Astrid recoiled, shoving the chair back and rising to her feet. Darkness seeped from the seams, sharp and pointed insidiousness.

"Hold," Velma said quietly. "I had to glamour the box to keep the guards from finding it. We only have a few moments before they come sniffing around for it."

Astrid's eyes snapped to Velma. "How do they sense it if they are without magic?"

Velma's eyes darkened. "I cannot say. These guards are not from Thornewood, and they are..." She paused and exhaled. "Off. They cannot sense the Luna stones, but they can sense this. Whatever this is. I believe the same thing infecting the stones is beginning to influence some of Thornewood's people."

Astrid came closer to Velma who opened the box. Three gleaming Luna stones sat nestled on a bed of royal purple silk. But that wasn't what caught her eye. Veins of ebony black darkness pierced the stones' gleaming iridescence, pulsing with corruption. Where the darkness touched, the stones flaked away, leaving behind a shiny, obsidian finish.

Astrid reared back. "What—" She cleared her throat. "What is it?"

Velma snapped the box shut, murmured a few words, and shielded the box in a new glamour. The choking malevolence lessened, allowing Astrid to take a full breath once more.

"Something is corrupting the stones." Velma's voice was hushed and serious, her eyes darting to the front of the cart to ensure no one listened.

"Celestine?" Astrid questioned.

Velma shook her head once. Her lips twisted. "I can't say. It doesn't feel like it. Whatever this is feels almost other-worldly." She shuddered and slid the box underneath her once more.

Astrid didn't want to touch the corruption, but sometimes her gift worked better when she did. From the brief glance Velma had given her, Astrid knew whatever it was would spread and might even be able to communicate. Now that she'd felt it, she sensed the same thing, on a much grander scale, coming from inside Thornewood castle.

Astrid exhaled, sinking back into the seat she'd pushed away.

Velma leaned forward. "That's not all. Meet me tonight, and I will explain more." She whispered a location and rose, adjusting her brightly colored caftan around her and read-justing her glamour. "Be there," she hissed. "Show yourself out the back."

Velma slapped a smile on her face and headed back to the

front of her cart, greeting a man and woman who'd come up to the booth and peered in.

Astrid sat there for a long moment, her thoughts whirling with the revelation. If she ventured closer to the castle, she might be able to gauge how bad the corruption was. Whether they could burn it out remained to be seen.

The sounds of Velma haggling with the two hapless customers made her snort. Astrid rose, her bright gaze sweeping through the back of Velma's quarters. With a smug smile, she snatched two of Velma's higher quality wines and tucked them inside her cloak before vanishing through the back door and into the marketplace once more.

CHAPTER FOURTEEN

A SURPRISE & A WARNING

Dusk fell several hours later allowing Astrid freer rein around the square. Most of the shops had closed, but a few still had customers milling around. One such cart smelled of something fried, and Astrid turned to it almost as if she were in a trance. It had been hours since she'd eaten, and Velma's wine had long soured in her stomach.

A man with a round face and a bright smile greeted her.

"What do you have left?" Astrid asked, digging in her coin pouch, deft fingers searching for a coin of small denomination.

"Fried venison and an elephant ear," the man said, his eyes taking in her curled red hair and glamour-dulled green eyes.

"I'll take one of each." She hesitated. "Though I admit, I don't actually want to eat an elephant's ear. What is it?"

The man laughed. "No need to worry. It's a pastry my wife came up with–fried dough smothered in wildflower honey and cinnamon."

"Oh," she breathed. "Do you have two then?"

"Two coming up and a stick of venison?"

"That will do." She pressed two coins on top of the cart—enough to pay for her meal and a little extra for the kind vendor—then stepped to the side to wait for her food.

Peace stole over Astrid as she watched the vendor greet several people in line with smiles and hearty hellos. She'd rarely felt peace since the moment magic had been ripped out from underneath them. While they still had power, they were all diminished, even when the bards left this kingdom and traveled to other faraway places. The queen's command had done something to the land, Magnus indirectly responsible for his spell.

Astrid knew he had no choice, but it didn't negate the fact that every day the spell went on was one more day the land, and its keepers, the bards, suffered.

Divulging their suffering would give too many of their precious secrets away, so Astrid and others of her kind worked every single day since the fall to restore balance to the land and its people. One day she would experience peace again, and on that day, she would go home, to the land of her people, and never leave again.

Astrid's senses sang with delight at the first bite of the fried venison. The meat was crisp, tender, and juicy. Her stomach growled with each bite until finally settling, content like a cat. She sighed and sat back against the tree trunk, reaching for the elephant ears. Her eyes might have been larger than her stomach, but she planned to finish off as much as she could before meeting Velma.

Bards ate and slept when they could, and from the foreboding feeling rising through her veins, Astrid suspected it might be a long time before she had such respite again. She ate every bit of the pastry, and when she was finished, Astrid leaned her head back and let her eyes drift shut.

Just for a moment.

The world swayed underneath her—a jarring, rocking motion, and for a moment, Astrid thought she might be back on the ship that took her from her homeland to here. Her eyes flew open, heart pounding as sharp screams rang out through the town. Senses dulled with sleep, Astrid staggered to her feet, lurching as the earth bucked and jarred below her.

Long shadows fell over Thornewood, the time when the first sun had long set and the second was not far behind, leaving just enough light to wander by. But the shadows jumped and swayed along with the world, long furrows opening in the ground, and people scrambled to get out of harm's way.

A muttered curse exploded from her as she stumbled away from the tree at the edge of the market and further into the forest, running as fast as she could to reach Velma. Trees cracked and crashed behind her, disturbing dead leaves and foliage and sent it up into the sky in a whirlwind of debris. Astrid drew her cloak over her face, keeping her eyes on the ground and slightly in front of her as she moved.

As soon as it had happened, it stopped, the only sound the snapping of limbs and trunks as the forest finished falling behind her.

She came to a staggering stop, turning in one swift motion to look behind her before she fell to the ground. A trail of destruction lay before her, dozens of trees upended, their trunks pushed up and spilling from the ground. No birds chittered, no snakes whispered, no woodland creatures rummaged.

The world was still as death.

Astrid's breath tore from her chest ragged and irregular. Crouching, she shoved both hands into the earth, fingers first, sending her senses through roots and mud and dirt, and the long-discarded carcasses of creatures passed long ago.

There. A thread of darkness pulsing into the heart of the world. She sent a tendril of magic toward it, seeking and questing. When she got close to it, she hesitated, instead choosing to circle around it, investigating it without touching.

It was the same corruption Velma had found, a rotting, pulsing thing of malevolence, sent only to destroy. Everywhere it touched, the earth perished, similar to someone upending a massive load of salt onto fertile farmland. New green roots shriveled and died, the loamy soil turned into hard crusted sand, shattering like glass as the magic passed through.

But then, it stopped, the magic still, but throbbing like a heartbeat. Astrid froze, heart beating like a rabbit. She was vulnerable right now, as all bards were when they communed with the world, and though the magic was far away from her location, she'd allowed her own to gather too close to the foreign entity.

Sucking in a breath, Astrid retreated, pulling her magic back to her as fast as she could. The magic lunged, sentient and hungry, and Astrid just barely snapped back into herself before it caught her. She scrambled to her feet, limbs tangling together. Astrid caught herself, twisted, and hurtled away from the power and straight into the heart of the forest where she hoped Velma and whatever dark surprises awaited her still stood.

By the time Astrid made it to the meeting point, she was covered in a fine sheen of sweat made of fear and exertion. Her cloak had long fallen from her face, red hair streaming away from her like a bloody ribbon.

Velma stood alone on an outcropping overlooking the castle. Wind whipped her dark hair into a wild tangle. A pang of heartache struck Astrid as she watched her. There would never be another beginning for them. Only an end.

A branch snapped as Astrid stepped out from behind the tree cover.

Velma turned, lips twitching when she spotted her. "You did that on purpose," she said with a smile. "Astrid the famous bard would never alert someone to her presence."

Astrid *had* done it on purpose. Velma's senses weren't as honed as her own, and she'd startled the other bard numerous times in the past. She shrugged off the memory and focused on Velma, ignoring the warmth in her tone. "What do you want to show me?" Astrid turned in a circle. "And where is the prince?"

Velma's eyes flashed with annoyance, but she turned and beckoned Astrid forward. "He claimed other obligations a little while ago." She shook her head and pointed in the direction of the castle. "You can only see it from this angle, and only from this high up. The false queen has gone to great lengths to conceal this from her people."

Fear shivered within Astrid. For a moment, she longed to turn and go, return to the Shadow Kingdom and live out her days there. Weariness crept through her bones, a soft sigh escaping her as she settled next to Velma. Her eyes scanned the back of the castle, frowning as nothing revealed itself. Just as her lips parted to question Velma, a sparkle of ebony glitter caught her eye.

Astrid's jaw snapped shut.

"There," Velma breathed, fingers extending toward the darkness. "Do you see it?"

Astrid wasn't sure what she was seeing, only that whatever it was shouldn't be there. She nodded, creeping forward to try to get a closer look.

Velma gripped her arm. "No. It's...aware." Fear trembled in her voice. Astrid's attention snapped to her.

"Aware?" But she wasn't surprised. The entity she'd encountered a little while before was the same, but she had been much closer. If they were this far away...

"What does it do?" Astrid asked.

Velma frowned. "I've never stayed around long enough to find out," she said dryly.

Astrid snorted. "Fair enough."

The castle backed up to the Thornewilde mountains, a place the bards had long suspected of hosting the vast majority of the Luna stones. For one person to hold such power was untenable, but no solution had ever shown itself besides flat out war.

Perhaps that's what it had come to now.

The thought should have unsettled Astrid more. Instead, a sense of rightness filled her, a knowing that while the bards employed peace in most of their dealings, sometimes war was unavoidable. Tyrants had to be dealt with like an infestation. A total cleansing and burning.

If they had to wipe out Celestine's entire bloodline...well, if it brought magic back into balance and ended this, it would be done.

Astrid would do everything in her power to make it so.

Her gaze drifted back to the glittering darkness seeping up the mountain, winding its insidious corruption through the Luna stones and poisoning their magic supply. Soon, Celestine would no longer be able to hide it. Even if the rot never revealed itself from here, there were too many things going on for people not to pick up on it. The earthquake from before had to make people nervous. Superstition drove villagers, sometimes in dangerous ways.

She'd need to find an alternate path from the kingdom tonight. With magic faultier than normal and her prior difficulties with maintaining her glamour, she couldn't risk being spotted in the town square. The presence of a bard marked change and upheaval.

In the past, towns welcomed them as harbingers of progress, messengers of goodwill and hope.

These days, their presence marked yet another thing no one wanted to face.

"What can we do?" Velma asked, her gaze trained on the same place Astrid's was.

"We call in the others," Astrid said, her tone grim. "I must leave tonight."

Velma snapped her head to Astrid. "Leave?" she blurted. "Why? The problem is here, Astrid, not in any of those small towns you so enjoy frequenting."

The nastiness in Velma's tone wasn't a surprise. Astrid's long absences were one of the many things to tear them apart. She could never understand why Astrid never settled in one place. Astrid couldn't explain it herself. Something kept her moving, kept her traveling from place to place, always searching for something she couldn't define. She had never been lost, not quite, but the world had a pull on her and had since magic fell—tugging, pulling, beseeching her to travel far and wide, searching for something she couldn't explain.

Was it this? This final piece of the Luna puzzle? Astrid didn't answer Velma for a long moment, her eyes still trained on the mountains. "Magic pulls me," she said after a long silence. "Every time I think about settling down, it tugs me to a new place, a new puzzle." This last time she felt it, the power led her to Harlow. And now, to this.

Velma scoffed. "Magic pulls nothing."

Astrid's faint smile sent color pooling in Velma's cheeks. They'd had this argument dozens of times. Astrid always insisted magic was alive. Velma insisted while it might respond to a mage's ability, the mage ultimately controlled it.

Astrid knew without a shadow of a doubt Velma was wrong. "We all have different abilities," she allowed, to spare the other bard's feelings. "Magic responds to all of us in different ways."

Velma crossed her arms over her chest. "Then leave, Astrid," she snapped. "Leave and let this kingdom fall."

Astrid snorted and gathered her cloak around her, concealing her dirty hair and face. "This kingdom will fall regardless of whether I stay or go. If you were wise, you'd leave this place and not return."

Velma paled, her lips parting in surprise.

Astrid didn't wait for Velma to ask any more questions. With her glamour pulled tightly against her skin, every tug of magic like gritting teeth to control, she strode back through the forest, away from her former lover and to the Shadow Kingdom to warn them all.

CHAPTER FIFTEEN

DEATH OF THE VIRAGO

D aylight still streamed glowing fingers over the horizon. Astrid crept through the forest, away from Velma, but not yet on her way back to Harlow. There was one more thing she had to see. Taking the long way around, Astrid pulled her cloak of invisibility tight against her skin and moved to the training grounds. Celestine had kept the remaining Virago, the ones who hadn't perished in the wilds of the forest, but there were rumors the women were disgruntled and displeased with their new leadership.

Not that Astrid would trust any of them after what they'd done, but one of them in particular was still missing. One who had not been involved in the uprising. Melara was too smart to be back here, but if Celestine had caught her during the escape, it was possible they'd taken her back here. Or worse.

On silent feet, she slipped through the new guard, none of them familiar from the former Kingsguard. They noticed nothing amiss, none of them even slightly sensitive to magic.

Just the way Celestine wanted it. The less she had to share, the better.

Seven girls stood in the training ring, their leather armor cracked and worn. A few looked familiar, but one stood out the most.

Kalen, if she remembered correctly.

Astrid crept closer, careful to keep her footsteps light and her glamour tight around her. The girls stood in a line formation, swords held lightly at their sides. Kalen stood in front of them, her gaze sweeping the motley crew. "We are behind on our training. Celestine requires us to practice four times a week."

"In addition to everything else she has us doing?" one of the girls from the middle snapped.

Kalen's lips thinned. "This is what you asked for," the girl said lightly. "A new way. Pity it isn't the way you wanted."

The other girls shifted, one looking away, eyes shining with tears.

The sun highlighted her profile, gleaming against the pale cream of her skin.

And the veins of corruption shooting from her chin to her temple.

Astrid gasped, taking an involuntary step back.

Kalen was the only one to hear it. The girl's eyes focused in Astrid's direction, a faint furrow on her brow. Quiet as a mouse, Astrid stood, not daring to move until Kalen looked away.

This one was sensitive to magic, and Astrid would bet Kalen kept that tidbit to herself.

When Kalen's attention redirected to the last of the

Virago, Astrid crept around the ring, her focus on each and every one of the girls. Half bore marks of corruption, dark, gleaming veins pulsing with their skin.

There was, however, no sign of Melara. Relieved, but also worried, Astrid took a few steps away, settling onto a pair of rocks to watch the training session.

For all her faults, Kalen was a good leader, but even she couldn't suppress her disgust at the girls' obvious exposure to the rot. What Astrid didn't think Kalen saw was the power lending extra oomph to the strikes against the practice dummies.

It was almost like it was responding to their needs and their desires. Why wasn't it attacking them like it had Astrid?

Frowning, she watched for a few more minutes and was about to stand when Kalen called a halt to training, dismissing every girl in the ring. She stayed behind her eyes trailing over the area where Astrid sat.

Curious, Astrid waited.

"I know you're there," Kalen said quietly. "Who are you?"

"Come closer and I'll show you," Astrid said in a teasing voice.

Kalen frowned. "If you're looking for Harlow, she is long gone."

Astrid snorted. "And why would I be looking for her?"

"Everyone strange who comes here seeks the Heir of Magic," Kalen said with a sigh.

Intrigued, Astrid stood, allowing her footsteps to make noise. "Everyone strange?" she inquired.

Kalen nodded. "At least three people have come since her absence."

"Walk with me," Astrid commanded.

The Virago laughed. "I am not so inclined to lose my life today, stranger."

"I am no stranger," Astrid said quietly. "I am the one who first came for Harlow."

Kalen stilled. "You are the bard."

Astrid halted. How had she known? "Who knew of my presence?" she demanded.

Kalen snorted. "Celestine knows far more than you think, bard." Her voice lowered. "She holds more power than she should."

"Come," Astrid said again, her voice quiet. "You will come to no harm with me."

Kalen looked around before offering a short nod. "I do not have much time. Celestine will expect me within the hour."

"It will take far less than an hour," Astrid said. She allowed Kalen to lead her out of the training area toward the back of the castle, the forest offering cover and privacy.

"Why have you returned?" Kalen asked when they were both sure they had not been followed.

"Intel," Astrid said. If Celestine already knew she was here, there was no reason to hide her reason from Kalen. The liar queen would already expect spies to have infiltrated her court, especially with Shade's absence. The man had no weakness she could see, unless you counted the Shadow Queen, and Astrid wouldn't exactly call her a weakness. She held more power in her veins than most people Astrid had ever met.

Except for Harlow.

The thought made her shift uncomfortably. All they could hope was Harlow learned how to deal with the power simmering in her veins before the darkness creeping their way affected all of them.

"Harlow is alive then?" Kalen inquired.

Astrid's lips curved, though Kalen couldn't see her. While she had no plans to harm Kalen, dropping her cloak would give Kalen far more information than she planned to give. When she didn't answer, Kalen quietly snorted.

"I hold no loyalty to Celestine," she insisted. "I am here for my Virago and no other reason."

"Most of your Virago are lost," Astrid observed, "corrupted by the force growing inside the castle."

Kalen stiffened. "You've seen it?"

Surprised, Astrid studied the Virago. "You have not?"

Kalen turned away. "Celestine allows no one within the royal wings. Not even guards." She stiffened when she realized how much intel she'd given Astrid. Intel the bard could use to her advantage when it came time to take Celestine out.

"So she's hiding something."

Kalen's laugh was bitter. "That woman is always hiding something. She's two steps ahead of everyone and I can't figure out how she does it."

"Perhaps she's a Seer," Astrid mused. Even with magic fallen, Bloom held onto some of her powers.

Kalen's eyes flickered. "I don't think that's it. She's never revealed to anyone what her powers are, but I've never seen any indication of precognition."

If Celestine were a Seer, it would be difficult to hide. Of course, Bloom had lived among the Virago and kept her power hidden, but it wasn't all that hard to do with how little magic trickled through the world, and her mother had trained her for years on how to stay hidden and keep her power secret. Seers didn't often come from the Kingdom of Roses, but it wasn't out of the realm of possibility. Tucking that tidbit away for further research, Astrid pressed Kalen.

She still needed to see Lucien. The magic pressed this need against her and had for a while, but getting close to him was turning out to be impossible.

"Tell me where I can find the prince."

Kalen laughed again and shook her head. "No one sees the prince without Celestine's permission."

Astrid allowed a little of her face to show through her glamour. "She won't know I am there, Kalen. I need to speak with Lucien in all haste."

The Virago leaned against a white barked tree, a strand of dark hair falling onto her forehead. She was pretty, even with circles of exhaustion darkening the undersides of her eyes. When Kalen didn't answer, Astrid tried another tack. "Why aren't you affected?"

Kalen's eyes flicked to hers. "By the rot?"

Astrid made a mmmm noise.

"I am not loyal to Celestine," Kalen said, a laugh cracking through the trees. "It doesn't actively attack me because I do nothing disloyal."

Astrid blinked. "And yet you stand here with me in a copse of trees?"

Kalen sighed. "This is, strangely, the only place free of corruption inside of the castle grounds. I do not know why, but there is power here, deep-seated into the earth. Almost as if someone knew what would happen and protected this area for someone who might sense it."

Astrid frowned. She'd been distracted by Kalen and hadn't probed the area. Tentatively, she sent her senses to the earth, touching the surface at first, before allowing a trickle of power to seep lower.

Kalen was right.

This area *was* protected by strong magic. "How do you know this?" she asked Kalen.

The Virago shrugged. "I'm sensitive to magic, I suppose." She said nothing further.

"You sensed me," Astrid said quietly. "You've known about the corruption far longer than anyone else, haven't you?"

"I've done awful things in my time here," Kalen whispered. "Things I'll never be able to forgive myself for. But I will never be able to forgive myself if this...darkness takes over Desminda's people. My people."

"And now you try to be a hero," Astrid said dryly.

Kalen scoffed. "I've never been a hero, bard. Only a survivor. Celestine suspects and always has suspected I'm not as loyal as I should be, but I remain uncorrupted, and Celestine is unsure of what it means. She keeps me around because she's curious."

"Curiosity is never good," Astrid muttered.

"Not when it involves Celestine." She sighed. "Lucien travels to the gardens in the evenings, right when the sun goes down. The corruption lurks there, so it might be impossible to reach him without it sensing you."

"It didn't sense me on the training grounds," Astrid remarked. In fact, it only sensed her when she reached out with her power. She'd need to investigate further.

"Whatever it is, it's sentient. And multiplying." Kalen rubbed a hand over her face. "You say my Virago are lost?"

"They no longer hold loyalty to you," Astrid said. "Their loyalty remains with Celestine and will stay that way until they are cleansed."

"Cleansed?" Kalen inquired. "How does one cleanse another if we don't know what it is that has invaded them?"

Fire, for one, but Astrid held her tongue. "I suspect you know, little mage."

Tears shimmered in Kalen's eyes. "I risked everything to keep them safe, and you tell me it has all been for naught?"

"Nothing is ever for naught." She settled on the ground a few feet away. "It will always lead you to the right path."

Kalen stared in her direction, a look of incredulity on her face. "I followed the path I was meant to take, and it has led me to nothing but despair. There is no other path for me. If I try to leave, I will be hunted. If not by Celestine, then by whatever this is lingering in the heart of this castle."

"If you move swift enough, the power will not catch you."

Kalen's lips thinned. "And how would you know?"

Astrid grinned. "Because I outran it."

CHAPTER SIXTEEN

A ROSE-COLORED MEETING

E ven Astrid had to admit Lucien cut a striking figure sitting amongst the pale white and pink flowers of the queen's former gardens. Celestine, for all her faults, had ensured they'd been kept up to standards. Every vine and stem bloomed heavy with scented flowers, a riot of pale perfection.

Mixed scents of jasmine and lilies, roses and verbena, drifted over to her, and Astrid inhaled, a smile curling her lips. Strange to find a place of peace in a kingdom of pain.

The prince sat stiff-backed, brilliant green eyes roaming over the lands as if searching for something he was sure he'd never find. His lips were pressed tight, and his jaw clenched, fists pressing against the seam of his fine cut breeches.

The Prince of Thorns was unhappy. Unbearably so. Astrid didn't need her magic to tell her so. A strange tug pulled inside of her stomach, a whisper of a thought so insane, Astrid almost gasped out loud.

Suicide, she thought. *What you are asking of me will bring certain death to me and anyone else involved.*

Magic never spoke back to her. She wished it would sometimes, if only for her to deliver the blistering lecture it needed.

She'd used her strongest glamour spell for this incursion, wrapping it around her so tight it felt like a second skin. A slippery second skin with the way magic was reacting to her, like a fish trying to wiggle away from her.

However, even though the corruption lurked around the garden, its touch evident in the blackening stems of some of the roses, it did not touch her, nor did it seem curious like it had last time. If her glamour fell, Astrid would be in peril, but she couldn't think that way.

It would hold.

It had to.

She crept closer to the prince.

"You've been following me," Lucien said mildly, his voice so low it was almost a whisper.

Astrid froze.

Inside the palace grounds, his guards kept a wider berth. Still alert but not as watchful.

Foolish.

"You smell of roses, bard." Lucien allowed a small smile to curl his lips. "The flower of my homelands. But not quite. Your scent is a rare rose, one I have not been able to cultivate successfully, even in the fertile soils of the Rose Kingdom."

Intrigued in spite of herself, she moved closer.

"It's called the Anais Rose. Pale orange and white in color, with multiple petals. Much like a peony." He inhaled deeply. "The scent is unexplainable. Like honey and jasmine and lotus all mixed together. It's proven impossible to grow anywhere except for the soil of a kingdom weeks away from here. Perhaps months." He lifted a shoulder in a shrug. "I've tried multiple times and have squandered many cuttings in my efforts. Perhaps it senses the despair in my blood and refuses to root for a coward such as I."

Astrid stood so close she could reach out and touch his shoulder.

"Are you here to kill me then?" He chuckled. "It seems fitting I should die at the hands of one who smells like one of my greatest personal failures."

"I would think a greater failure is your presence here, under the thumb of your sister."

His lips twitched. "Yes, though I count the rose as second."

Lucien's tone was droll and a little sad.

"You didn't answer my question," he said.

There had been many times in Astrid's life when a path appeared in front of her, forked into more than one direction. She'd never been so fortunate as to have a blinking arrow highlighting which path to take, but she saw just enough to show her the immediate outcome if she took one over the other.

It happened now, two shining roads ahead over her. One dark. One light.

But darkness didn't always mean failure. Every night ended with the day. In sunlight, one could see destruction, despair, hopelessness laid bare.

In the dark, if one were very lucky, one could see the stars.

With trembling fingers, Astrid allowed her glamour to drop and lowered her cloak.

Shouts of the guards rang out. The corruption rotting the earth woke up and turned its attention to her.

Lucien swore, his eyes widening when he saw her. "You must leave immediately," he hissed.

Astrid shook her head and held out her hand. "Your sister plans to execute you tonight, Prince. You will not escape it if you stay here."

Lucien sucked in a breath, his eyes wide. "We won't make it out of here alive," he hissed. But he eyed her open hand with the look of a drowning man.

"I am a bard, Lucien." A smile spread across her face. "The original magician."

The prince took her hand.

Astrid swept an arm around his waist, pressing herself close to his body. "Hold on," she whispered in his ear.

With a jerk, Astrid *tugged*.

And the magic, sated and happy with her decision to save the errant Prince of Roses, obeyed.

Once they made it out of the castle grounds and into safe territory, Lucien quiet as a mouse behind her, Astrid dropped their cloaking.

The prince's pale complexion had turned chalk white sometime during the white-knuckled ride. To his credit, he did whatever Astrid told him to do and questioned nothing. For all his faults, Lucien had a rock-solid sense of self-preservation, a trait he and Astrid shared.

She slid off the horse and held out a hand to the prince. He looked at it, a dour expression on his face, and snorted, sliding down after her.

Lucien lurched and swayed, throwing out a hand to steady himself. Astrid didn't offer further help, sensing his pride would be wounded if she did. While he regained his composure, she stretched, first her legs and then her neck, working out the tightness from the last few hours.

The ride had been tense and quiet between them, Astrid struggling to hold onto the magic as they rode deeper into the Thornewilde Forest and Lucien rigid and stiff behind her, neck craned over his shoulder as he searched the woods for pursuers. The prince had acted a coward for a long time. Astrid hoped once he realized what was at stake and what they could all have if they worked together, Lucien would come around.

Otherwise, rescuing him would be a great waste of her time, magic, and resources.

When the prince straightened, he exhaled a long breath. "I can't believe we made it out." His voice was tinged with awe, eyes wide as he looked around at the dense canopy of trees above them.

They stood about an hour outside of the castle grounds, still in the thick of the forest. Soft loam and brush squished against her boots as she walked around, checking to ensure they were completely alone, no presence except the critters and creatures watching through the hidden cover of the trees.

"You have never been in the presence of a bard then, prince," Astrid said mildly.

Lucien snorted. "Our kingdom thought your kind died out long ago."

A pang shot through her heart. "It wasn't for lack of trying. We've been hunted ever since magic's fall."

Silence fell for a moment. "I'm glad they failed," Lucien said quietly.

She stared at him. Golden light sparked against his wine-red hair and his pale skin, highlighting his profile with soft luminescence. He was handsome in the way a god was, untouchable and aloof. But Astrid felt the loneliness inside of him, the desire to reach out and clasp something or someone to him if only to allow him to feel for a moment.

"To get us to this moment? So I could save your life?" she asked. Astrid wasn't sure why she said it. It felt unfair, but she couldn't help it. Harlow had told her Lucien had twice stepped in to save her, so Lucien wasn't always a coward when it counted.

A faint smile appeared on his lips. "To save us all, I think." He glanced toward her, brilliant green eyes studying her in a way that made her feel bare. "What do you plan to do with me?"

Astrid sighed and plunked down to the forest floor, leaning against a tree. Her face tilted up to study him. "I suppose I could kill you."

A laugh cracked from Lucien. "I suppose you could, but saving me would have been a grand waste of time then, wouldn't it?"

"Time will tell about that," Astrid muttered.

Lucien patted the horse and stepped out of its path,

lowering himself to the ground. He sighed and dropped his head in his hands. "Why did you get me out?"

Astrid had no plans to tell him because magic told her so. "I'm not sure." The call to save him had felt so urgent, Lucien had to be important in the grand scheme of things. How it would play out was anyone's guess.

"We can only stay for a few more minutes," Astrid said, uncomfortable with Lucien's perusal. "It is a long way to our destination."

Lucien made a noncommittal noise and fumbled through the pocket of his vest, pulling out a small slice of jerky.

Typical prince. He didn't offer any to Astrid.

With a soft laugh, Astrid focused her attention inward, gently reading the earth to better plan their route. She wasn't hungry anyway, and they had a lot of road to cover before they reached the Shadow Kingdom.

CHAPTER SEVENTEEN

COURT ETIQUETTE. OR SOMETHING

Desminda stared at Harlow, ill-concealed impatience drawn in the slight furrow of her brow. "No. No." She sighed and adjusted Harlow's hands to the exact angle Desminda thought they should be in order to touch the spoon.

Harlow groaned. This all felt so stupid, and why should court etiquette matter when all but certain death loomed over their heads?

Her sister, the queen, couldn't conceal the gleeful grin she wore. Nova sat at the back of the room, facing Harlow, watching as Desminda manhandled her with increasing frustration.

"Why does this matter anyway?" Harlow groaned, voicing the thoughts she'd had since the second Nova suggested this ludicrous endeavor.

"Because Shade isn't the right person to teach you things like this," Desminda snapped. "In Thornewood, I thought your lack of social grace endearing. Now, it's dangerous."

A snort escaped Harlow. "Dangerous?" She looked down at her crooked fingers, Desminda still adjusting them, and laughed out loud. "The deadliest thing that might happen is my soup spilling onto my skirt and upsetting the laundry staff. Why can't I hold it the way I want to?"

Desminda's nostrils flared. "Because there is the proper way to hold it. Like a lady. And then there is the ill-bred country folk way to hold it."

Nova's eyebrows flicked up, the smile dropping from her face. They'd both once acted as "ill-bred country folk." Her sister might have never truly been one, but it didn't stop her from once eating in the same manner Harlow did.

To break the tension, Harlow exhaled. "You might hold your soup spoon properly," she said quietly, "but your manners are just as ill as mine sometimes."

Nova grinned at Desminda's shocked inhale.

"How dare you?" the former queen breathed.

Harlow let the soup spoon clatter to the bowl. "You are a terrible teacher," she said mildly.

She scooted her chair back and rose, forcing Desminda to take a few steps back.

"I am your *queen!*" Desminda snapped.

A month ago, Harlow might have felt great fear at the words. Now she just felt tired. "Once, perhaps."

She turned to Nova, dismissing Desminda in a way she never would have dared before. "Do you have another courtier who might instruct me?"

Nova pressed her lips together. "Of course." She rose and gestured for Desminda to walk out. "I thought perhaps the former queen's presence might make this easier for you."

Then it was obvious Shade had not mentioned their... history, if Nova wasn't aware of the current tensions between them. It made her feel a little better, but even seeing Desminda in the hallways made her heart hurt in the most awful of ways.

The former queen lingered behind for a moment, hurt darkening her golden eyes. "Very well," she said after a long moment. "I will retire to my chambers." Desminda turned, her skirts swishing and crinkling as she sailed through the door, her head held high.

When she was out of hearing distance, Nova sighed. "I'm sorry. I didn't realize something happened between you."

"Nothing happened," Harlow snapped.

Nova snorted. "Which means something did." She held up a hand at Harlow's muted protests. "It doesn't matter. Desminda is...lost right now. I merely thought doing some-thing productive might help her. Instead, I'm afraid I've made it worse."

Shade came through the door a moment later, a bemused look on his handsome face. When he spotted Harlow, that expression cleared. "Ah," he said.

Nova's laugh bubbled and spilled over, amusement making the stormy color of her eyes spark like lightning.

"Not funny," Harlow muttered.

Shade spread his hands out. "It's evident every time you two are in a room together, one of you leaves angry."

Nova covered her mouth and turned away.

"Can we please stop talking about this?" Harlow muttered. She and Desminda had a couple of stolen moments, but the queen had made her feel special in a way she never had before. Like Desminda had actually seen her. But her naivete in those moments made Harlow want to curl up and die. Desminda was trained from birth to be deceitful when in the pursuit of a goal. Or anytime really. Being a queen meant becoming a skilled liar and politician. Her goal had never been Harlow at all, only to ensure loyalty and obedience. If Harlow thought she actually meant something to Desminda, she would have willingly thrown herself in front of a moving carriage to save the queen if she stood directly in its path.

Now she couldn't help but feel stupid every time she saw the princess.

Words stuck in her throat, and all she could do was stare at Shade balefully. He was different here. Lighter. More prone to laughter and fun. And it all had to do with the woman standing by his side.

"It doesn't matter," Shade said. "We are leaving soon. Desminda will ride with us for a while, but I suspect our paths will diverge after a while."

Nova watched Harlow, the amusement gone from her face.

Harlow digested the words. "I don't understand," she said when Shade didn't elaborate.

"The training with Magnus is going well. He will ride with us and stay with you to continue your training. Reports from Thornewood are concerning. Something evil stirs there. We can wait no longer to gather allies to our sides. You are important to that goal."

But there was something in his eyes...something he wasn't telling her.

Harlow was so very tired of secrets. "What is it?" she demanded. "What else?"

Nova's brows drew together. "Shade?"

So he hadn't told her either. "It's nothing."

Harlow snorted. "That's what you always say."

"It is merely a thought. I am bothered by something that has not yet and perhaps will never come to pass. It's nothing to be concerned about."

But Harlow had been around Shade long enough to know when he worried about something, there was a strong likelihood of whatever it was turning into reality. For that, she always wondered if he had a touch of precognition talent in his blood. Nothing like Bloom or an actual Seer, but perhaps a knowing that made him such a great strategist.

His gaze skimmed over the table setup. "I've already instructed you in the ways of a court dinner," he mused.

Nova chuckled. "Desminda told Harlow she ate like an ill-bred country bumpkin."

Shade's eyes widened. "What's there to know other than what utensil to use with what course?"

Her sister burst out laughing. "Perhaps Harlow learned it honestly, then."

Shade's look of perplexity almost made Harlow laugh, too.

Nova looped her arm through Shade's. "Come. I will bring a courtier in to instruct Harlow on the proper way to act, and perhaps I will bring in one for you as well."

Shade's dark muttering followed them out the door, as they left without so much as a polite goodbye.

Harlow let out a breath and flopped onto the couch,

grumbling about ungrateful sisters, surprised she had an actual moment to relax. She'd been on edge for over a week now, constantly surrounded by members of Nova's court, Nova herself, or Nova's inner circle. It was maddening keeping her posture erect at all times or having to measure every single word she said.

While it was more relaxed than Thornewood, this was still a court where every word she spoke reflected on her sister or could have dire consequences. Granted, Nova didn't appear to be the kind of queen who would call for someone's head over a perceived slight, but practice from Thornewood had made Harlow cautious.

With good reason.

"The queen would be fit to be tied if she walked in here and saw your boots on her velvet couch," a mild feminine voice said.

Harlow lurched up, a few of her hair pins snagging on the crocheted throw underneath her head. It caught and dragged with her as she stood, weighing her head down and concealing her eyesight with creamy lace.

Evara stood in front of her, one eyebrow hitched up at Harlow's frantic efforts to free herself. "Boots on the couch and destroying one of her most precious throws?" The guard tsked. "For shame, Harlow."

Harlow glared at the guard, her fingers frantically moving through her hair to find the errant pins snagged in the throw. Her curls had always been a source of annoyance for her, but she'd gotten used to them and had learned to properly braid after Nova showed her not long ago. But this morning,

Harlow had opted for a looser braid because Magnus had given her the day off from training.

Poor decision given her current predicament.

Evara clicked her tongue and snorted. "Let me," she said briskly and reached for the throw.

Harlow took a step back. "I've got it."

Evara's lips twitched in amusement. She folded her arms over her chest. "Do you?" Her head tilted, hazel eyes sparkling with suppressed laughter. "By all means then."

Harlow ignored her, fingers steadily working through her mass of curls. After an excruciatingly long minute of making things worse, she sighed. There must be a hundred pins in her hair.

"Please." Harlow gestured to the lace throw.

"Please what?" Evara asked, her lips curving up.

Harlow blew out a breath. "I require...assistance."

"Oh? Would you like me to call someone?"

"Evara," Harlow growled in impatience.

Merry laughter rang from the guard. "Come here, fool," she murmured.

Harlow dutifully stepped toward the guard, stopping when they were still a little too far away. Evara exhaled a laugh and moved into Harlow's space. "Bend your head," she ordered. The difference in their heights was almost negligible, so Harlow bent her knees and tilted her head downward. Part of the throw had stuck to the top of her braid, and the rest was pinned through the bottom.

Evara studied it for a long moment. "Right. This might take a minute."

Harlow stiffened.

"Unless you'd like me slice off your braid?" Evara's tone was filled with amusement at her plight.

"No," Harlow snapped.

"So ungrateful," the guard said lightly, seconds before nimble fingers dug into Harlow's scalp.

The touch sent goosebumps rising on Harlow's arms. Someone touching her head had always felt intimate, but with her sister, it was a gesture of trust and love.

This...this didn't feel like that. Her scalp prickled with warm electricity as Evara's fingers moved through her hair, plucking random pins here and there.

"Your hair is beautiful," Evara murmured, her warm breath gentle against Harlow's forehead.

Crimson heat touched Harlow's cheeks.

"Thick and curly, painted with all the colors of the sun."

Harlow swallowed, heat spilling through her veins. "Are you almost finished?" she croaked.

Evara's husky laugh shivered against Harlow's skin. "Why? Is my touch that repulsive?"

"No. No. I—" Harlow swallowed. It was the opposite of that, in fact. She felt like a flower straining toward the sun, reaching for Evara's touch. And why? The guard had been nothing but sarcastic and borderline rude to her.

"Relax," Evara commanded. "I'm almost finished. Then you may scurry away and pretend like my fingers never sullied you."

Harlow's face jerked up. "Sully?"

Evara's hazel eyes met hers through the lace. "You act like I possess a pox."

"That. No." She shook her head, Evara's fingers stilling against her scalp. "I'm sorry," she said after a long moment. "It's just embarrassing. I—I find myself constantly feeling inept here."

Evara's brow furrowed. "Inept?" She shook her head. "You are a light of dawn in a kingdom of darkness, Harlow."

Their gazes held. Evara finally broke it, dropping her eyes and plucking the small throw from Harlow's head. "There," she said lightly. "All done."

But the guard didn't move away. And neither did Harlow. Her fingers itched to reach out and touch Evara, to coil her fingers through the guard's midnight curls. The young woman looked nothing like Desminda. Acted nothing like her. There was little evasive about Evara's open nature, but Harlow knew people were much deeper than how they appeared on the outside, and the urge to explore Evara's secrets made Harlow's breath catch.

"Th—thank you," Harlow said after a long silence.

Evara's hazel eyes darkened. Her open expression closed down until the mask of castle guard was firmly back in place. "You are welcome, young princess." With a slight bow, the guard turned on her heel and walked out of the room.

"Why does everyone keep calling me princess?" Harlow muttered, flopping back onto the couch before she jerked up and looked around for another throw to get caught in.

She laughed at herself, her gaze snagging on the one Evara had removed. It was a pretty thing, well-crafted with delicate embroidery. The guard hadn't even been gone half a minute and Harlow couldn't stop thinking about Evara's warm, nimble fingers scraping through her hair.

With trembling fingers, Harlow reached over and took the decorative throw, folding it carefully and tucking it into her inner vest pocket.

So she could have it cleaned, she told herself, cheeks burning with the absurdity of her behavior.

CHAPTER EIGHTEEN

THE BARD RETURNS WITH AN UNPLEASANT SURPRISE

A flash of familiar red hair turning the corner made Harlow's breath catch. She hurried toward the figure, hoping it was Astrid, but she was too far away to tell if it was her or someone else.

Few people had that color hair in this kingdom, but what was odd was the man following behind her. He had a familiar build with hair the color of a fine red wine, but that was impossible, wasn't it?

Frowning, Harlow picked up her speed, all but flying around the corners, but the bard, like always, proved elusive.

The thought made her smile. It had to be Astrid. But if it was, who walked with her?

The answer revealed itself when she skidded to a halt before Nova's sitting room.

A strangled sound came from her throat when she saw the dusty but fine clothes, and the sparkle of light through the rare red colored hair.

"Prince Lucien," she breathed, forgetting a moment to bow in his presence.

His eyes traveled over her, widening when he saw her in the dress of the Shadow Kingdom. "Harlow!" He took a step toward her, hesitated, and Harlow belatedly remembered to bow.

"No need for that," Lucien said, his voice a touch rough. "I am a guest here, and I'm afraid I'm not here as a representative of my kingdom."

Harlow rose, a frown curving her brow. What did he mean by that?

The doors opened, revealing Evara and Tristan. She hadn't seen the guard since the incident with the hairpins, about a week ago. Harlow had carefully avoided her but had forgotten in her excitement to see Astrid.

The bard smiled widely and opened her arms, drawing Harlow into a cloud of dust, and the scent of roses and light sweat. "It is good to see you, friend."

Harlow let Astrid squeeze her and returned the gesture. "You've been gone so long!"

The bard let her go and stepped back, curling her fingers around the crook of Harlow's elbow. "Come. I have news affecting everyone." She drew Harlow into the room, passing by Evara without a sound. The guard's eyes didn't leave their position, but Harlow's breath caught as she let Astrid lead her past, her blood pounding through her veins at Elara's presence.

Get it together, she told herself. This felt different from her infatuation with Desminda. More dangerous. How it could be, she had no idea. Loving a queen could be deadly to even the most powerful. Evara was a guard, technically below Harlow's station, but there was something about her that made Harlow nervous. As if she could lose herself.

She'd done it once before and had no plans to do it again.

Astrid's fingers squeezed her arm before releasing her, and the bard looked down at her with an odd expression, but thankfully said nothing.

Nova and Shade were already in the room, a tea service spread between them.

Shade stood by Nova's chair, the queen settled with her skirts situated around her in a perfect pool of wrinkle-free silver satin. Her dark hair was piled into a neat coronet around her head, a small crown of sparkling black stones set atop the style.

Lucien's eyes widened when he spotted her, his lips parting at her presence.

Nova did not rise. Lucien and Astrid stopped a few feet away, both dropping into a deep bow at the same time.

"Please," Nova said. "You must be exhausted from your trip. Sit and have refreshments."

Astrid groaned in thanks and sank into the offered seat. Lucien gave her a strange look, taking the seat in a much more dignified manner.

"Prince Lucien," Nova acknowledged with a slight tilt of her head. "I'm afraid your presence here has me at a loss."

Harlow never fully realized what a silver-tongued liar her sister could be. She hadn't been here long but felt the presence and remnants of Nova's shadows soaked into the very foundations of the castle and grounds. Nova had known about Lucien far longer than she pretended. Her shadows would have told her long before they'd arrived, giving her time to prepare for his "sudden" arrival.

Lucien, to his credit, seemed oblivious to Nova's magic and expected his presence to take her by surprise. "For that, I must apologize. I'm afraid I'm just as surprised." His eyes slid to Astrid. "I met the bard in...unique circumstances, and we did not have much time to communicate about my departure."

Always the careful courtier, Harlow thought.

Nova's face remained passive. "I see," she murmured. "Astrid, please tell me of your journey and your decision to bring a foreigner into my kingdom."

Astrid's eyes sparkled with amusement at the queen's words. She'd been at this game far longer than most of them had been alive, and Harlow envied her ability to adapt to any situation presented to her.

"I'm afraid I didn't have much choice," she began. "The prince was in mortal peril from the moment I stepped onto the castle grounds. I had to choose to take him with me or have his death on my conscience."

Shade, dark and looming behind Nova, kept his expression carefully blank, but there was no love lost between the prince and the former Kingsguard Commander. Nova could execute Lucien with zero recourse if she chose to.

From the light sheen of sweat on Lucien's brow, he was more than aware of his precarious position.

Astrid flashed a grin and straightened in her seat, lowering the cookie she'd snatched from the tray to her ceramic saucer. She brushed the crumbs from her finger with a napkin. "Lucien proved himself eager to abandon his duties at Thornewood to come here."

The prince's mouth dropped open.

"Astrid," Nova said, an exasperated note in her voice.

"Fine, fine," she said with a laugh. "There is a presence in Thornewood." Her expression darkened. "It is foreign. I've never felt its like. My counterpart believes it originates within the Luna stones."

Shade's attention snapped to Astrid.

Nova set her teacup down. "Have you seen this presence?"

Astrid nodded. "It is aware. Sentient almost." She shook her head. "I ventured too close to it and it...responded. Vehemently."

Nova's eyes flicked to Lucien who sat pale and rigid in the chair beside the bard. His expression showed no surprise.

"Prince Lucien?" Nova prodded.

Lucien inhaled and shook his head. "I cannot tell you what it is. But your counterpart is correct. It appears to have started within the stones."

"There is rot within Thornewood, Your Majesty. Hidden by Lucien's sister. But she will not be able to hide it for much longer. If it still remains hidden," she added darkly.

"Explain," Nova commanded.

"The earth moved," Astrid said. "I can't explain what happened, but one minute, everything was as it was supposed to be. The next, the trees shook around me, the ground lurched from its rest, and I was forced to flee. When I was able to later examine it, the presence had seeped from the castle into the village."

Lucien cleared his throat. "Impossible."

"Oh?" Astrid said, eyeing him. "Were you there? Or were you in your pretty little pampered prison?"

Nova blinked.

The ride from Thornewood to the Shadow Kingdom must have been interesting. Harlow looked between them. Lucien's jaw tightened, but Astrid remained as she always was—placid and amused. They must train bards from a young age to remain unflappable in stressful situations because Harlow was sure she'd be a blubbering mess in the presence of two monarchs, one asking difficult questions.

"Prison, yes," Lucien snapped. "There was nothing pampered about it."

Astrid smiled, a slow sardonic grin. "Few have leave to sit in the garden drinking tea in contemplation, guarded from harm by several trained soldiers."

Nova held a hand up. "Please. We have enough to worry about without getting dragged into petty arguments."

"I utter nothing but truth," Astrid said mildly.

Lucien sighed. "I was unaware of this presence until Celestine showed me. My sister seemed bothered by it, so I do not think she is the cause of it."

"She has no idea what it is?" Shade asked.

Lucien's gaze flicked to the former Commander. Harlow thought for a moment he wouldn't deign to answer, but Lucien thought better of it. "If she does, she hides it well."

"Then we must find out what it is," Nova said.

"Your Majesty," Lucien interjected, his eyes sliding to the bard, "there is...more."

Nova's eyes fluttered shut for a brief second. "Continue," she said.

"It shows an intellect, much like Astrid felt, but Celestine has been..." He paused, his expression pained.

"We cannot help if we don't know everything," Nova prodded.

"It's easy for you to say. I am in an enemy kingdom with no protection, only the mercy of your hearts."

Nova's smile was faint. "You saved my sister twice. For that, I always planned to spare your life if I had the chance to."

Lucien's brow furrowed in confusion. "Sister? Who is your—?" His lips parted. "By blood?" he blurted.

"Does it matter?" Nova asked, her tone mild but edged. "Harlow is my sister in every way that matters."

"I didn't know," Lucien breathed, his eyes finding me, curiosity and something else lurking in the emerald depths.

"I know," Nova said. "It shows me you are not always driven by gain."

Lucien's lips tightened at that, but he nodded. "Harlow is unique. One cannot help but want to help her."

Shade snorted which made Nova laugh. "I've heard such," Nova agreed. "Perhaps it is those guileless blue eyes."

Harlow frowned at her sister, but that only made Nova laugh harder. "Continue, Lucien. Please."

He gave Harlow one more look before he continued. "Celestine has not been herself."

"She's worse?" Harlow blurted. "How is that possible?"

Nova's eyes sparkled. "Spoken with the subtlety of an axe falling, but valid."

Lucien's pale cheeks colored. "You've met before."

"Many years ago. Celestine did not know who I was." Nova poured herself another cup of tea. "I found her to be loathsome, quite honestly."

The laugh burst from Lucien. His hand reached to cover his mouth, but he couldn't hold in his amusement. "You are the first person who's spoken true of my sister. She is quite awful." He slumped in his seat. "I do not know what she is doing anymore. Celestine has become someone I no longer recognize. Her fascination with Thornewood was not unexpected, but Celestine, as she usually does, took it much farther than anyone expected. I never thought she'd go this far to try to restore her power. But this rot, whatever it is, she seems to have an affinity for it."

Shade's posture went rigid. "Elaborate, prince."

Lucien's gaze locked on Shade. After a moment of intense staring, Lucien rubbed his face with the back of his knuckles. "She was always intent on regaining magic, but lately she is convinced it needs a keeper."

"The same as the former queen," Harlow mused. "Except she wants to control it all."

"Desminda's mother controlled magic with an iron fist and let almost no one have it. Except for Magnus," Shade said.

"Magnus?" Lucien blurted. "I haven't heard that name in a long time." He shook his head. "Shame what happened to him."

"Even though Magnus was the one who ripped magic away?" Nova inquired.

Lucien flicked his fingers. "I always assumed there was

more to that than met the eye. He never would have done it if he had a choice."

Perhaps Lucien was smarter than he let on.

"He would appreciate the sentiment," Nova said mildly.

Lucien stilled. "Excuse me? How would a dead man appreciate anything?"

The thought of her father dead and cold in the ground sent a spear of hurt through Harlow's heart. It had always hurt when she thought about his death, but now that she knew him, the hurt had turned icier, more painful.

The doors behind them opened, revealing Magnus Stone-hand, larger than life and cloaked in golden magic.

Lucien sucked in a gasp and slowly rose to his feet.

"Prince," Magnus barked, "it's about time you came to your senses and dumped that bitch of a sister."

Lucien moved toward Magnus so quickly no one had time to react. Her sister shouted, shadows tearing from her hands.

The metallic sound of a sword tearing from Shade's scabbard registered, but Harlow stood frozen watching as Lucien held out his arms.

And embraced her father.

CHAPTER NINETEEN

AN UNEXPECTED FRIENDSHIP

Nova's shadows floated in mid-air, waiting for their mistresses' command. But Nova was as stumped as the rest of them.

The two embraced, murmuring low and gruff words of greeting, back-slapping until they stepped back and clasped hands.

"You're the only one ever brave enough to call my sister a bitch," Lucien said wryly.

Magnus laughed. "It helped that she had no magic."

Nova sat back down, studying the two with confusion. "How do you know each other?"

Magnus shrugged. "Lucien and I grew up together. Somewhat. Our fathers knew each other, and I did some work for him. Lucien was nothing more than a snot-nosed teenage boy."

Lucien shook his head. "And Magnus was an overbearing, ill-mannered oaf."

Magnus only laughed. "I am surprised to see you here. It

appears I've missed some things, so I expect you'll fill me in over dinner?"

Lucien looked to Nova who shrugged. "The prince is a guest here," she said faintly. "I am not sure how long he will stay."

"I expect he's homeless," Magnus said mildly. "Celestine won't take being abandoned kindly."

"I should say not," Lucien said before he blew out a breath. He bowed to Nova. "I thank you for your hospitality."

"Don't thank me yet," Nova said. "Shade will oversee your visit, and you will be required to assist us when he or I, or Magnus, deem it necessary. You have free rein of the grounds, but you will be apprehended if you try to leave the city."

Lucien's eyes flashed. "So I am a prisoner?"

"Not at all," Nova said, her teeth flashing in a savage smile. "You are a monitored guest. It is gracious considering you come from a usurped kingdom, wouldn't you agree?"

He tilted his head in acknowledgment. "Yes, Your Majesty."

"One more thing," Nova added. "The former Thornewood queen is here. I remember you two had a betrothal?" It was phrased as a question, but everyone in the room knew Nova was already aware of their impending marriage.

Harlow thought it might hurt more to be reminded, but there was only that dull ache when she remembered her history with the former queen. Still there, but more like a healing bruise and not a sharp, stabbing wound.

"Desminda is here?" Lucien blurted. "She lives?"

"Complicated for the Bitch Queen, eh?" Magnus needled.

Lucien shot him a dark look. "I wasn't sure she made it." His lips twisted. "I expected Harlow to, but whether Desminda made it with her was unknown. Celestine assumes she is dead."

"She is not," Harlow interjected. "Does this mean the betrothal still remains?" she asked Nova.

Her sister's gaze was heavy against Harlow's skin. She always saw too much. "It depends. Ousting rulers through force is not against the laws of the land. If Celestine can hold Thornewood and its territories, Desminda is no longer a queen. Blood does not overrule might."

Lucien's expression changed then. "She plans to return?" he breathed. "It would be a death sentence."

"She would not return alone, prince," Magnus said mildly. "Desminda has not yet decided what she plans to do. Your presence will complicate things, and you will not do anything to sway her in any direction. Understand?"

Lucien's lips thinned. "You always were far too much of a busybody for your own good," he groused. "I have no plans to influence anyone while I am here." He stretched his hands out in front of him. They trembled slightly. "I feel magic stirring in my veins for the first time in so long." When he looked up, tears shimmered in his eyes. "Perhaps you have gardens I might tend to?"

Nova inclined her head. "The ministrations of a Prince of Roses would be an honor."

Lucien's smile was so brilliant it made Harlow's breath catch.

"I know you and the bard are exhausted. Please retire to your chambers. If you wish to visit the gardens, Shade or Tristan will escort you. We will meet again for dinner here in six hours." With that, Nova rose, dismissing them all.

Harlow was the last to leave. Shade had brushed past them in an effort to get to Lucien, nudging Magnus to follow. Astrid stood and stretched, weariness etched on her face, before she yawned and left without a word.

The guards shut the door behind them, leaving Harlow alone with her sister.

"Everything is changing quickly," Nova said, picking up her skirts with both hands and shuffling over to one of the couches. She kicked off her slippers and sat down with a sigh, picking her legs up and curling them under her. With nimble fingers, she pulled the crown from her head and set it gently on a table beside the couch.

Nova gestured for Harlow to sit.

When she was situated, Harlow asked the question itching at the back of her throat. "What do you think it is?"

"The presence?" Nova asked.

At her nod, Nova shrugged. "Hard to say. I've never heard of anything like it, but magic is sentient, so I'm unsurprised this entity is as well. Perhaps it's a different type of magic."

"Dark magic exists?"

Nova shrugged. "Magic is magic, Harlow. It's the intent of the wielder." She frowned. "But Astrid makes it sound like maybe it is. If it attacked her and tried to attack Lucien, maybe we should consider it." Nova leaned over and snatched a cookie from yet another tray.

Harlow hid a smile. She was starting to think her sister needed a snack intervention. Everywhere she went there was a tray of food. Berries or veggies, cheese and nuts, cookies and crackers.

"Magic needs will, though. Something to direct its purpose. This is why I'm having trouble believing this rot is sentient. If it is, it's far beyond anything I've experienced." Nova munched on the cookie, lost in her thoughts.

"Maybe we should try to take a piece," Harlow said.

Nova blinked. "From what Astrid said, she and Lucien barely escaped."

"We don't have the entire story yet. Astrid held many things back."

Nova smiled. "You know this for sure?"

Harlow snorted. "I've found few people speak the entire truth when court is involved."

Nova pressed her lips together. "And I'm sorry for that. I really am. Lucien might be here of his own volition, but I will never forget what he did to you. Or to Desminda's kingdom. He cannot be trusted until he proves his worthiness." She took another bite and chewed. "Astrid was wise to refrain from telling us everything. I will have her return here before dinner to provide a full accounting."

"Astrid uses powerful glamours to escape notice." Harlow reached for a cookie. "It is interesting she was able to sneak onto the grounds and snatch Lucien right out from everyone's notice."

Nova laughed. "You think far more than some of my nobles," she said fondly.

Harlow hadn't slept a full night since she arrived. All she

did was think. About the past. About the future, still so uncertain. About herself. Where she belonged. She felt far too young to be this worried, but Nova had been a queen her entire life. Maybe she'd been worried for far longer.

The thought didn't comfort her. Did Nova sleep as poorly as she did?

"Spit it out, Harlow," Nova said with amusement. "I can see your brain whirling like a mill."

"Are you happy?" she blurted.

Nova stopped chewing. Her brows knit together.

"Like really happy. With this? With everything?" Harlow waved her hand around. "This is all so much, and we—" Her throat worked. "We used to be so happy. Weren't we?" All the time they spent together. All the things Nova had taught her. The laughter and quiet moments spent together. They were the happiest times of her life. As Harlow grew, things had changed between them. It was the natural order of things, but never once had she doubted how Nova felt about her. Never had she felt unloved or unwanted. Not until the moment she found Nova's note and her world had come crashing down.

Nova dropped the cookie and rose to her feet, hurrying to where Harlow sat. She gathered her in a flower and storm-scented hug. "Of course we were happy," she whispered against Harlow's hair. "I've never been happier than I am here." Nova sighed. "But I have responsibilities that surpass my personal happiness now. I neglected them when I took you from the village." She tilted Harlow's chin up to look at her. "It was a decision I never regretted. Not once. But I have a kingdom to maintain." A hesitant smile crossed her lips. "It is a different kind of happiness. But so much better and fulfilling since you came back into my life."

"And Shade?" Harlow sniffed.

Nova laughed. "And Shade," she acknowledged. "One day I shall tell you everything. How I came to know him." Her voice dropped. "And how I came to love him."

Tears filled Harlow's eyes. "You truly love him?"

Nova nodded. "He is a man worthy of love." She sighed. "And I plan to make sure he knows it."

And for a few moments more, it was just Harlow and Nova. No warrior. No queen.

Only sisters.

CHAPTER TWENTY

THE CRANKY BARD

Astrid's wet red hair had been slapped up into a high, tight bun, highlighting the rings of exhaustion around her eyes.

"I apologize for calling you back in," Nova began. "But I believe there are things you left out."

The bard snorted. "You are right. Bards never show their hand before they are ready."

With that cryptic note, Astrid said nothing else.

"Bard," Nova warned.

"Our paths converge for a while longer," Astrid finally said. "Harlow and Desminda will need to gather allies to secure her bid to retake her throne. But it will not be as easy as she expects. Harlow is the daughter of a traitor, and Celestine's goal is to reunite mages with their power." Her lips twisted. "Or should I say, that is what she *says* she wants to do."

"Shade and I have made plans for Harlow to travel very

soon. We could not speak openly with Lucien, but Bloom made us aware of the corruption before you arrived, though she had little information."

Astrid nodded. "Speaking to spirits is a frustrating exercise."

It was a strange thing to say, but Nova didn't press it.

"They will travel to the Kingdom of Witches, our closest allies."

Astrid snorted. "You think the witches will be amenable to any proposal from Desminda? After what her mother did to the—"

"Astrid," Nova snapped.

The bard's eyes narrowed. Harlow sat forward. "What?" she breathed. "What happened?"

"It is nothing," Nova said.

Harlow's frustrated sigh rang through the room. Astrid chuckled. "You cannot keep the wool over her eyes forever, Your Majesty."

"Enough," Nova commanded. "Harlow will find things out when the news is ready to be delivered. Not a moment sooner."

"News?" Harlow pressed. "About me?"

Nova gave her a dark look. "Enough. Certain things are not mine to speak of." She shook her head. "Astrid. Report."

Astrid gave Harlow a sympathetic glance before starting at the beginning of her journey.

Even at the end, Harlow knew Astrid hadn't told Nova everything, but even the queen couldn't compel the bard to spill her secrets.

"I will travel with them," Astrid said. "Our paths will

split soon afterward, for there are other places I must go. The news of this rot, whatever it is, must be spread far and wide."

"You will spread panic," Nova protested.

"No," Astrid said, bright eyes sparkling. "I will spread hope."

CHAPTER TWENTY-ONE

WEDDING BELLS AND SHADE'S PERSONAL HELL

The third missive this month sat discarded on Nova's side table, a crisp, cream-colored envelope with a flowery handwritten note begging for a merger. Every time Shade saw another, rage bubbled in his veins.

Not at Nova. Never at her.

At this. Whatever this was.

Kingdoms from all over the lands fought for the Shadow Queen's hand in marriage. Nova never mentioned them, never spoke about the potential to add a king, never said a word about the offers she had, the borderline begging notes and gifts they showered her with.

In fact, Shade wasn't even sure she read them.

She had a competent man named Clevan handle her mail. He read everything she received, took care of what he could, and what he couldn't, he met with Nova about at least once a week.

The betrothal notes sat piled on the side table for weeks now, seemingly untouched.

But Shade couldn't help himself.

He read every single one.

His fingers hesitated as he reached for the newest one, addressed only to the Shadow Queen. It was from a kingdom he'd only heard of in books, one far away from the Lands of Lunamoor.

Seamist. The only thing he knew about the place was the legends of the turquoise seas surrounding most of it. Other kingdoms envied Seamist for its easy access to water and fertile soil.

The kingdom would make an enviable ally for Nova.

Despite his mouth going dry and his heart thudding painfully against his chest, Shade slid his thumb against the bottom of the vellum flap and pulled out the card.

Shade sat at the side table, a cup of tea long cooled in front of him, when Nova entered the room. Her face brightened at the sight of him, and she closed the door firmly behind her, clicking the lock into place before picking up her skirts and rushing over to him.

He grunted when she flopped onto his lap, a smile tugging against his lips as the overwhelming smell of jasmine and night assailed his senses. Nova peppered him with kisses, her warm mouth rousing him the way it always did.

"I missed you," she breathed against his skin.

Her arms tightened around him. Shade let his head fall against her shoulder. He inhaled, his lungs tightening at the thought of what he must do.

"Shade?"

"We're leaving tomorrow," he murmured against her velvet dress.

"I know." She blew out a breath. "My shadows will be with you."

Nova was careful not to intrude on his privacy, something he appreciated, but he was so in tune with her and her magic that he felt her shadows everywhere now. "We will be gone for months."

"Harlow deserves to see more of the world. She needs to know where she came from."

He made a noise of agreement.

"What is wrong?" Nova tilted his chin up, silvery eyes peering into his.

He forced a smile. "It is nothing."

Nova snorted. "It's never nothing. Something is amiss. Is it the trip? Harlow?"

"None of that. Astrid and Lucien have made great strides in the preparation. They do not like each other, I think, but they work well together."

"He is unused to powerful women," Nova mused.

"Even with Celestine?"

Nova chuckled, the low sound tightening Shade's groin. How could he still want her all this time even knowing what she was and who she was meant for? He should set her aside, take the tattered shell of his heart, and leave her to her kingdom of dusk.

But she leaned against him, soft and willing, her eyes full of hope and love.

And Shade had never been strong when it came to his own weak heart.

He rose in a single, fluid motion, drawing her against his chest, and brought her to the bed a few feet away. Shade laid

Nova down and came to rest above her, staring at her pale, wild beauty.

"Shade." Her hand came to his cheek, a finger stroking down his face. "What is it?"

He would leave her tomorrow. For good. For both their sakes.

As he brought his mouth to hers, he whispered against her lips, "I am overwhelmed by you, body and soul."

Tomorrow he would go.

But tonight, he would allow his soul a moment of brief respite.

Shade awoke in pitch black, Nova draped across his chest. He lay there for a long moment, enjoying the silken feel of her against him. It took everything in him to gently roll her away and rise, softly padding over to his bag. He dressed swiftly, careful not to wake her, but as he finished and picked up his pack, Nova shifted and rolled, her bright eyes glowing in the darkness.

"You're leaving?" she murmured.

"Yes. Go back to sleep."

"Nonsense." Nova sat up and pulled her dressing gown on. "I will help you."

"No." The word sounded like a gunshot.

Nova stilled. "I knew it. Something is wrong."

"I do not require any assistance." Grief filled his veins at the thought of leaving her behind. But he could not come back here, not knowing what she was giving up for him. He would not be the reason she did not reach her potential.

Nova frowned, her starry eyes studying him. She could see much better in the darkness than he could, but the moonlight highlighted her dark hair and pale skin, magic giving a luminescence to her eyes that made her look like a creature from a fairy tale.

"I know you do not. But I can offer my presence." Her lips thinned from displeasure.

"I do not want it." His voice cracked.

Nova inhaled. Her eyes narrowed before they fell away and onto the table where the betrothal missive still lay. Shade's attention moved there as well, and a grave silence fell between them.

"Those mean nothing," Nova said quietly.

Shade snorted. "You spurn opportunity and prosperity for a man who is nothing."

Nova shook her head. "A man who *thinks* he is nothing," she snapped.

Shade's jaw tightened and turned away.

"To me he is everything."

He shook his head, his heart cracking into a million pieces. Nova was rarely angry, but her slight form vibrated with rage as she regarded him. This was the better way.

No tears. No grief. Only Nova realizing she should have let him go.

The queen snorted. "Foolish man. How can one be so powerful on the outside, and so clueless on the inside?"

He looked away. "You are a queen. I am a commoner."

"Which means nothing. You still understand so little about me."

"Being a queen means power. You must seek it to hold onto your lands."

A wind stirred in the room. "The wrong queen has influenced you for far too long."

Shade's shoulder's tensed at the sound of shattering glass. Shadows wrapped around his hands and waist, forcing him to turn and face her. He struggled, but it was obvious within a few seconds he would not win.

"Power is internal," Nova said, gliding toward him on an invisible wind. "I command the shadows. There is no secret out of my reach, no door or window I cannot access, no whisper I cannot hear. The darkness answers to me, the dusk is my friend." Her smile was sad. "You see power through the lens of fear. I see it through the lens of hope. We are not and have never been vulnerable. You may leave me, Shade Montello, but we both know we hold each other's hearts. But I will not hold yours hostage. Your fear is a weakness, but I see my love as a strength." She shook her head and dropped her power. Shade swayed when the shadows left him as if he'd lost a part of her. "If you ever have need of me, call to the darkness." With those haunting words, Nova tugged on the belt of her dressing gown and brushed past him, her scent lingering behind as she closed the door.

It took him a long time to walk out the door, his fingers gathering a strand of dark hair from the pillow and tucking it into his vest pocket as he did.

At least...at least he would have a piece of her as he let the winds take him wherever they would.

CHAPTER TWENTY-TWO

WHO'S THE SADIST NOW?

Harlow groaned as she got into the saddle, every muscle aching and bruised. Magnus, her father, had put her through the wringer this week, intent on her finalizing her lessons with the axe and her magic.

Finalizing being an attempt to make her feel a little less hopeless.

She hadn't finalized anything except getting more confused. Magic was hard.

And, thanks to her father, super hard on her body too.

Next to her, Astrid snorted, her wild red hair swinging as she mounted her horse. She'd taken her lute this time, a risky move considering music was still seen as forbidden in the other kingdoms and magic wasn't cooperating as well as it once had. But Astrid would know best what she needed for the trip and whether the instrument would become a burden. She'd traveled far more extensively than others, especially Harlow.

"Do you think you'll play?" she asked Astrid.

The bard shrugged. "Depends on where we end up. We are safe for a while. The queen's territory is vast. Once we get into the witch kingdom, things will be a lot more dangerous."

Harlow frowned. "Aren't they allies?"

Astrid grinned. "Allies with Nova. Not us." With that, she gently nudged the horse forward, leaving Harlow behind.

Luci was nowhere to be found. Again. Harlow visited her every time she could, brushing the night-dark mane until it glimmered. But sometimes she couldn't find the beast, even when Harlow knew she should be in her stall.

Luci wasn't exactly a normal mare, so Harlow had stopped questioning it after a while because she always seemed to come back.

Except for now when Harlow wanted to take her to the witch kingdom.

In Luci's place, she rode a friendly, chestnut brown mount with a sweet disposition and a tendency to stop no matter where she was if she found a delicious-looking patch of grass or weeds. Not ideal for someone riding into dangerous territory, but Harlow wasn't the best rider either, and Nova had declared this mount safer than the rest.

Luci was a nightmare given mare form, but for some reason, she tolerated, and perhaps even cared for Harlow. Though Luci seemed a little more partial to Nova, perhaps it was the darkness they had in common rather than any real dislike toward Harlow.

"Come on," Harlow nudged. Flora was the mount's name, probably due to her preferred food source.

The horse snorted and took two steps forward, abruptly dropping her head to munch.

"Come on," Harlow muttered.

Shade, Magnus, Desminda, and Astrid were already several feet away, riding into the darkness.

The horse didn't budge even when Harlow tapped her sides with her heels.

"Nudge harder," her sister said.

Harlow yelped. "Nova! I didn't know you were here."

"I wasn't. I decided to come down last minute and see you off." Her sister wore a plain grey dress and a blue scarf wrapped around her shoulders. Nova's eyes were tight at the edges, her lips pursed as she watched the others ride away.

"Nova?" Harlow questioned. Her sister was rarely in a bad mood, but there was a tension in the air she'd never sensed before.

Nova shook her head and reached up to hug her sister. Harlow leaned down to snag an arm over Nova's shoulders. She breathed in the familiar scent and smiled against Nova's hair.

"I will miss you," Nova breathed. "Take care of yourself. Stay with Magnus and...Shade." Her voice broke. "They will keep you safe."

Harlow pulled away and frowned down at Nova. "I can keep myself safe," she groused.

Nova laughed. "I know you can. But you still have much to learn." Her sister reached a hand up, and Harlow took Nova's cool fingers. "Many surprises lie in wait for you. Some good. Some...not."

Harlow blew out a breath. "If this is ever over, I never want to be surprised again," she muttered.

"Don't I know it," Nova said, sadness in her voice. "I will see you again soon."

"Try not to be such a little spy," Harlow said, unable to help herself. She'd sensed Nova's shadows again this morning, slipping under her door frame.

To her surprise, Nova laughed. "Or be sneakier?"

Harlow rolled her eyes. "I'll keep you apprised of events."

Nova grinned.

"Oh hush," Harlow grumped. "I know you think you're quite the spy, but if I can sense those things, don't you think others can too?"

Nova's eyes narrowed. "You underestimate the power of darkness."

Harlow grinned. "Made you think, didn't I?"

Her sister snorted and swatted Flora on the hind end. The horse startled and took off at an awkward canter. Harlow squawked and lurched for the reins, Nova's laughter tinkling behind her.

"That's how you get that lazy beast to go!" Nova shouted.

Harlow turned and glared at her sister, her body jostling all over the place. Nova wiggled her fingers in a goodbye gesture.

The smile slid over Harlow's face before she could stop it. She'd missed her sister so much. Today felt like the first sense of normalcy she'd had in a long time.

Too bad she had to leave so soon.

She caught up to the others quickly now that Flora was moving faster than the pace of a ground snail. It helped that the grass was behind them. For the next few miles at least, they'd be on a stone road, the grass several feet away from where they rode.

Lucien had stayed behind. The prince would only act as a complication when they rode into the witch kingdom, and Nova suggested he stay with her while they strategized on how to regain Desminda's throne.

If the former queen even wanted it back.

Desminda had said nothing for days, avoiding Harlow when they passed each other in the hall, even going so far as to make an abrupt turn down a hall Harlow knew she didn't mean to go down in an effort to avoid her.

Harlow's courtly lessons never commenced again, Nova busy with Lucien's arrival and other things.

Other things possibly being the stiff-backed former Commander riding silent and stewing ahead of them all.

Harlow had no intention of asking any questions. She didn't want to know about their affair, or whatever they were doing. It all felt too much for her overwhelmed brain.

So she did what she was good at lately. She kept her mouth shut and her head down.

But as they rode, the urge to ask questions itched at her. Where exactly were they going except for the witch kingdom? Who were they there to see and why were they going? Would they actually ally with Thornewood? It seemed a risky ask to her.

She nudged Flora and the horse actually responded, picking up the pace into a smoother gait, until she caught up with Shade.

His gaze slid her way. "Good morning."

"Morning, Shade." She didn't miss the shadows under his

eyes, but wisely kept her opinions to herself. "How long are we riding?"

His lips twitched. "We are at least a few days away. The ride should be relatively safe since we will stay on Nova's lands for most of it, but we must still be wary of bandits and other ne'er-do-wells."

"Bandits?" Harlow asked. "Nova has them too?" She blushed as soon as she finished the question. Of course her sister did. Just because she was a good ruler, it didn't mean everyone who lived here was good.

"They're everywhere," Shade said mildly.

She liked how he rarely took the bait she offered him unwittingly to make her feel stupid. When he deigned to answer her questions, he did so with no mocking tone or ridicule.

"What exactly are we going for?"

Shade huffed a laugh. "I suppose it could be confusing for someone who is first entering into politics."

Harlow grimaced, making Shade chuckle. "I'd rather not be here at all," she muttered.

"Yes, well," Shade sighed and sighed. "Sometimes fate has plans in store for us other than those we want."

Harlow's eyes lingered on him.

He cleared his throat. "We go to seek their help in ousting Celestine. Though now, with the new information we have, we also seek information. The witches are well informed, much like Nova."

A thought occurred to her. "Why doesn't Nova have more information about Thornewood?"

"Most magic dies when it enters the Thornewood lands.

The Kingdoms of Crystal, Roses, and Light are most affected by Magnus's spell, but there are parts throughout the forest and close to the border of the Kingdom of Wolves who also suffer. The shifters who live there lose much of their natural magic when they get too close to the Thornewilde Forest." His expression darkened. "They may not be much help to us unless they stay in their beast forms."

Harlow gaped at him. "Beast forms?"

Shade glanced at her with a furrowed brow before his expression cleared. "Ah. Yes. We never got that far in our classes, did we?"

She blinked. "Uh. We graduated."

Shade snorted. "It wasn't the end of your education."

"The red x's," Harlow murmured. The map from the classroom instruction during her Virago training swam in her mind, some of the images hazy. Certain kingdoms were x'd out on the maps, denoting Thornewood's adversaries. "They are our enemies?"

Shade shrugged. "The witch kingdom is also x'd on our map."

"That's not an answer."

Shade's teeth flashed in the dim light. "They are enemies to the former Thornewood queen. Perhaps not us."

"So...we're going in and hoping for the best?"

Shade laughed, the sound lighter than she'd heard in a while. "Welcome to politics, young Harlow."

She fell silent, her thought spinning as she thought about how this could possibly work out for them. It seemed they were on a fool's errand.

But wasn't that how things had seemed for the last few months now anyway?

Harlow sighed and let her horse fall back into a slow walk.

Astrid came up beside her a few minutes later. "Doing okay?"

"Did we really have to leave so early?" Harlow grumbled.

Astrid laughed. "That is usually the way of journeys," she said easily.

"It's Nova's territory. We could have left after breakfast, couldn't we?"

"Spoken by someone who's never been on a true journey before," Astrid said as she dug in her pack and tossed Harlow something wrapped in parchment.

"I came here, didn't I?" Harlow grumbled. The smell of bacon and eggs made her stomach growl. Her eyes widened when she realized what was in the parchment, and she unwrapped it so quickly it tore.

"Easy," Astrid said. "I only brought a few, so I wouldn't eat the entire thing at once. It will hold until this afternoon, so I'd eat half for now and save the other for lunch."

Harlow shoved a huge bite in her mouth, sighing through her nose as the salty, still warm, meat-filled biscuit hit her taste buds. "Thank you," she muttered through a mouth full.

"You're welcome. Surprised you didn't raid the kitchen and get your own."

Harlow swallowed. "I was trying to sleep as much as I could."

Astrid snorted. "Next time, remember food is more important than sleep the night before. It won't seem so, but you'll sleep like the dead once you get off that horse from riding all day."

Harlow gave her a suspicious look, but Astrid merely shrugged and rode ahead.

The climate was gentle, a slight wind teasing Harlow's neat braid. She took a few more bites of the biscuit, reluctantly folding it back up when half was gone, and tucking it into her pack.

The Shadow Kingdom didn't see the sun like other kingdoms, but as they rode, light grew until the road and everything ahead of them was visible for at least a mile or two. Not clear, exactly. The Shadow Kingdom always had an odd form of fog around it, but good enough.

The sound of thundering hoofbeats coming from behind them, made Harlow turn in her saddle. Shade let out a shout ordering them to halt.

Flora reluctantly stopped, huffing in annoyance when she bent her head and found no grass to munch on. Harlow patted the side of her neck. "We'll break in a few hours, I'm sure. Then you can find as much clover as you can stomach."

The rider grew closer, a dark braid bouncing against the woman's shoulder. She wore dark leather and a sword strapped on her back.

Harlow's stomach fell when the rider came into plain view.

Evara wore a smug smile when she spotted Harlow. "Hello, princess," she cooed as she brought her well-behaved horse up beside Flora.

Shade eyed the warrior. "Why are you here?" His words fell like rocks.

Evara's eyebrows rose. "The queen sent me as extra help."

When Shade opened his mouth to protest, Evara shook her head. "You are riding into hostile territory. The queen thought it best you had a representative of her kingdom to help foster positive relations." She smiled thinly. "Or at least force them to hesitate before they murder all of you."

Astrid cracked a laugh. Evara grinned back, her hazel eyes sparkling. Harlow thought she looked far too pretty to be up so early. Strands of dark, curly hair had escaped from her braid, and her cheeks were flushed a rosy pink color from the wind.

When Evara caught her staring, she winked at Harlow, who looked away quickly. Color heated her cheeks, and Harlow cursed inwardly at her fair complexion and how easily it gave her feelings away. Even with all the lessons and lectures Shade had given her, Harlow still couldn't keep her facial expressions under control.

"Is it really that dangerous?" A quiet voice said from in front.

Desminda.

"Yes," Evara said with zero hesitation. "Few enter into the Witch Kingdom and return the same."

"What do you mean?" Desminda pressed.

"You have never traveled," Evara said and nudged her head toward Harlow. "Much like her. The other kingdoms are vastly different from your thorny one. Your mother ruled by fear and control. The others do the same, but the difference is they still have their magic, and they are not all human. And they do not rule their people by fear. They ensure others fear *them*. There is a difference." Her teeth flashed in a savage smile. "Things lie underneath their skin you'd rather not see."

Desminda's shoulders stiffened. "I am not my mother."

Astrid stared at the former queen. "Then you best show them quickly who you are."

"You'd best show all of us," Evara said. "Hiding under your cloak of former privilege serves no one, *queen*."

Harlow couldn't see Desminda's face, but from the rigidity of her spine, Harlow knew it wasn't positive. She kept her mouth shut and focused on the road ahead. There would be a better time for all the other questions she had.

And she had enough of them to make even Shade weep.

CHAPTER TWENTY-THREE

A FLOWER-MUNCHING NIGHTMARE

E vara made for a lively if annoying travel companion. There was rarely silence when she was around, and for every crack of a branch or moan of the wind, Evara was there whispering tales of murder and mayhem.

Even Harlow found herself entranced by her storytelling ability and wondered to herself if the guard had once been a part of Astrid's people, a secret bard.

But Astrid had shown no indication of knowing her any deeper than when they all arrived bedraggled and exhausted on Nova's doorstep. Then again, everyone kept so many secrets it was no wonder Harlow saw subterfuge behind everything.

They rode for hours, stopping only once to let the horses drink and eat, and Flora had happily trotted off to a patch of bee-covered clover, abruptly shoving her nose into it and tugging flowers up with her broad, flat teeth.

How she didn't get stung seemed a miracle.

Harlow sat cross-legged on the soft earth, idly tracing a

trail in the grass. Heavy fog had rolled in an hour or so before, coating the land with a mist of grey. Most of their party wore black or grey, so they all looked like pale spirits, the dead walking in a land of charcoal, except for Astrid whose brilliant hair looked like windswept blood. Even Harlow's golden hair had taken on a dull sheen with the fog's humidity.

She let her mind go blank, focusing on nothing except the touch of the breeze and the smell of a foreign flower. Bees buzzed around her, fat and heavy with summer pollen, though it never felt like any season here, only perpetual dusk. While it wasn't always dusk, it was nothing like the sun-drenched lands of Thornewood. Memories assailed her of her and Nova running barefoot, sunlight caressing their shoulders and browning their noses, much to their foster mother's chagrin.

A smile curved Harlow's lips. As much as she wanted to find Nova, she wasn't sure she belonged in her kingdom. And again, the thought arose...where did she belong if not with Nova?

"The bandits won't bother us on the way out," Evara said, coming closer to where Harlow sat. "Nova sent shadows out earlier warning them away. She might tolerate them, but they all know she could wipe them away for good if she wanted to."

Harlow frowned. "She allows her people to be robbed?"

Evara snorted. "Bandits leave most people alone, and there are few who dare venture into our kingdom. Those who do?" She shrugged. "They usually are not here to wish Nova well."

A shiver ran down Harlow's spine. "Fair enough, I

suppose," she said quietly. Her sister appeared to have an unfathomable amount of power, but she held it tightly to her and rarely used it. What kind of magic lurked under her sister's skin?

"I saw Luci earlier," Evara added.

Harlow's attention perked up.

"She's pretending not to follow us." Evara rolled her eyes. "I'm not sure what kind of creature that horse is, but she's no normal mare."

Harlow had to laugh. "She's not," she agreed.

For once, an easy silence fell between them. Evara settled herself a few feet away and pulled out an oat bar, broke it in half and offered the other piece to Harlow.

"No thanks." Harlow dug the biscuit out from her pocket. "Astrid gave me this earlier and warned me to save the rest for lunch."

Evara brightened. "She raided the kitchen?" Regret flashed in her eyes, tugging something in Harlow's stomach.

Harlow broke half of her half and handed it to Evara.

The guard hesitated. "You'd share?"

Harlow shrugged. "Why not?"

Evara took it before Harlow could change her mind, pressing the half of her oat bar in Harlow's hand to make it even. "Thanks."

Harlow didn't respond, instead taking a bite of the oat bar. It was surprisingly good, and it held up well for travel, but they all knew they'd be sick of oats by the time they crossed the border.

Evara groaned as she chewed. "I've asked Cook several times how to make this and she refuses to part with her recipe. The biscuits." She held a small piece up and shook it. "How does she get them so moist?"

A smile tugged Harlow's lips. They were amazing, and Harlow wasn't unfamiliar with the kitchen, but even she hadn't succeeded in making biscuits quite that light or fluffy. "Buttermilk?" she guessed.

Evara glanced at her. "What is that?"

Harlow's brow furrowed. "Um. Sour milk, I think."

The guard's lips curled in disgust. "Funny."

"I'm serious," Harlow protested. "It makes baked goods quite delicious. Pancakes too."

Evara eyed her biscuit with a little less pleasure. "That sounds disgusting," she murmured more to herself than Harlow.

"It's the liquid left over in the churn once butter is made. So maybe not milk exactly. Made from it, I guess." Harlow shrugged and popped the last of her biscuit into her mouth.

Evara snorted. "I'm going to make Cook tell me," she vowed, her eyes sparkling. "And if she doesn't, I'll threaten to tell Nova she's using spoiled goods to cook with."

Harlow gasped. "Evara!"

The guard laughed and took a bite of her oat bar. Harlow rolled her eyes and got to her feet, muscles groaning as she stretched.

Shade wiped his hands off and rose as well. "Let's get back on the road. We have at least four more hours until we stop for the night."

Groans sounded from all around. Shade rolled his eyes and mounted his horse, gesturing for all of them to hurry up and move. Harlow's thighs screamed as she plodded over to the still munching Flora. "Come on," she urged, taking the reins in one hand and gently tugging toward the party.

In another life, Flora must have been a mule. Her head didn't budge even with harder tugs and some blistering insults from Harlow.

"You stubborn old—"

"Get on and slap her in the ass," Evara said, leading her own horse over.

"Easy for you to tell me what to do," Harlow said. "You have a nicer one."

Evara laughed. "I have a well-trained warhorse. You have a flower-munching mixed breed mutt."

"Well then why did Nova give her to me!"

One of Evara's brows rose. "Because you are quite awful at riding," she said matter-of-factly.

"Am not," Harlow muttered under her breath, tugging the horse again, who again refused to do anything but stick her nose in the flowers.

Evara took the reins from her hands. "Up," she commanded, checking the saddle straps.

Harlow blew out a breath. "Fine." She climbed on and took the reins back, just as Evara drew her arm back and slapped the hell out of Flora's rump. Once again, the horse went nuts, lurching into that awful canter/walk/lurching gallop.

"You're an awful thing," Harlow whispered in Flora's ear.

The horse twisted its neck around and tried to bite her.

Harlow screeched and jerked her leg back, Evara's low laugh following them as girl and demon mule lurched away.

S hade set a breakneck pace for the rest of the day. By the time he finally gestured for them to stop, Harlow felt like all her teeth had rattled right out of her head thanks to Flora's mulish personality and inability to walk like a normal horse.

She led Flora to the creek and a patch of fresh grass, loosely tying the reins around a tree in a knot that would loosen if she had to flee. Right now, Harlow wished she could flee back to a soft bed and three meals a day.

Weakling, she chastised herself. She'd been with Nova for weeks now, and even though she'd trained, the fear she felt while living in Thornewood had all but disappeared, even with Desminda in close quarters.

Perhaps it was because the young former queen had become diminished, and Harlow no longer felt her life hanging in the balance every time Desminda looked at her. Her golden eyes were dull, and she rarely said anything other than to respond to a direct question. Harlow only spoke to her when she had to, still holding on to a grudge she didn't quite understand.

The queen led her docile mount to a tree several feet away, unhooking the small saddle bag before she left her there and found a shady spot underneath a copse of trees.

She acknowledged no one and nothing, simply rummaged through her bag for something to eat. A pang of sympathy went through Harlow at how beaten down Desminda looked, but none of this was her fault.

Nor was it Desminda's.

Sighing, Harlow snatched up her own bag and walked over to Desminda who glanced up in surprise, before her expression closed down. "What?" she snapped.

Harlow rolled her eyes and sat down beside her.

"I wish to eat by myself," Desminda said.

Harlow ignored her, taking a bite of deer jerky and washing it down with a small bag of water.

"Harlow." Desminda's golden eyes rested against Harlow's face, heated with anger.

"You don't," Harlow said mildly.

Desminda snorted. "Oh? And you would know?"

"You don't like being alone." Harlow chewed on the stiff jerky, grimacing at the amount of salt in it.

"I am fine being alone," Desminda huffed.

Harlow made a sound of not quite agreement.

"Leave me," Desminda commanded.

"No."

The former queen gasped in outrage. "How da—"

Harlow rolled her eyes. "How dare I, yes, I know. Apparently, I dare very much."

"You are impertinent!" Desminda hissed.

"Is this a surprise?"

Desminda fell silent.

The former queen's fingers trembled as she broke off a piece of the oat bar.

"You are being a brat," Harlow said quietly.

Desminda's jaw dropped. "Are you serious? Can't you just leave me alone?" Her voice rose at the end, drawing Astrid and Shade's attention. The latter's dark eyes rested on them for a moment before he returned his attention to dusting off his boots.

Astrid watched them with a faint smile before turning to say something to Evara.

Magnus hadn't said a word the entire trip and had ridden ahead hours ago. Shade hadn't seemed concerned about it, so Harlow assumed he'd catch up later.

Harlow ignored Desminda. "You sought refuge in an enemy queen's kingdom and turned your nose up at everything you've been given. Nova had every right to throw you in a cell and let you rot there." The words bubbled up from a place Harlow had long been tamping down.

"An enemy?" Desminda spat. "I am no one's ene—"

"You are everyone's enemy," Harlow interrupted. "I don't know much about politics and how things work or how to be a smooth courtier, but I do know your family wiped magic away and devastated the people in your queendom. My mother and father died in their efforts to save me during the Thornewood raids. And my sister, the *Queen* of the Shadow Kingdom, suffered a fate not many of us would survive." Her voice had dropped into a low hiss.

"And you still think you're the victim. *None* of us are victims."

"Your father," Desminda said with a harsh laugh. "Your *father* is responsible for all of this."

Even after all this time, Desminda deflected blame. Harlow smiled, but it wasn't friendly. "At your mother's behest. The same woman who killed my mother. The same woman who forced him to rip power away from those who had it by right of birth so your family could stay in power." Harlow snatched up her food and started to rise. "You are no queen of mine."

Devastation flashed over Desminda's face, there and gone in an instant, before her expression shuttered into one of bored indifference. "And you are nothing but a dead whore's get—a bastard of magic and witches. A mongrel with too much power and not enough sense to make it in my guard."

The slap rang out in the clearing so loud it sounded like a crack of thunder. Harlow's hand stung as she rose to her feet. "Speak of my mother again, and you will find your throat at the end of my sword, royal blood or no."

Desminda's cheek glowed an angry, bright red. Tears shimmered in her eyes. "Harlow—I—" She reached out, but Harlow turned on her heel and walked away, tossing the oat bar to the ground in her fury.

The thought of Desminda's touch made her skin crawl. How things could change in an instant felt unfathomable to her. Hot, angry tears spilled from Harlow's eyes.

The ground rumbled underneath them, dark boiling clouds tumbling in from the west.

Shade rose to his feet, his face a mask of concern.

Harlow held up a hand. "Please," she whispered. "Just a moment. That's all I need. I promise."

His eyes held uncertainty, but Shade nodded once, sharp, and sat back down, though his eyes lingered on her back as she walked away.

She found a spot close enough to see them but far enough for the quiet sob to burst from her throat with no one to hear it. Harlow breathed in and out like Astrid showed her, slow and steady. It took her several minutes, but the fury boiling in her veins settled into a deep, rushing roar of blood in her ears. The dark clouds had disappeared back into the sky, and a shaky breath expelled from her lips.

Harlow lost track of time after a while, her gaze focused on the horizon and her mind carefully blank of anything that mattered. Despite how silly she felt when she did this exercise, it helped clear her mind. Since her emotions appeared linked to her magic, Harlow tried to practice the technique every single day.

But Desminda's words came spilling back, poisonous and vicious. The words of a queen to a nobody. Harlow gritted her teeth and sighed. There'd been many ways to handle it, and Harlow had gone straight to violence.

"She *is* a brat," came a voice to her right.

Harlow jerked, only to see Evara walking toward her, loose hipped and swaggering. She smiled and tossed a water sack to her. "Take a few drinks. It helps."

Harlow eyed it but opened the container and took a long swill of fresh ale. She coughed in surprise, then tilted it up again.

"Good." Evara sat down beside her. "Someone should have told her those things years ago."

Harlow snorted. "No one wanted to die."

Evara chuckled. "Yes, I suppose not." She shrugged. "Someone related to her then, though her bloodline seems a little sullied with people like her mother coming out of it, no?"

"You don't like her," Harlow observed.

Evara shrugged. "I like few people." The guard lay back against the soft, cool grass and plucked a long piece, folding it between her long pale fingers.

"Why is that?"

The guard's hair had fallen out of her loose braid and curled against the grass. She looked both lovely and deadly, and Harlow felt herself drawn to Evara's darkness.

"People are a disappointment," Evara said simply, the blade of grass whirling between her fingers. "Most will let you down." Her gaze lifted to Harlow. "There are few who will stand beside you in a storm when they have nothing to gain from it except getting wet."

Point taken.

"Desminda is a queen," Harlow murmured.

"Was," Evara said. "She is only a girl now. A lost, vicious little girl."

Harlow huffed a laugh. "She's older than me."

"And yet you are not the one spouting poison." Her head turned to study the area where everyone else still sat. Shade had moved positions and appeared to be trying not to make it seem like he was watching them. "Such a mother hen," Evara tsked. "I like him."

"Shade?"

"Mmm."

Harlow snorted. "Most women like him."

Evara frowned. "No. Not like that. He is handsome, but it is something he can't control. What he can control is his courage, his bravery, and his obvious love for our queen."

Harlow studied him, his profile sharp and edged. He was quite handsome, dark and lean, intelligent and observant. She understood why Nova cared for him. But she didn't realize how much he cared for her sister. "He loves my sister?"

Evara's laugh sounded surprised. "He is the kind of man who would set himself on fire if she were cold, Harlow." She shook her head. "Love like that does not come often. He would be a fool to let it go."

Harlow's brows drew together. "He is letting her go?"

"You did not observe our queen this morning?"

"Your queen," Harlow murmured.

"Mmm." The noise sounded noncommittal. "There is something going on between them, none of it good."

Harlow laughed. "You're gossiping like a hen."

A dimple peeked from Evara's cheek. "Only to you. Shade is a man used to being alone. Nova is a queen, and he is common born."

Harlow studied him closer. There was an edge to his expression, his jaw clenched tight. "You think he's left her for good," she breathed.

"The idiot packed twice what we did," Evara said, lazily lifting one hand and pointing it at Shade's mount. Harlow turned her attention and spotted the extra bag and water sack.

She started to stand, but Evara stopped her with a firm grip on her hand. "No. Not now. Give him some time to mull. Nova is still with us. She will watch over him until it seems hopeless. Your sister will beg no man to love her."

"She is the best of us," Harlow whispered. "He'd be an idiot to leave her."

"Yes," Evara agreed. "Say nothing for now. Let us speak of you and the former queen." She rolled onto her stomach, her messy hair falling around her face.

Harlow's lips pressed together. "There's nothing to say."

"Considering you threatened to kill her during a two-minute conversation, I'd wager a guess there's some history."

"There isn't," Harlow snapped.

Evara rolled her eyes. "I'm not a fool. You may think I'm just a guard, but I see more than you think."

Harlow felt exposed, like Evara saw too much. She felt the same about Desminda, but the former queen had always been more interested in something when it affected her or her plans, never when it was just Harlow being Harlow. "I never said you were a fool," she murmured. Harlow crossed her fingers together. "It really was nothing. I saw something that never existed."

"You cared for her."

She had. Was it ever anything more? Harlow had never fallen in love, or if she had, she'd never recognized it for what it was. But she was okay. She felt okay. A little bruised, maybe, but it didn't feel like she couldn't go on. She had to go on, and she was okay doing so without Desminda. "I...did." Harlow snorted. "But I don't think I loved her."

Evara's expression grew serious. "You would know if you loved someone. Love can consume you."

Harlow's gaze slid to Evara. "You love someone?"

One of the guard's dark brows lifted. "I am not some hundred-year-old elder. I've been in love before."

"What was it like?" Harlow asked, a wistful note in her voice.

"When it's with the wrong person, it feels like walking on glass barefoot. A thousand tiny cuts that sting when you least expect it."

Harlow blinked. "That sounds...terrible."

Evara huffed. "It is."

"Have you loved the right person?" she asked hesitantly.

The guard grinned and rolled over before coming to her feet in a fluid motion. She dusted off her pants and vest before winking at Harlow. "Now that is the real question. How do you ever know if it's the right person?"

Harlow shook her head. "I suppose I would never want to be without them."

Evara jerked her head toward Shade, still sitting alone. "Would you set yourself on fire if they were cold?"

When Harlow didn't answer, Evara chuckled. "You know it's the right person when the other one would do it first because you were cold, too."

Evara turned and walked away, leaving Harlow to ponder her words. Duty wasn't love. Once, she would have jumped in front of an arrow for Desminda because she had to. Now she didn't have to do anything but survive.

And she realized maybe Desminda wasn't and maybe had never been part of those plans even from the beginning.

CHAPTER TWENTY-FIVE

STRETCH IT OUT

S hade insisted on sleeping on the outer edge of the camp. Everyone suspected he wouldn't sleep at all, but no one argued with him. He assigned guard shifts. Harlow took the first, even though she protested, Evara the second, and Astrid the last. Shade didn't give Desminda a shift at all, and no one commented on that either.

The former queen looked like a ghost and had retreated into herself even further, if possible, after Harlow's harsh words.

But Harlow wasn't sorry. She'd meant every word of it. Could she have phrased it better? Softer?

Yes. She could have responded in many ways, but anger had won. Desminda had taken her pain, minimized it, and thrown it back into her face with an insult.

No one chastised Harlow over it either, but they'd silently ostracized Desminda for it.

It was the only thing Harlow regretted. Desminda had lost a kingdom and struggled with it, but it had also made her vicious in her words. Being ostracized by everyone wouldn't help her. It might even make her worse.

She'd worry about it tomorrow. The fire still crackled cheerily as everyone settled into their sleeping rolls. Harlow sat at the edge of the road, several feet away from the others, her senses open like Magnus had taught her. No one said anything to each other as they prepped for sleep. Astrid stayed close to Evara, though far enough for propriety. Shade chose to sleep away from everyone else, and Harlow suspected Desminda didn't have a choice on being alone.

Magnus was still gone, and Shade hadn't mentioned him when they stopped. If he was due back tonight, Harlow wasn't aware. So she waited and watched with both her eyes and her other senses, the sounds of the fire, wind, and critters going about their evening luring the others into a deep sleep.

A TOUCH on her shoulder jerked her out of her reverie a few hours later. Harlow startled and looked up to see Evara standing over her, one finger against her lips.

Harlow nodded and pushed up, wincing at the pull in her muscles. The worst thing she could have done was sit there for hours without walking around, and that's exactly what she'd done. Evara held up a hand, looked at the others, all still sleeping, and gestured for Harlow to follow.

She took Harlow across the road but within sight distance.

"Do this," Evara said and launched into a fluid set of moves, swaying and bending. Harlow blinked and frowned as she tried to emulate her. Evara grinned and held up a finger, then did the same set of motions but much slower.

"Try again," she whispered.

Harlow shrugged and mimicked her movements. It took her a few tries, but she finally got it, and as soon as she did, Harlow felt the gentle stretch and pull of her muscles, almost groaning as she worked the soreness out.

"Ten times," Evara whispered. "Next time you're on guard duty walk around."

Harlow smiled her thanks as Evara crept across the road. She moved as quietly as she could and soon felt like a willow reed moving with the touch of the wind. When she hit ten stretches, she straightened and lifted her arms above her head, feeling surprisingly better than she had when she first stood.

Evara nodded when Harlow walked back across the road and over to her own mat.

Within minutes, Harlow was fast asleep.

CHAPTER TWENTY-SIX

SOMETHING AWAKENS

Something felt off. Harlow awoke slowly, disoriented at first until she spotted Shade's still figure not too far away. He'd finally fallen asleep. She stirred and rolled onto her side, brushing her hand through the heavy, dense fog that had rolled over their camp while she slept.

Her breath felt heavy and wet, the humidity curling her hair into damp strands that stuck against her face and neck. She eased from her roll and stood, quickly gathering her hair into a messy braid. The fog rolled over her skin, obscuring everything and everyone around her.

A shiver rolled down her spine. The fog was lighter closer to the ground. She couldn't see a foot in front of her and hesitated to investigate, but a feeling she couldn't explain urged her forward. Harlow put her hands in front of her and took a few steps, wincing every time her foot hit the ground, fearful she'd step on someone. But the wind and the fog urged her on, guiding her in a strange but knowing way.

It wanted her to go somewhere. Harlow looked over her

shoulder, but there was only mist. Blood roared through her ears, but she kept going. The power didn't feel malicious, more curious and urgent. So Harlow let herself be led and hoped she wouldn't regret it later.

She lost track of how long she walked, the fog a constant, damp reminder of how easily she could step off a hillside or fall into water, but Harlow trusted the presence guiding her forward.

Until suddenly it stopped, pushing against her front to hold her in place. Harlow halted and looked around but saw only mist.

See, a voice whispered through her mind.

Harlow's magic pulled and pulsed inside her, sinking through her feet and down into the damp, loamy earth. She gasped at the tug of it, the warmth in her veins as it responded to the command. Harlow liked being in control, and her life over the past several months had been a tangled mess of fate and chance. Her magic was one more thing she couldn't control, and the feeling of helplessness raged in her as her magic explored and rushed through the earth to wherever the voice had directed it to go.

One day she'd be able to control it. She was better, but there was still so much she had to learn.

There was so much life underneath her feet. Animals burrowed deep, warm and safe in their dens, snakes and bugs, and other critters rustling through the earth, busy living. The magic split and branched, heading all different directions. She gasped as it hit something warm, alive, and far more powerful than she'd ever seen before.

But something about this felt familiar. Like...home.

Harlow gasped and tried to reach for it, but the magic stopped just at the edge, touching only the barest border. It felt like sunshine and mystery and...love. Tears fell down her face, but the power refused to budge as if it wasn't quite time for her to discover whatever it was that loomed so far away.

Her attention snagged in the other direction, toward familiar soil.

Thornewood, Harlow thought. It felt the same as it had when she left except...

There.

The magic stopped, hesitated, and branched again, surrounding something it wanted her to sense.

Harlow sank to the ground, feeling with her fingertips for the softest part to sink into. The second she did, a picture cleared in her mind.

Darkness.

Corruption.

Hate.

Harlow gasped and tried to pull her back, but that darkness lunged, slicing through her magic like a hot knife through butter, surrounding her with its aura.

Lines of ebony wrapped around the gold of her magic, and she felt...Harlow screamed.

She felt her magic *die*.

THE SCREAM TORE Magnus from his thoughts. He jerked his mount to a halt, focusing his senses toward the direction the cry had come from. He'd ridden ahead several hours to scout the path they planned to take. All was clear, but there was a concerning amount of magic gathered at the borders of the Kingdom of Witches.

Passing over it might be an issue, but their kingdom could no longer ignore Celestine's growing threat or the darkness encroaching on the stones. On the personal side, Magnus had plans to try to find Harlow's relatives while he was there. He thought it was a long shot, but the kingdom was tight-knit. Someone there had to know something.

Harlow deserved to know her mother's people. *Her* people.

The sound cut off abruptly, but it had come from the north, around the area he and Shade agreed to meet up. Magnus swore under his breath and spurred his mount into a gallop.

All he could pray was that he wasn't too late.

The presence of evil held her in a stranglehold. Cut off from her magic, unable to move, Harlow moaned low, squeezing her eyes shut against the images whatever it was soaked into the soul of the Luna stones showed her.

Never-ending night. An army of pale skinned, dark-eyed males, not a single one of them human. They moved too gracefully, their limbs a touch too long. Harlow's eyes skimmed over their figures, a deep sense of unease unfurling in her stomach. They marched toward something in the distance, a towering castle flying a single white flag.

A circular symbol made of thorns adorned the center.

Your power tastes of the earth, little girl. Bring it to me.

What are you? she asked. Its power was a sibilant hiss through her mind.

I am the Original. The Walker. And I am awake.

Fear bleated through her veins. She tugged her wrists against the dark veins holding her hostage, knowing she couldn't escape, but the desperate need to free herself over-ruled all other thought.

What do you want?

The army in her mind parted, revealing a tall, pale-skinned man with dark hair and dark eyes. His features were finely made, with high cheekbones and a broad unlined fore-head. No longer an *it*, Harlow thought. He wasn't quite handsome, but he was far from ugly. Something sinister lurked in his eyes, a sense of satisfaction curving the side of his lip up.

You aren't real, Harlow whispered.

It's only a matter of time.

Pressure pulsed against her mind, the darkness seeking entrance to her innermost thoughts. Harlow gritted her teeth, unsure how to battle the intrusion. She imagined a wall of thorns and vines, tightly interwoven. Buds formed at the end of the vines, blooming flowers in a riot of color.

The man laughed, a thing of shadows and horror. Razor-tipped claws shredded the barrier in her mind and ripped her secrets free.

CHAPTER TWENTY-SEVEN

TRAPPED

The fog had lasted too long to be natural. Astrid and Evara walked through the camp, the mist a silent shroud. No sound echoed in the forest. Even their footfalls were a silent sweep through the leaves and loam.

Evara carried two daggers, one held loosely in each hand. Her gaze swept back and forth, attempting to penetrate the mist. Astrid walked beside her, hands empty and loose, a thin thread of power circling around her palms.

"Harlow is missing," Evara whispered.

Astrid's attention snapped to Harlow's empty bedroll. She uttered a soft curse and gestured for Evara to follow. The guard obeyed, her gaze lingering on Harlow's discarded blanket.

"Watch your step," Evara whispered. She reached for Astrid's arm, stopping the bard. "Look." Evara pointed with the toe of her boot at a barely visible sole print in the ground that disappeared when the fog rolled over it.

"We'll never track her in this fog." Astrid blew out a

breath and stared ahead. "Stay still. I'm going to try something."

Evara stilled, watching as the power pooling around Astrid's palms brightened. The bard closed her eyes and tilted her head up to the invisible sky, mouth moving as she uttered soft words. Evara strained to hear her, the language almost musical.

Slowly, ever so slowly, the fog began to swirl around their feet, lifting just enough for them to see the ground. A fine sheen of sweat glistened against the bard's skin, her mouth pulling into a grimace.

"I can't part it completely," Astrid breathed, sagging against one of the many birch trees around them.

Evara peered at the ground. "It will do."

Astrid exhaled, a sigh of relief as the fog around their calves separated, revealing not only Harlow's path but the still forms of Shade and Desminda.

"It's unusual for Shade to still be resting," Evara observed, a slight frown on her pale face.

Desminda stirred, her dark hair sliding over her back as she sat up. The mist concealed her face, leaving only the view of her from the neck down. Astrid's lips twitched at the sight.

"Princess," Astrid whispered. Desminda jerked in surprise.

"Astrid? I can't see you! Where are you?"

Evara turned toward Shade.

Astrid headed toward Desminda, eager to catch her before she stood and got lost in the never-ending fog. "Wait. Stay there," she urged.

Desminda stilled obediently.

Astrid reached the princess just as Evara's alarmed shout rang through the wood. "Come," she urged Desminda. She tugged the princess by the arm over to Evara.

The guard loomed over Shade's prone form. A sense of dread unfurled in Astrid's stomach.

"Is he alive?" she whispered.

Evara crouched and touched the pulse in Shade's neck, her face grim. "Slow but steady." She blew out a breath of relief. "This fog is unnatural. Someone or something is keeping him asleep."

"Why only him?" Desminda asked, wrapping her shawl tighter around her shoulders. The princesses' face was drawn and tight, eyes darting around wildly.

"Magic," Evara murmured. "It's the magic in our blood."

"Shade is human, through and through," Astrid said before a laugh bubbled from her. "I always wondered if he had a touch of fey in him."

Evara shrugged. "Still possible. He's more human than mage, at least." She stood and brushed off her hands. "He will be fine here. Harlow is more important."

Desminda's brows drew together. "She isn't here?"

Astrid shook her head. "I can't move the fog completely. Watch our feet and stay close."

The princess looked at her bedroll longingly. Evara snorted with derision and started walking, Desminda's dark look following her.

Astrid sighed and jerked her head. "Come," she demanded.

Evara slowed, allowing them to catch up. "I can't hear anything," she whispered.

"Something is very wrong," Astrid agreed.

Silence fell, the oppressive weight of the mist soaking their skin and hair. Every breath felt like sucking in water. Astrid grimaced as Evara led them through the path Harlow took, carefully avoiding the girl's footsteps as she tracked.

Desminda followed meekly behind, so close to Astrid she could feel the princesses' aura melding with her own. Astrid's footsteps hitched when Desminda's power touched her own. She glanced back at the princess, but Desminda had her head down, carefully watching where Astrid stepped.

Her lips pursed, Astrid tucked the strange feeling away, and focused on Evara.

Thunderous hoof beats broke the silence, a low male shout cracking through the night.

"Harlow!"

Evara motioned for them to hurry and picked up speed, racing through the fog toward the voice.

"Magnus!" Evara called.

The hoofbeats came to a stop. Evara stumbled onto the stone path, Astrid and Desminda behind her. Magnus loomed like a golden god, blue eyes ringed with magic and narrowed in concentration.

"Where?" he demanded.

Evara pointed back toward the camp. "Her steps stop at the road. I haven't had the chance to pick them up again."

Magnus swung from his mount and drew the axe from his belt. "Wait here."

His eyes glowed as he stepped to the other side of the road. A whisper of golden power trickled from his fingers, and he sent it searching through the fog.

Astrid marveled at the ease in which he used his power, envious at his abilities. Hers used to be like that. Before magic had fallen. Bards had more access to their power than others, but it was a trickle of what it used to be. She shook away the thought, focusing on the here and now. There was a plan for all of them. The bards would regain their former glory, and Astrid would be able to rest, if only for a little while.

A golden path lit up before him. Magnus lowered his hands and frowned at Harlow's glowing footsteps. "Why would she leave the camp?"

Evara came up beside him. "Something called her. Harlow doesn't seem the overly adventurous kind."

"Overly curious," Astrid added dryly. "Perhaps there was something shiny in the forest and she went to investigate."

Magnus snorted. "I don't know my daughter as well as I'd like yet, but I'd say you're both correct." The amusement dropped from his face. "Keep your weapons out. Harlow isn't too far ahead."

They fell in behind Magnus, each armed with their weapon of choice—Magnus radiating magic, Astrid's glowing palms, and Evara with two daggers. Desminda had no weapons of her own, though her face remained drawn but watchful. Astrid eyed the guard's back curiously. Evara had magic. Astrid was certain of it. So why did she choose mundane weapons over her natural power?

She'd overheard Nova calling her the Queen's Shadow more than once. Never where others could hear her, but Astrid, like all bards, was adept at hiding in plain sight. However, she'd never once seen a hint of Evara's magic.

Magnus held up a hand, eyes tightening around the edges as he looked in both directions.

"She's here." He took a few steps forward and fell to his knees, swearing under his breath.

Evara gasped and came around the other side of Magnus, careful not to touch either of them. When Astrid came close enough to see through the dense fog, her magic sputtered and died.

Dark, glittering threads of magic held Harlow to the ground. The girl was on her knees, her teeth bared in a grimace. Her eyes were squeezed shut, effort apparent on her face. Tears streamed down Harlow's cheeks, soaking into the dark earth below her.

Astrid had never seen anything like it, but she'd recognize that power anywhere.

The Thornewood presence.

"Magnus," she murmured, her voice low and urgent, "whatever this is, it's dangerous. The power comes from Thornewood, the same thing I escaped while I was there. It might be better not to touch your bare skin to the earth."

Magnus looked up at her, brows drawn together. "I will not let my daughter suffer while I still have breath left in my body." Dismissing her, Magnus touched Harlow's arm, right where the threads lay.

A hoarse shout tore from the mage's throat before his eyes widened and an eerie silence settled over the wood.

Astrid locked eyes with Evara.

"We give them five minutes," the guard said. "That's all."

Astrid nodded. "Five," she agreed. "Should we look around?"

Evara shrugged. "There can't be much other than the woods around here. I'm familiar with the area, but the damned fog is screwing with my sense of direction. I think it's best we stay here and wait."

Astrid frowned. "Shade is unattended."

"And asleep. He should be fine. Nova periodically checks on him."

The bard's brows lifted. Evara waved her hand, looking away from Astrid's curious expression. "She does it to everyone she cares about. Shade is aware."

What an odd and dangerous power the queen had. "She controls the shadows everywhere?"

Evara shrugged and refused to answer. Which, in Astrid's opinion, meant yes.

Desminda stayed behind Astrid, her lips pressed tight. Eyes lingering on Harlow, she inched closer to the bard.

Astrid shook her head. Taking Desminda's crown had done the princess no favors. Sometimes flowers bloomed. Sometimes they fell off their stem and died. Desminda was very close to the latter.

"Come," she said, taking Desminda's arm. Astrid led the princess to a visible tree and stopped. "Stay here. Do not intervene. Understand?"

Desminda's eyes flashed with annoyance. There was the princess Astrid remembered.

"If you act witless, people will treat you as such," she said softly.

Desminda's lips parted. "I am not witless!" she insisted.

Astrid shrugged. "Then you must not act like it."

Even covered by the mist, Astrid could see Desminda's

cheeks flush with fury. Covering a smile, Astrid returned to Evara.

"You deliberately goad her," the guard whispered.

"As you do to Harlow?" Astrid said.

Evara snorted. "Harlow has no airs. She has no lost kingdom, no riches torn from her."

"Only a great destiny unknown by any of us," Astrid warned. "We do not know what she will become."

"Desminda has been on her path for years now. Even with her life torn away, she remains."

Astrid sent Evara a sharp glance, eyes narrowing. "How would you know such?" she hissed. Astrid's thoughts went back to the walk over when their auras tangled, but she said nothing.

"None of us are without gifts," Evara said cryptically. "Now hush. The mage is almost out of time."

Astrid snapped her mouth shut, vowing to discover Evara's secrets. But the shadow was right.

Magnus' time was almost up, and Astrid didn't have a clue how to save either of them.

CHAPTER TWENTY-EIGHT

SUNDERED

Magnus stood in a field of nothingness. Every ounce of life had been sucked out of the ground by a force darker than any he'd ever encountered. He stood on fallow ground. No. Not fallow. *Dead.* Magnus crouched and touched his fingertips to the soil. It shattered under his fingers, cracked and broken, no sign of any life in the once fertile loam. Puffs of brittle yellow grass dotted the landscape. Piles of bones here and there, white and bleached, lay undisturbed.

Heat itched the back of his neck, thin pearls of sweat forming before rolling down his neck.

Even worse than the hellscape in front of him? There was no sign of his daughter.

Magnus stood, brushing the dead soil against his pants. Sending his senses out, he searched for any sign of life. Any critter, mammal, person, tree...anything with a touch of life in it. He could communicate with anything, though preferred to speak only to the warm-blooded. Barring the absence of those, Magnus' second choice was the earth and trees.

Nothing revealed itself but the same presence of evil wrapped around his daughter. It seeped into the soil, the sky, the rocks and dead grass. Everything it touched withered and perished, unable to fight against the absolute corruption leaking from its tendrils.

With nothing else to do, Magnus started forward, his footfalls silent against the dead earth and went to search for Harlow.

Covered in sweat, Magnus wiped the back of his arm against his face. Grimacing at the dust and filth it came away with, Magnus sighed and put his hands on his hips. He tilted his head and looked up at the sky, squinting at the red and yellow circles. The second sun burned like a ball of fire above him. The first was dimmer, subdued somehow. It was the same world they lived in, yet not quite.

There was still no sign of Harlow. He had no idea how long he'd been here searching, but it felt like hours had passed. His throat clicked when he swallowed, and every inch of him was soaked with sweat.

The search was proving fruitless, but he had no intention of leaving without his daughter. Magnus sent his magic out once again, spiraling through the dead lands in search of Harlow, expecting to once again come up empty-handed.

But...there. There! A sign of life pulsed against his power, recognizing it.

Harlow.

Magnus pulled away before the darkness sensed it and

covered himself with a strong glamour before turning in her direction and hurrying toward her.

A few minutes later, he spotted her in the same position he'd left her kneeling in the Shadow Kingdom's forest. But the veins of darkness here had wrapped around her body completely, leaving only her golden hair and face exposed.

Worry turned his stomach as he came closer, stopping in alarm when he spotted the presence crouching next to her.

A man, tall, pale, and glowing with an aura of insidious darkness.

One white hand rested on his daughter's shoulder.

Rage such as he'd never known flooded his veins. His nostrils flared as he sought to tamp the power burning through his soul, eager to reach out and destroy this thing that dared touch one of his blood.

He silently exhaled, mind whirring at how to get closer without the being sensing his power. As long as he kept it tightly cloaked, he thought he might get close enough to deliver a deadly strike. But time was not on his side. Harlow grew paler every second she stayed kneeling, her power a stuttering glimmer of gold, much like his own.

He crept toward them, an agonizing slow pace. Magnus' heart raged within his chest, the thought of losing her more than he could bear. It was bad enough losing Marion, but to make the choice to send Harlow away...every single day he regretted his decision, even knowing it was the only way she could survive to adulthood.

Even so, she hadn't made it yet.

He gathered his power tighter, cloaked in an impenetrable glamour, careful not to let any bare skin touch the ground. Magnus watched every footfall he took, ensuring he wouldn't stumble over an exposed root or pile of buried bones. Somehow this thing had the ability to sense things through the earth, but it could only do so through bare skin or contact from something living, though not human. An animal's paws, the roots of a tree, or the belly of a snake were all conduits for the creature's power.

The possibilities staggered Magnus. Could this thing be spying on them all the time through the land? Had it realized Thornewood was one of the few places without magic? Magnus shoved those thoughts away. Plenty of time to think about this later.

The only thing that mattered now was Harlow.

Magnus gathered his power, concentrating on the one blow he could land before the thing, man, *creature*, whatever it was, realized his presence. He had to land it with a hundred percent accuracy while also keeping Harlow safe. With one hand he sent out a tendril of magic, careful not to touch the ground. The being stiffened, eyes opening.

So it could sense things through the air too. Magnus bit down a curse. With the other hand, he sent out an additional tendril heading straight for it.

When the thing's head turned in Magnus' direction, pinpointing almost the exact spot he hid, Magnus struck, shielding Harlow while sending a blast of raw power straight for its face.

The strength of the blow sent the thing reeling back, snapping its tendrils from his daughter's body. Flame rolled over its body, encompassing it in his magic. Magnus lunged toward Harlow, snapping her slight frame up in one scoop, and shielded them both, sending an additional blast back toward the creature.

A shriek of pain and rage shattered the quiet, but Magnus didn't look back. The most important thing he needed was to gain space so he could concentrate enough to get them back to the forest. They would need to stay on the road for the foreseeable future and ride without stopping.

His daughter lay like a corpse in his arms, pale and unconscious. A frisson of fear snaked down his spine, but he couldn't worry about it now.

When they were safe, or as safe as they could be, he'd try to wake her up.

For now, he had to keep them both alive.

CHAPTER TWENTY-NINE

THE BARD & THE SHADOW

They stood over Harlow and Magnus, both of their comrades locked in an invisible battle. "If you have any way to help, now would be the time," Astrid said her voice tight and strained.

Evara's expression shuttered. "I know you spy on me, bard. I won't give up my secrets so easily."

Hmm. Few sensed a bard's presence if they didn't want to be detected. "Not even to save Harlow's life?" Astrid rarely saw the guard pay attention to anyone, though she knew Evara was aware of everyone, especially when Nova was around.

But when she was with Harlow, Evara seemed different. Not like Desminda. The princess had used poor Harlow for her own devices, but before she had the chance to discard her, the girl had realized what was happening. Astrid was relieved when it happened. Little good would come of loving someone of royal blood, at least not in Thornewood.

Nova's kingdom and Nova herself might prove the opposite of that. The queen and Shade had found something special together, if Shade ever put aside his self-defeating notions that he was not good for Nova.

Even Astrid could see they strengthened each other.

Desminda weakened Harlow. They were fire and fuel together, an explosive, perhaps deadly combination. Astrid thanked her lucky stars the girl had finally realized the potential for damage Desminda could have wrought on Harlow's heart. She'd escaped just in the nick of time, and credit to her, had been smart enough to realize it even at her tender age.

Evara rolled her eyes and sank carefully to the ground. "Take care, bard. Don't touch the ground with bare skin."

"Not sure it matters. I only plan to touch Harlow."

"The princesses' healing magic could help," Evara observed.

Astrid blinked. She hadn't thought of that. "She's like a frightened rabbit. Do you think she'll help even if we ask?"

Evara's expression darkened. "You and I are far more powerful than the former queen. She will acquiesce or I will force her."

Astrid gave her a long look. But Evara, despite her bloodthirsty words, was right. Desminda could help them. Healing magic resonated with the world and all its living things. Mages with Desminda's type of power resembled bards in that their magic responded to the world around them and sought to heal the wounds people and other sentient things incurred.

The tendrils wrapped around Harlow and now Magnus were a rot in some way, a disease Desminda might be able to cure them of, or at least temporarily disable so they could untangle them both.

Astrid stood and motioned for Desminda. The princess pushed away from the tree and took hesitant steps over, stopping several feet away from Harlow.

Evara snorted in disgust. "We require assistance, Princess," she said, a sneer curling her upper lip.

Astrid sent her a warning look.

"I don't see how I can help," Desminda said, golden eyes darting between Evara and Harlow.

"You can stop acting like a damaged flower, first," Evara snapped. She jerked her head toward Harlow. "Come. Kneel beside me. Be careful not to touch your skin to the ground."

Desminda flinched before the familiar haughty expression Astrid had seen so much of appeared on her face. But Astrid saw the hurt and despair behind it. She kept quiet, though. Evara had little patience with someone of Desminda's tender personality, but she was right. They did need help.

Astrid didn't like forcing anyone to do anything, but Harlow and Magnus were imperative to their plans, and losing them would kill any chance they had of uniting their kingdoms and freeing magic.

Desminda's eyes slid to Astrid, but the bard stayed silent, waiting for the princess to decide.

"And if I refuse?" the princess asked quietly.

A savage smile slid over Evara's face. "A refusal is only words. Meaningless if the other party is more powerful."

Desminda paled. "You wouldn't."

The smile didn't drop. "I would. I'll slice into your mind like butter and rip out your power if you refuse to help us."

A chill slid down Astrid's spine. Could Evara really do that? Was this a bluff? Astrid couldn't tell, but Evara's gaze held Desminda's. If she were bluffing, Astrid would never play cards with her. Bards could usually sense a lie, and Astrid smelled no deceit in Evara's words.

Desminda's gaze flicked to Harlow. "You'd violate me to save her?"

Evara's eyes flashed with pure rage. "I'd violate a coward to save someone who saved a traitor queen and brought hope to my queen. I'd do worse if it meant saving Harlow's soul. Decide now, coward. Before I decide for you."

Desminda's golden eyes flared. "You care for her." Jealousy colored her tone.

Astrid blew out a soft breath. Desminda was a fool.

A dark chuckle came from Evara. "Decide, liar queen," she said softly. Crimson darkness flared around the guard, tendrils of blood-colored night curling over her skin and hair.

Astrid drew back an inch, fascinated by the sight. The power wasn't the same as Nova's. Similar, but different.

Desminda swallowed hard, her tanned throat working in fear, before she hurried over to Evara's side and sank beside her.

"Good choice," Evara murmured.

Desminda shut her eyes for a brief moment, resignation in her posture.

Astrid took over. "I will guide your magic. We need to sever the tendrils holding her. As soon as we do, we need to separate them and pull Harlow up from the ground."

Evara grimaced.

"I know," Astrid said in understanding. Magnus was not a small man. It would take all three of them to lift him from Harlow. If he fell, it might be all over for them.

"How am I supposed to do that?" Desminda said with a tremble in her voice.

"You heal them," Astrid said.

Desminda's eyes snapped to her. "Heal this...sickness?" She shook her head. "It feels far too powerful for me."

"It is," Evara said. "We don't need you to heal it all. Just the pieces touching them both."

Astrid nodded. "Are you ready?"

Desminda's jaw tightened. A long moment stretched before she gave a short nod.

"Good. We should all touch her at the same time." She met Evara's eyes, then Desminda's. "On the count of three."

Evara exhaled.

"One. Two. *Three.*"

Power exploded in the clearing.

CHAPTER THIRTY

A BEACON OF EMERALD AND BLOOD

Magnus' breath stuttered as he ran. He'd been running for a while now, Harlow's slight weight feeling like he carried a boulder three times his weight. There was no shelter anywhere he could see, only a desolate wasteland.

He'd have to stop soon. If he didn't, he would be too tired for the amount of magic it would require to leave this hellish place. Magnus couldn't sense any presence behind him, but most of his focus was on his daughter, monitoring her pulse and the flicker of her magic.

A flash of emerald and crimson appeared in the distance. Magnus stumbled, an alarmed shout tearing from his throat, as he struggled to keep them upright. He stopped, ragged breath the only sound in the dead world.

There. Another flash. Magnus sent a tentative thread of power, a soft sob breaking from him when he recognized at least one part of it.

Astrid. He'd recognize her power anywhere. The crimson

magic was unfamiliar, but if it was with Astrid, then the bard must trust whoever it belonged to. With single-minded determination, Magnus tightened his arms around his daughter and ran like the wind toward the bard.

Rarely had he ever needed saving. He couldn't recall a single time he felt overwhelmed by a threat except for Marion. The threat then hadn't been magical, but he'd felt the danger deep in his soul and he'd been powerless to stop it.

This was something different. An absence of life existed here. That creature had sucked everything good and green from the world and had tried to do the same to his daughter. He never was afraid for himself. But when it came to the last thing connecting him to this world? He'd do anything to save it. Even if it meant running away.

Jagged breath exploded from his lungs as he ran.

Mage. I wish to bargain.

The voice slipped into his mind, sliding right through his defenses.

Magnus stumbled to a halt, shock freezing his veins. He looked around but saw nothing alarming. Besides the land of death, nothing stood in his way, no creature of darkness, no magical threads of darkness.

How had he slipped into Magnus' mind?

Who are you? Magnus sent a thread of seeking magic out, desperate to find where it was.

I am The Original, the voice said.

Magnus' veins turned to ice water. He'd heard that term once whispered in hushed tones from one of his old mentors. The only other time he'd come across it was in an old text he was studying for Marion.

I have nothing to bargain, Magnus said. His heart beat so hard he felt it in his throat.

He sensed it a second before the thing struck. A thin tendril of darkness a few feet away.

It exploded from the ground and whipped toward his foot. Magnus dodged, spun on his heel and ran like his life depended on it, making a zig-zag pattern leading to Astrid. It didn't seem like the creature had taken note of her yet.

If he could get Harlow to her...

A sibilant chuckle rasped through his mind. *You may save your daughter if you stay*, the voice said.

I will save my daughter either way.

You overestimate your power in these lands. Your daughter's power is ripe for the taking, mage, but you are a fruit heavy with seeds. If you agree, I will release her back to your companions.

Why? Magnus didn't slow his pace.

Because your kingdom has stolen something from me. And I want it back.

What is it?

The creature laughed again.

Everything.

He was so close. "Hold on, baby," Magnus whispered. His eyes focused on the horizon, and he put on a burst of speed even though his lungs felt like they might explode.

A rumble in the earth slowed his steps.

Magnus dodged the cracks forming in the ground and went left, tightening his grip around Harlow.

Her eyes fluttered open.

"You're safe," Magnus breathed, his voice cracking as he ran.

Harlow's eyes widened. She reached up and gripped Magnus' arm.

"Danger," she said, her voice hoarse. A tear rolled down her temple, golden hair streaming behind them.

"We're almost there."

Harlow's face crumpled. "He's too strong. We won't make it."

Magnus' lips pressed together, his expression turning carefully blank. He wasn't sure they'd make it either, but he'd die before he left her here. "We will," he said grimly.

"Father," Harlow whispered, her fingers tightening around his bicep.

A broken sob escaped from Magnus, his arms tightening around his little girl. "Hold on, Harlow. Whatever happens, do *not* let go of me."

She nodded, resigned blue eyes meeting his.

He would not get this far only to let her down.

Magnus gathered every single bit of power he possessed, coiling it around him like a set of armor.

If this were to be his final stand, he'd make it one worthy of song.

CHAPTER THIRTY-ONE

A QUEEN'S MISGIVINGS & A BARD'S DELIVERANCE

"There he is," Astrid whispered as Magnus flew across the horizon. She, Evara, and Desminda stood in a desolate wasteland, arms linked together, desperately trying to remove the rest of the taint from their comrades. Most of it had fallen away seconds before they touched her, but a small thread of darkness remained wrapped around them.

Magnus eyes widened in fear at something none of them could see. Astrid's stomach twisted. "Desminda," she said urgently. "Hurry. Up."

The princess sobbed, eyes wide with terror as she watched Magnus holding a prone Harlow in his arms, desperate to reach them. "I'm tr-trying. I ca-can't get a hold of it."

Evara's eyes flashed with power. "Try harder," she hissed.

Astrid frowned at Evara, but she agreed with her. Desminda had never been pressured like normal people, never been expected to perform in a time of urgent need. "You can do this," she said quietly. "You *must* do this."

Desminda's nostrils flared. Her eyes fluttered shut and power flooded from her body, straight toward Magnus. Pure magic, the color of a morning sunrise flooded the inhospitable wasteland and headed straight for their comrades.

Astrid guided it with her own magic, a bright emerald green. Desminda's magic was untrained and wild, slippery to hold on to, but Astrid coaxed it toward Harlow and Magnus, whispering a prayer under her breath Desminda could hold onto it for that long.

Magnus was so close she could see the white of his eyes. Astrid murmured under her breath, willing him to pick up speed, praying this wasn't all for naught.

A moment later, Desminda's healing magic reached him, covering them both in a wash of golden power. He didn't halt, his jaw tight with fear, but Astrid felt the moment the darkness relinquished its hold.

And from the look of relief on Magnus' face, he felt it as well.

A hoarse shout tore from his throat as soon as he reached them. Evara reached out and gripped his arm. "Hold on," she barked.

A moment later, Harlow's body shuddered in the Shadow Kingdom's forest and she collapsed to the ground, completely unconscious, Magnus' prone body beside her.

Desminda keeled over with a grunt. Unable to hold herself up, she fell sideways. Neither Astrid nor Evara caught her. Astrid winced when she hit the ground, but Desminda would be alright. Only soft ground had met her, and Harlow and Magnus were the ones in the most danger.

Evara knelt beside Harlow, her hands running over the

girl's body, meticulously checking for wounds or bruises. She let out a soft exhale when she found nothing other than dirt and sat back on her haunches, looking over at Astrid. "She will be alright."

Astrid nodded and sank down beside Magnus to do the same. "Exhaustion. That's all."

Evara sank the tip of her finger into the soil. Astrid inhaled, but Evara shook her head. "Whatever it was, it's gone."

"For now," Astrid said grimly.

"For now," Evara agreed. "Just don't touch bare skin to the ground." She squinted at the sky. Soft rays of morning light poured through the fog. "It's lifting. Best to rouse Shade before he wakes up and sees all of us missing."

Astrid glanced at Desminda. Her eyes were open and unseeing, but the princess still breathed. Evara snorted. "She will be fine. I'll watch over them all."

Astrid nodded and jogged back toward the campsite, relief spilling through her. Too close of a call. They could not afford another one so soon. Getting to the Kingdom of Witches had to take priority.

Shade stirred as soon as she stepped into the campsite. He blinked and jerked awake, a look of confusion on his face as he scrubbed a hand over his jaw. Astrid stayed back and lifted a hand in greeting.

He scanned the campsite and the road ahead, the fog finally lifting enough to see several feet ahead. "What—what happened?" he croaked.

"Many things have happened." Astrid took a few steps closer to him.

Shade had a wild look about him, eyes wide and bloodshot, his normally pristine hair stood up in all directions. "I slept all night," he said in wonder.

Astrid winced. She understood. Sleep was a rare commodity in her line of work, and she couldn't remember the last time she'd gotten a full night's rest. Shade's work promised more danger than hers, so it wasn't surprising to see the awe on his face. Empathy stung her eyes, and she looked away.

Shade sighed and rose to his feet with a grunt. "Magic?" he asked.

Astrid snorted. "More than magic. Get dressed. We can talk on the road."

Shade gave her a long look but didn't argue. "Give me five minutes."

Astrid nodded and left him there, jogging back across the road to Harlow and the others.

By then Magnus and Desminda had roused. Harlow lay prone on the ground, still unconscious. Evara stood close, hazel eyes scanning the horizon. Her expression lightened when she saw Astrid, and she jogged over, gesturing for her to follow.

"There's something wrong with Desminda," she whispered when they were out of earshot.

Astrid's brow furrowed. "Wrong? Is she injured?"

Evara frowned. "Nothing physical. She seems... different."

"Has Magnus noticed?"

"He's the one who pointed it out." They both looked over at the mage. Exhaustion pulled his mouth down, and his eyes were drawn and heavy. Power blinked and sputtered around him before it finally went out like a spark dying in the morning light. Magnus slumped against a boulder, his eyes resting on Harlow.

"Is it something we need to worry about right now?" Astrid asked.

Evara shrugged. "Who's to say?"

The laugh that bubbled out of Astrid was tired and ragged. "Indeed," she agreed. "Help me get Harlow. We'll worry about Desminda when we have to."

Magnus protested when Evara and Astrid scooped Harlow up, slinging her arms over their backs, half carrying, half dragging her back to the campsite.

Desminda pushed herself up, magic drained and scared, but she managed to walk on her own. Magnus did the same, his stance far removed from the powerful stride he'd had before.

Whatever this presence was, this foreign magic assailing them, they had to burn it out at the root before it destroyed them all.

Shade eyed them as they stumbled back into camp, his brows lifting a hair when he saw the state of his ragged band of comrades.

"Eventful evening?" he asked dryly, strapping his bag to his mount's saddle before giving it a firm pat on the neck.

Magnus snorted, groaning as he reached around to tie the reins of his mount loosely around a tree to prevent the sweet thing from wandering off in search of grass. "Everything hurts," he said with a wheeze.

Shade stilled, his gaze falling on his friend. His friend

only had one weakness, and she had died in Shade's arms years ago. For him to admit to pain, whatever happened must be serious.

Magnus took a water sack from his bag and drained it, grimacing at the taste. "We will speak on the road."

At Shade's protests, Magnus shook his head. "On the road. We can dally no more."

Evara stood off to the side, her back turned. Shade had no doubt she spoke to the shadows, keeping Nova apprised of events. He'd felt her presence lurking, but she stayed away from him, refusing to engage or get too close.

His heart ached every time he noticed the shadows, even if he knew they were only the normal ones and not her magic. He felt her like a phantom ache, always present in his heart.

Cursing himself for his behavior would do him no good. He'd made the right decision. Who was he to disobey the advice he'd long given others? No good would come of getting involved with a queen. Or a king. Or anyone who wore or would one day wear a crown.

Too much heartache and trouble followed them.

Desminda stood by herself, a desolate look on her unusually pale face. Her hair hung in a lank braid, dark shadows etching a permanent home on her face. Harlow lay close to Magnus, curled on her side and totally oblivious to the world around her. If they didn't look so serious, Shade might laugh.

The once mighty crew who rode into the Shadow Kingdom looked more like a bunch of down-on-their-luck bandits forced to live off the land.

And something had kept him sleeping last night to do this to them.

"Eat while you can," Magnus advised. "Once we get on the path, we won't stop much until we reach the witches."

Desminda gave Magnus a sharp look, but the big mage only paid attention to the bread and jerky in his hand. Magic burned through energy reserves, and none of them had brought enough provisions for a major battle. They still rode through Nova's lands and had wrongly assumed they'd be safe from all but bandits.

"Should we gather berries?" Shade asked.

Magnus shook his head. "Everyone still has their reserves, I assume?" Nods all around. "We'll be fine then. Once we start riding, I'll have time to recover."

Shade wasn't so sure, but he didn't argue with his friend.

Evara turned to them and strode over to her mount, unwrapping Harlow's lazy beast as she did, and fought with the stubborn horse while trying to saddle her own.

Astrid snorted. "Luci will be here soon. I'd love to see how she deals with this flower-munching nightmare."

Evara glared at the mount. "Maybe she'll eat the thing and leave its carcass for the crows."

The mount stared at her balefully.

Shade chuckled and led his mount closer to the road. His was well-behaved enough to wait for him, but he took no chances and tied him close to Magnus'.

"Is she alright?" he asked, peering down at the still unconscious Harlow.

Magnus' jaw tightened. "The thing trapped her magic and fed off her like a siphon. Harlow will need time to recover. Help me with her?"

Shade nodded and lifted Harlow in his arms, marveling

at how light she was. Her head lolled back, golden hair falling away from her sallow face. He sucked in a breath at how ill she looked.

"We will talk on the road," Magnus said again, his voice low enough for only his ears to hear. "Getting to the Kingdom of Witches takes priority."

Shade's nod was a jerk of his head. He waited for Magnus to mount, his friend wincing as he settled into the saddle, and shifted Harlow so Magnus could maneuver her into the saddle in front of him. Once his arms were wrapped around her and he'd gently settled her against her father's chest, Shade stepped away.

Magnus' eyes were haunted, a shimmer of grief reflecting in the hazy morning. Shade clapped a hand on Magnus' knee. They both had memories, some not good, of the witches and their treatment of Marion, but Harlow was of witch descent and deserved the chance to know her family. On the political side, he hoped this was enough to secure their assistance in freeing Thornewood from its oppressors.

But now, Celestine seemed the least of their worries. Whatever had happened to them during the night had shaken everyone, and Shade had an odd feeling Celestine had nothing to do with it.

If he and Nova were communicating, he could ask Lucien, but it was best for everyone if they kept their talks to a minimum and only when absolutely necessary.

Evara swept past. "You are a fool," she whispered.

Shade jerked his attention to her, but Evara didn't turn back. The guard wasn't ignorant and had no doubt noticed how much time he'd spent with her queen. But there was no way she knew what had happened the morning he'd left her.

Was there?

Frowning, Shade stepped away and mounted his own horse, muttering a curse when he realized he hadn't bothered to help Desminda. He turned to see how the princess was doing and was surprised and heartened to see she'd secured and mounted her own horse and was following behind.

Oh, how the mighty had fallen, he thought. Once, his entire being revolved around seeing to her needs. Now, he'd almost forgotten she was there.

Desminda's eyes glimmered with gold, a remnant of power simmering in their depths. She gave Shade an unreadable look before going around him, stopping her horse at the path and waiting. Her face had lost some of its chalkiness, but her body still held a fine tremor.

Magnus turned his mount toward the west when they'd all gathered at the path. "We must all stay on the road, even when we break for meals. If we ride hard enough and skip lunch, we should reach the witch border by nightfall. It's in our best interest to pass into their kingdom immediately."

On that happy note, they set off at a breakneck pace.

CHAPTER THIRTY-TWO

LIBRARY THIEVERY

"What happened?" Shade murmured when they finally stopped for an afternoon meal. Harlow had finally woken up, but she'd dozed on and off for hours, communicating little.

She sat cross-legged on the path, munching on a biscuit, eyes trained ahead of her.

Evara and Astrid sat together, heads bowed close discussing something in earnest. Neither smiled.

"I don't quite know," Magnus began. "I was on my way back when I heard Harlow scream. As soon as I rode within a mile of the sound, fog thicker than porridge appeared everywhere. Astrid and Evara came out of the woods and intercepted me."

Shade listened as he spoke of the events of the past night, stopping to ask for clarification when there were things he didn't understand.

"How did it grab her?" Shade asked.

"I'm right here," Harlow said, her voice hoarse.

Magnus glanced at her. "Then speak."

She sent him a dry look. "Something called me. It woke me up out of a sound sleep and led me to the clearing." Harlow sighed and shook her head. "Touching the ground was stupid. Everything was fine until I put my fingertips in the earth."

Shade nodded. "You think it has power when someone's skin touches the ground?"

Magnus grimaced. "I do. There's a connection to a mage's power when we connect with the earth. Somehow it accesses that, even far away. It sucked Harlow into its grip." He sighed and shook his head. "It took all four of us to escape."

"Four?" Shade inquired.

"Desminda was the catalyst. Her magic seems anathema to the presence."

Harlow frowned. "Desminda saved us?"

"Group effort," Magnus said. "But her power, guided by Evara and the bard, is what freed us from the darkness."

Harlow shivered. "It..." She licked her lips. "It took my magic away." Her brows furrowed. "No. It suppressed it somehow. And then it ate it." Harlow's lower lips wobbled. "Will I get it back?"

Magnus' eyes tightened at the edges. "Yes. Of course. It may take a few days depending on how much it took. But your magic is a well and will constantly replenish."

The relief on her face sobered Shade. "And yours?" he asked Magnus.

"The place it took us to weakened me. Nothing living exists there. It is a barren wasteland." Magnus shuddered. "But it was familiar. Too familiar."

Harlow shivered. "It was Thornewood."

Shade's attention snapped to her. "Thornewood? How?"

Harlow shrugged, one too thin shoulder lifting. "In the past, I think."

Magnus nodded. "He called himself The Original. The Walker."

"He said my kingdom stole something from him and he wants it back." Harlow shifted, trembling hands lifting to rub her arms. "I don't understand. What does it want?"

Magnus' expression went grim. "Everything."

Shade swore under his breath. "But what is it?"

Magnus took a hunk from his jerky and chewed before responding. "There is reference to this...being in some ancient magic texts. If it's the same, and I suspect it is, the thing existed at the dawn of our kingdom's birth."

"Is it a mage?" Shade asked.

Harlow blew out a breath. "It's magical. I can feel its presence everywhere. But it's not a mage in the same way you and I think about them. I don't think the thing has any humanity."

"No," Magnus agreed, pushing another biscuit over to his daughter. "It comes from below. But I don't think it originally existed there."

"You think it's from another realm?" Shade asked.

"No way to tell," Magnus answered. "But its power level is far vaster than anything I've ever seen."

"I didn't stand a chance," Harlow said, a hitch in her voice when she said the words.

Magnus watched his daughter for a moment. "The thing about magic is that it's flexible. It almost had me too and I've spent my life training my power. But I've learned that everything can be beaten. To do that, though, you must understand it."

Harlow studied him. "And how do we understand something we've never seen before?"

Magnus smiled. "Books, my daughter. Texts. Scrolls. Stories. Information is how we arm ourselves against the unknown. We study it the best we can and then we experiment. I wounded it briefly with my power, so we know it isn't immune."

Harlow's expression brightened a small bit. "Books," she murmured. "Thornewood has many banned texts."

Shade sent her a sharp look. "And how would you know that?"

A flash of a smile formed and disappeared just as fast. "I broke into the library when I was training."

Magnus' booming laugh at Shade's incredulous expression broke the somber air.

"She didn't get that from Marion," Shade said, lips twitching.

"No," Magnus said, still chuckling. "My wife was brilliant, but she left the troublemaking to me."

Harlow watched them, a hungry expression in her eyes. Shade knew what it was like to live without a mother, but he hadn't lost his as soon as Harlow had. She'd grown up with kind women, thankfully, but there was nothing that could replace a true mother's love.

"What did you find?" Shade asked against his better judgment.

"A book about religious control."

Magnus' eyes flashed.

"And then another about old magical families." Harlow shrugged. "Both were boring."

Shade snorted. "You left them behind?"

Harlow shrugged. "We left in a hurry."

"Hmm," Shade acknowledged. "Perhaps the witches have a library."

Magnus laughed. "Marion lamented the loss of library access often after she came to Thornewood. If it's as wonderful as she says it is, there may be a plethora of knowledge to help us."

"Good." Shade rose. "Then let us hurry."

Harlow had perked up considerably a couple of hours later. Emboldened by the food and drink and the handy pillow she'd found against her father's chest, Harlow requested to ride.

Shade didn't think it was a good idea. The mount led behind Evara stopped every ten minutes when it got even a hint of flower pollen in its stubborn nose. He'd never heard a female curse quite as soundly as Evara had the last few hours.

"We're a few hours away," Shade advised. "Are you sure you're strong enough?"

Magnus winced. Harlow sent him a baleful glare. "I'm fine," she insisted, sliding off Magnus' mount toward Flora. The horse spotted her coming and let out a shriek worthy of a kitchen maid.

Harlow stopped in surprise, a hand clutching her chest in fear. "Flora!" she shouted a moment later. "What on—"

A high whinny from behind caught Harlow's attention. She gasped, and a wide, happy smile graced her face. "Luci!"

Harlow took off at a sprint toward the nightmare bearing down on them. Shade went to call out, but Magnus gave him a look and shook his head.

How that man could not be afraid for his daughter with a hell horse bearing down on her, he couldn't say, but Luci ran at a full-on gallop straight toward her.

The horse loomed above the slight girl, skidding to a stop far closer than Shade was comfortable with. Harlow stood on her tiptoes to hug Luci, and the horse bent down to allow it. Her fingers stroked through its night-colored mane as Harlow murmured to it.

When Luci lifted her head, she studied them all with an intelligence far too keen to be animal. Shade shifted under the mare's gaze, but Magnus swung off his mount and came up beside Harlow, reaching a hand toward Luci.

Luci investigated Magnus, and apparently seeing something she liked, sniffed his hand. Magnus tousled Luci's mane and leaned forward, speaking in low tones.

Shade shook his head. Madness. His friend spoke to a horse and magic was out to get them.

How had his life gone from predictable to complete chaos in such a short time?

CHAPTER THIRTY-THREE

THE DARK REACHES IN

The stones grew darker every day. Celestine had shut off access to the room, allowing only herself and her most trusted guards to enter. After Lucien's abandonment, Celestine realized there were few she could allow into her inner circle. At first, she wasn't concerned. Yes, something influenced the stones, but there had been no influence other than the way it looked.

Over time, the thing started making its presence known, whispering to Celestine when she entered to allow the stones to soothe her lack of magic and her frustration at not knowing how to free the power she was born with as well as the one who could help her regain it. She'd consulted the libraries, brought in mages from outside of the Lunamoor, and even resorted to bribery.

Nothing had worked.

Perhaps it had been a foolish move to kill the queen before she got her answers.

Celestine sighed and pulled the blanket tighter. Moonlight streamed into her room, outlining everything in a watery silver glow.

Some people regretted their actions. Celestine rarely made a decision she looked back on later and wondered if she should have taken another path.

Until now.

So eager to regain her lost power, she'd worked behind the scenes to crush a kingdom and had succeeded. Somewhat. While the kingdom still stood, its rulers were gone. The king and queen were bone dust, and the princess was either dead or in hiding.

Celestine smiled to herself. Even if Desminda hid, she wouldn't stay gone forever.

And when she came back, Celestine would take the knife to the brat herself.

She stretched and rolled onto her side, away from the window.

I can help you...

Celestine stilled, her heart beating so loud it sounded like a drum in her ear. It was the same voice she heard every time she entered the room of stones.

I know where the princess hides.

I know her secret.

Let me in, Celestine, and I will show you. I will elevate you to greatness.

Oh, how she wished the voice could. Was it her mind playing tricks on her? Was this her penance for her deeds? To lose herself in her cursed mind and slowly go mad?

She'd never spoken back to the voice, never gave sound to the fear plaguing her.

Speak to me, Celestine.

Her breath was a roar between her ears.

I know you hear me, Queen of Roses.

"I am Queen of Thornewood," Celestine whispered.

No. Not yet. You are their usurper. Not their queen. You hold no true power. You only hold their precious stones. Let me in, Celestine, and I can tell you how to become their true queen.

"I want more than Thornewood," Celestine said, giving voice to the darkness in her heart. "I want it all."

The dark chuckle caressed her skin, worming its way into her psyche. A smile curled her lips at the decadent sound.

I can give it to you. I can show you why your stones lie dormant.

"Can you help me bring magic back?"

I can show you the way.

It wasn't yes, and it wasn't no.

Celestine rolled over, looking toward the direction of the sound. A male-shaped darkness loomed in the corner, a shadow not yet given form.

"What do you want from me?"

I need a form.

Celestine stiffened.

To share. You will still have your faculties, the voice insisted. Its sibilant hiss sounded like a dying fire.

"Why should I trust you?"

It laughed again. *Perhaps you shouldn't. Maybe you should run from this place and never look back. Thornewood is a poison upon the land. Its soil dies as we speak, magic starved for years.*

Celestine sat up. "What do you get out of this?"

My power is tied to those stones, it said. *A spell lies over them, over most of the stones in the surrounding kingdoms. I know who put it there.*

Celestine's heart pounded.

And I know where he is.

"Where?" she demanded.

Information comes at a cost, Rose Queen.

Celestine mulled over its words, wondering if she were being tricked. "What are you?"

The darkness in the corner flickered. Rage filled its voice. *I am The Original. The First Walker. I am Everything.*

Celestine stared. The words meant nothing to her. "A demon then?"

A huff of haughty amusement came from the corner. *Not a lowly demon, but close enough, I suppose. I walked this land far before the mages came.*

"Why do you need a form so badly?"

My form is...limited in its current capacity. My magic is contained to the earth. If I take form, there is no limit to what I can do.

Celestine didn't quite believe him.

"And what do you wish to do?"

I wish to seek revenge.

She tilted her head, narrowing her eyes at the wavering form. "Against whom?"

Those who've sinned against me, stolen my land, and my power.

Celestine waited.

I seek the heirs of the golden-eyed one.

Celestine shook her head. "I'm afraid I cannot help you. I know no one with golden eyes."

But as she said it, she realized she did.

There was only one person in the surrounding kingdoms who had eyes like that, and Celestine had killed her mother a few months ago. Or...maybe it wasn't her mother at all. Curious.

I smell her blood here, the being said. *She's been here recently.*

"Who is this golden-eyed heir?" Celestine asked.

My enemy, the voice hissed. *Help me find her and power beyond imagination will be yours.*

"And when it's over?" Celestine asked. "Will you relinquish my body? Return that to me which is mine?"

The being hesitated which told Celestine everything she needed to know.

I will.

Celestine kept her expression blank. "I would like time to decide. Give me two days."

Impudent wench!

Celestine's brows rose. "Two days or my answer is no."

I can take it, the voice hissed.

Celestine smiled. "I don't think you can. If you could, you wouldn't be in my chambers bargaining with an *impudent wench.*"

The voice hissed again in displeasure. *Two days*, the voice agreed.

A moment later, the oppression in the room faded.

Celestine drew in a ragged breath. Wiping the nervous sweat from her brow, she sank back onto the pillow, her mind spinning at the possibility. How could she protect herself but also get what she wanted? Letting that creature inhabit her body made her ill with fear, but it would help her reach her goals. *If* she helped him.

He sought Desminda.

What was so important about her, other than the demon's need for vengeance? The princess must possess something he badly wanted if he was willing to bargain with Celestine.

First, Celestine had to figure out what it was he so desperately sought.

Then, she had to figure out how to keep the demon, or whatever it was, from taking over her soul.

If she could fight him off when she realized her goals, she could have everything, including Desminda.

Smiling, Celestine curled onto her side once more.

She was asleep within a minute, the smile never leaving her lips.

CHAPTER THIRTY-FOUR

A SPARK OF DARKNESS

S he felt it, a spark of something in her chest. Squirming deeper and deeper inside, like a piece of food caught in her throat and she wasn't quite choking on it, but she couldn't expel it either. Desminda rubbed the area, concern wrinkling her brow.

They'd ridden hard today, stopping only once for a bite to eat. She'd said little since they'd left, and no one said anything to her. An overwhelming feeling of emptiness yawned inside her, present since they day they'd ridden out of Thornewood in a desperate race for their lives.

But today, that chasm seemed endless, and she couldn't see a way to climb out of it.

Harlow had written her off, anger evident every time the girl spoke to her. Shade had switched loyalties to Nova, the Shadow Queen, and Evara barely tolerated her. She no longer had a place with them.

Once she'd been on a road to glory and power. Now she was adrift, a princess with no kingdom.

The road ahead seemed endless, the hazy sky above them dragging Desminda's mood down even lower than this morning. Murmured conversation floated up, so soft she couldn't make out any words.

She couldn't seem to make herself care.

Sighing, she nudged the sides of her mount. The gentle mare picked up speed, putting some space between her and the people who barely tolerated her.

A question had burrowed into her mind a few weeks ago and hadn't left her. Did she want to take her throne back? Or did she want to leave, go somewhere no one knew her, and start over?

Neither seemed palatable, but one *was* less work. A huff of laughter escaped her. She could get a small little house tucked away in the woods and figure out how to live off the land. Her mother would be horrified if she were alive. That thought made her smile wider.

"Desminda!"

The sound of Magnus' voice tossed her out of her whimsical thoughts. She slowed her horse and turned.

"Up ahead is a fork in the road. Take the one on the right." Magnus had been looking at her oddly all morning. It bothered her less than it should. She shrugged and made a mental note. Right at the fork.

What would happen if she went left?

The thought made her smile.

The fork in the road marked two completely different paths. One was full of trees, shadows falling heavy on the ground. The other was brighter, as if the sun was bright only a few miles ahead.

Fewer trees existed on that path, only brush and plains. Desminda guided her mount toward the treed path, yearning to take the left. Pink flowers bloomed on the other path, dotting the landscape with a riot of color. Bees with fat pollen baskets buzzed low, circling around the flowers, searching for more sustenance.

Desminda envied them their easy lives. Holding in her sigh, she turned in her saddle and faced the road ahead.

The Witch Kingdom loomed before them, a forbidding castle made of dark stone rising in the distance. Desminda's breath caught when she spotted it, a shiver of fear rolling down her spine. Thornewood had always been so bright, its stained glass casting sparkling rays of colors down onto the marble floors. Her mother always kept fresh flowers in vases all over the castle, the scent of roses and jasmine never too far away.

A pang of grief struck her so suddenly it took her breath away. Tears swam in her eyes, and she blinked them away. The sound of hoofbeats came from behind. Desminda straightened, wiping the grief from her face and waited for whoever it was to approach.

Shade came up beside her. "Princess." He inclined his head. "You seem preoccupied."

Desminda snorted. "Hardly. I'm a pariah. Why would I try to fit in? I'm a thornbush in a field of chamomile."

To her surprise, Shade chuckled. "All your life, you trained to be queen. I am not surprised you feel you don't fit in."

She glanced at him in surprise, then laughed. "I should have known you'd notice."

They rode for a while in silence before Desminda sighed. "I am lost, Shade."

"I know," he murmured. "It is normal to feel lost." A sad smile crossed his face. "You must decide what it is you want. Your birthright lies an entire kingdom away." He waved a hand ahead of them. "Your destiny might lie ahead. There's no way to tell what the future holds. You are the one who decides what path to take."

Shade reached over and touched her arm. "Thank you for saving them."

Desminda started. "It was not only my effort."

"Magnus informed me. Your magic healed him. And Harlow. Despite the tension between you, it is evident you care."

Desminda huffed. "She hates me." She looked away from him. "And I deserve it," she muttered.

Shade laughed. "Harlow's heart is too tender for hate. She dislikes you, but that can change. Time heals most wounds, Desminda, but you do not make it easy for people."

Her lips parted. "You would not have said that to me a few months ago."

Shade inclined his head. "You are right. Things are changing whether we want them to or not."

She slid a glance at him. "And we head for an enemy's kingdom to convince them to be our friends."

Shade shook his head. "We do not have to be friends with our allies. The same goal has united worse causes before."

"You trust these witches?"

He chuckled. "I trust few people. What I know about the witches, I've read only in texts. This is a good lesson for you.

Your mother rarely let you leave your kingdom. She failed to teach you how to navigate true politics outside of Thornewood. If you wish to regain your throne, you'd be wise to listen and learn quickly."

Desminda nodded. "I will do my best."

Shade gave her a long look. "You must do more than your best. The fate of an entire queendom may rest on your shoulders."

Shade slowed his pace and turned his mount around, riding back to Magnus.

His words stuck with Desminda for the rest of the ride into the Witch Kingdom.

Freedom or her birthright?

The thing in her chest squirmed.

CHAPTER THIRTY-FIVE

AN UNWELCOME WELCOME

Harlow felt like she'd been locked inside a barrel and thrown into the ocean. Her head pounded, her mouth felt like the inside of a sock, and she could barely focus when anyone spoke to her.

She ate anything Shade, Evara, or her father gave to her, and drank so much water her bladder felt like it was about to burst. Whatever that thing had done to her, it had taken every ounce of energy out of her body.

Even though they were miles away from where it happened, a sense of dread still filled Harlow's veins. She was no stranger to fear, not after the last couple years of her life, but being so powerless...so *helpless* to do anything to save herself made her feel numb.

But it also hardened her resolve to learn her magic and embrace it, so she'd never feel that way again. Shade and Magnus had spoken in quiet tones for most of the journey, their voices low and urgent. Harlow tried not to notice how their eyes slid first toward Desminda, then toward her.

Desminda had saved her. The thought made something dark twist inside her. Harlow rarely had the energy to hate anyone. Why should she punish herself over someone else's actions? But Desminda had wounded Harlow's heart in a way no one else had ever done, and those wounds took a long time to heal. A tender place still existed inside her where Desminda once resided.

"Magnus?"

Her father stilled and slowed his mount, allowing it to drop back to ride beside her. His eyes were full of concern. "Everything alright?"

She nodded. "Still hungry and thirsty."

Magnus started digging in his saddlebag. She reached over and touched his hand. "But nothing that won't hold," she added with a smile.

"Magic drain," he said. "Regardless of how it's taken, magic use takes energy. You'll notice as you progress more, your appetite will grow."

He stared at the looming castle ahead. "No doubt the castle will have a bounty of food available."

An edge existed in his voice where none had been before. Her father was nervous about entering the witch kingdom.

"Do you know the queen?"

Magnus' eyes crinkled at the edges. "Not really. I've traveled to these lands before but was not allowed to stay." His face sobered. "I'm not sure I would have anyway after what happened to Marion."

Harlow nodded. She could understand that. Once her foster parents passed, all she wanted to do was leave that house and never return. Losing a husband or wife in the way he did...well, Harlow couldn't blame him. She'd never forget walking into the room and seeing her foster parents lying there, unseeing eyes and bodies still in death. But her mother's death came at the hands of a tyrant, when all Marion had done was try to save her daughter.

"You seem nervous," she said quietly. "Are we in danger?"

Magnus glanced at her, a small smile curving his lips. "You are far more observant than others give you credit for."

Harlow's cheeks colored.

He shook his head. "I do not know. They are not enemies of Nova's kingdom, but I am the enemy of many. And you, daughter, are from their kingdom in all the ways that count. I'm afraid I don't know what to expect. If they object to my presence, I will wait for you at the border."

Alarm rattled through her. "No!"

Magnus chuckled. "You are the safest out of all of us. You and the bard. Witch blood roars through your veins. Astrid has safe passage through all kingdoms. If it comes down to it, the bard will keep you safe."

Astrid, hearing her name, moved her mount closer. She dropped her voice as she approached. "We're in danger?" Her bright gaze scanned the horizon.

"We're discussing what-ifs," Magnus said.

She nodded. "I will keep her safe if only we are allowed inside." Astrid frowned. "I suspect it won't go quite like you expect it to, though."

With that, Astrid nudged her mount forward and sped to the front, slowing to ride next to Desminda.

Magnus frowned at her back. "Is she always like that?"

Harlow snorted. "All the time. She's worse than Bloom on occasion."

His brow crinkled before clearing a second later. "Ah. The Seer."

"Yes. Her power came in like an avalanche the first few days we were here."

"It can happen like that sometimes."

Shade chuckled, still within earshot. "Harlow's wasn't an avalanche." A flash of white there and gone was the only visible sign of Shade's amusement. "She blew the roof off the training quarters."

Magnus' eyes widened. "Well done!"

Harlow stared at him in surprise, but Magnus shrugged. "It could have been worse. You injured no one, correct?"

Shade confirmed.

"Then I say it was a success."

Harlow rolled her eyes. Men. Were they all like that? The destruction she'd wrought didn't feel successful, nor did she feel any more in control than she had the second it happened to her.

A shimmering bubble of magic appeared ahead of them, maybe a half mile to a mile away. Harlow gasped at the transparent riot of iridescence.

"The border is just up ahead," Magnus said.

Shade blinked. "How can you tell?"

Harlow's head snapped to him. "You can't see that?" she blurted.

Shade gave her an odd look. "See what?"

Magnus laughed and touched Shade's arm. "Look again."

Shade's shocked inhale and widened eyes made her

realize that no, Shade couldn't see it. The border was entirely magical in nature.

Maybe six months ago she wouldn't have been able to see it either. The thought saddened her more than she thought it would.

Evara and Astrid stopped their mounts, the bard turning back to them with a grim expression.

"We won't be able to pass through it unless they allow it," she said.

Magnus nodded. "Same as the Kingdom of Shadows. Every kingdom unaffected by the fall of magic put up a magical border. It's nothing to worry about. A safety precaution, that's all."

Harlow glanced at him. A few minutes ago, Magnus looked and sounded concerned. Now his tone had turned nonchalant. Harlow wished she had that ability to turn emotion off like he had. Like everyone else around her had.

He gave her an encouraging smile. "Almost there. We'll stop and rest again before we pass through." Magnus rode ahead and left her with Shade, who watched her father ride away.

When Magnus was next to Evara and Astrid, Shade cleared his throat. "Are you alright?"

"I'm fine. Still weak and hungry. Magnus assures me it's all normal."

He nodded. "When we get inside, it's important to remain silent unless you are asked a question, understand?"

Harlow smiled. "So just like back in Thornewood?"

Shade's expression sobered. "Unfortunately." He ran a

hand through his dark hair. "I've never been here either. We are riding into the unknown."

He so rarely confided anything in her that she straightened on Luci and hedged another question. "Do you think it's worth it? The danger we might ride into?"

Shade thought about it for a moment before nodding. "If it were only Thornewood, and this new threat had not reared its head, my answer might be different, but this presence, whatever it might be, will eventually affect everyone. Gathering allies to our side is our only hope." He glanced over at her. "If even Magnus, the greatest mage walking today, was almost caught in its web, then I'm afraid it isn't something we should tackle alone."

Harlow rubbed her wrists, still feeling that dark, oily magic holding her into the ground. She shuddered. "My mother's people are here," she blurted.

Shade nodded. "They are, but Marion was never forthcoming with information when it came to her parents. I'm sure Magnus has tried to discover who they are, but..." He paused for a long moment.

"Don't get my hopes up," Harlow concluded.

Shade winced. "I'm sorry, but yes. Try not to expect much. They might be hostile even with your presence. I don't expect them to harm you, but a daughter of their kingdom was killed by their enemy. It's possible they think you might have defected to the Thornewood side."

Harlow laughed. "Didn't I do that years ago?"

At that, Shade smiled sadly. "No. You were loyal to Desminda. Never to Thornewood."

Harlow sucked in a shocked gasp. "How could you—" she began but stopped.

Shade merely watched her as she grappled with his words. As much as she hated admitting he was right, Harlow had only gone to the castle out of desperation, following a trail of breadcrumbs her sister left. Her only goal had been to find Nova. Thornewood came second. Maybe even third when her heart had softened toward the irreverent princess. She blew out a breath. "Fine. I see your point."

"It's not only that. Perception is everything in political games. You ride in with Thornewood people and a mage, your father, who everyone thinks is long dead. They will mistrust us even more than usual, and so we will arrive with less bargaining power than we should. They are within their rights to imprison us on sight."

Harlow startled. "What?" she hissed.

Shade stared ahead, no longer able to see the shimmering border magic, but squinted as if he tried. "It is the way of things. I don't expect it to happen, but I will not be surprised if it does."

She slid a stunned glance his way. "You're remarkably calm about all of this."

He laughed. "I've been in many dungeons, young Harlow. As you can see, I've escaped all of them."

He nudged his horse forward.

"That doesn't make me feel better!" she called to his back.

Shade's dark laugh made her smile.

CHAPTER THIRTY-SIX

A TRAP!

True to Magnus' word, they stopped at the border to the witch kingdom, dismounted, and shared a meal.

Well...Shade called it a meal. Harlow called it a hodge-podge of stale bread, tough meat, and fruit that had seen better days. But it was sustenance, so she said nothing and took what she was offered. She'd cleaned out her own saddle bag during lunch, so Magnus and Evara shared their rations with her.

A fine tension had settled over their makeshift camp with Astrid the only one seeming even half relaxed. Desminda, once again, sat by herself, daintily chewing on a piece of jerky. Harlow envied her manners. She'd never met a single person who could eat jerky in a dainty manner until the princess. Normally, Harlow had to tear at it like a wild animal before getting a small enough piece worthy of eating.

She stood and wandered over to the princess, settling herself a few feet away. Desminda's chewing stilled, and she stared at Harlow warily. "What?" she demanded.

Harlow rolled her eyes. "I wanted company."

Desminda huffed a laugh. "You never want company."

It wasn't a lie. Harlow had always been content to eat by herself. It was Desminda who found herself constantly surrounded by people. Whether she preferred it, Harlow didn't know. She'd never asked. "Fine," Harlow snapped. "I wished to speak with you."

Desminda shrugged. "Then speak."

Anger filled Harlow at her callous disregard. "Must you always be so...so...sanctimonious?" she spat.

One of Desminda's eyebrows lifted. "That is quite a large word for someone with common blood."

The insult sank right where Desminda planned it. A dagger straight through her bones and right into her heart. Harlow sucked in a shocked breath, humiliation heating her cheeks and neck.

She'd tried. So hard. She'd tried not to be mean to Desminda. Harlow tried to understand. She wasn't always successful, but Desminda had never accepted responsibility for what happened, and she'd been almost impossible to live with since they'd left Thornewood. Harlow had come over to apologize for their fight and hoped to make amends, but she realized once again, she'd overestimated Desminda's ability for self-reflection and empathy.

She stood on shaky legs and tossed the extra hard biscuit she'd brought for Desminda right into the princesses' face. "I hope you rot in the hell you've built for yourself," she snapped.

To her chagrin, Desminda's hand snapped up and caught

the biscuit before it hit her. She tucked it into her shirt pocket and didn't acknowledge Harlow's words.

This was a mistake. At that moment, even though Harlow didn't hate her, something severed between them. Whether Desminda knew it didn't matter. Harlow felt the tear in her soul. Blinking back tears, she spun on her heel and went back over to Luci happily munching on some bright green grass. As soon as Harlow's fingers settled into her mane, the beast moved closer to her as if it could feel her inner turmoil.

Shade's disapproving stare settled on Desminda for a long moment before he turned his attention to Harlow. He pressed his lips together and looked away.

This was between them, he seemed to say, and he wouldn't step in.

Fair enough, but there was nothing between them anymore. Harlow had made a mistake in going over there, and she wouldn't try to reach out again.

"She doesn't deserve you," came the quiet words from Evara, watching her from a few feet away. The guard had shrugged off her armored vest and lounged on the ground like a tortured poet, her dark hair loose from its braid, and her eyes watchful. "Not even when she held the throne."

Harlow swallowed hard. "It doesn't matter," she whispered.

Evara jerked her head. "Come. Share with me."

From somewhere, the guard had managed to snag an apple that didn't look like it had gone through a battle. Next to it was a handful of unfamiliar seeds and a few bright red berries.

"I'm fine," Harlow said, stroking down Luci's powerful neck.

Evara shrugged. "I know. It doesn't mean you can't come over and try these berries. They're not poisonous. I promise." She grinned.

A strangled laugh bubbled from Harlow. Evara's teeth were stained bright red, seeds pocking the tops of her teeth.

Evara frowned. "What?" She touched her lips and looked at her fingers, eyes widening when they came away bright red. With a muttered curse, Evara scrubbed at her lips.

Harlow's laughter grew brighter.

Evara sent her a dark look and grabbed her water sack, taking a long drink that she swished around her mouth.

"You look like you've bitten into a raw piece of dirty meat," Harlow said breathlessly, laughter coming even harder.

Evara snorted. "Worth it," she said before she rinsed and spat again. "Those things are delicious." She held up a berry. "I think you should still try one."

Harlow held up a hand, laughter trickling away. "I'll pass this time. Maybe we can take some back to Nova when we return."

Evara's expression brightened. "We?"

Harlow blinked. "Um." Her fingers tightened against Luci's mane. "Yes. We can."

The guard smirked. "I'll hold you to it."

Harlow looked away and cleared her throat. *We*. It sounded like...something.

Was it something?

She brushed a hand against the mare and turned.

Evara stood less than a foot away, silent as a wraith. Harlow sucked in a surprised breath. The woman moved like a ghost.

Evara smiled, her teeth clear of seeds. "Listen," she said, her voice low. "Something happened back in that place. Wherever it was. Desminda isn't quite herself. As much as I dislike her, I don't think she's acting of her own volition."

Harlow frowned. "She seems fine."

"You have to *look.*"

Harlow didn't understand. "I just did."

Evara took a step forward. "No," she insisted. "Look." Her fingers reached out and clasped Harlow's wrist, and just like when Shade finally saw the border, Harlow saw what Evara spoke of. A small smudge of darkness lay within Desminda's chest, small enough to miss if you weren't looking for it. It pulsed with a malevolent beat, in time with Desminda's heart. That was bad enough, but a small, branched vein had broken away from the initial spot and reached upward, toward Desminda's collar bone.

"What is it?" Harlow whispered.

"A piece of that thing," Evara said. "I think."

"What do we do?"

Evara shook her head. "Nothing. We watch for now. Do not trust anything she says, and do not be alone with her, do you understand?"

Harlow swallowed hard and nodded. "She doesn't know?"

The guard shrugged. "We don't think so. She, like you, has never been formally trained on magic. It's very possible she has no idea."

"Why don't you tell her?" Harlow couldn't understand why no one had said anything about it.

"Because we need to understand it more before we help her. We don't want to tip her off to anything. If we wait, it might make its presence known. If that thing knows he left something behind."

Harlow grimaced. "How could it not?"

Evara exhaled. "Because that thing had *unfathomable* power. More power than I've seen in a long time. It's possible it hasn't missed it. Yet."

With those words, Shade shouted for them to saddle up again. Harlow rubbed her hands over her arms, trying to get rid of the sudden chill she felt.

When she slid a glance toward Desminda, the princess was watching her with those strange golden eyes.

The plan was for Magnus to approach the border, announce who they were, and ask for entrance. Shade thought the element of surprise and curiosity might make the witches more amenable to allowing them entrance. A legendary, supposedly long dead mage showing up unannounced might rattle even the most stoic of rulers.

As plans went, it wasn't the best. They were placing a lot of hope on things they couldn't possibly predict. Any worry Magnus showed earlier had slipped away into cold, hard resolve.

He gestured for them to stay back and approached on horseback, magic sealed tightly within. With his axe strapped to his back, Magnus looked more a warrior than a mage.

Harlow's heart pounded in her chest, fear freezing her veins as her father approached dangerous magic and requested entrance. Magnus stopped inches before the barrier.

A sharp scream rang out from behind. Harlow spun in her saddle, but she couldn't turn far enough to see what happened.

"Run!" Shade roared, whipping his mount around.

Luci didn't wait. She reared and took off at a thunderous gallop. Astrid raced beside her, Evara close behind.

"No matter what happens, don't stop," Evara barked.

A bright chartreuse shimmer appeared before them. Luci skidded to a stop, Harlow lurching in her saddle, hands slipping against the reins. Evara reached over, gripping Harlow's arm so hard she knew it would bruise. With brute strength, Evara settled Harlow before turning toward the bard. Before her eyes, Astrid disappeared, her body evaporating in a shower of emerald light. It happened so fast the bard didn't even have time to scream.

Evara swore underneath her breath, yanking Luci's reins to force her to turn. But the mare Harlow rode was massive, and there was no way for Luci to move that quickly. "Turn, damn you," Evara hissed. Tears shimmered in her hazel eyes when her gaze locked with Harlow's.

The light hit Evara, and even when her body began to disappear, she never lost that grim resolve to get Harlow to safety. A sob bubbled from Harlow's throat as she watched Evara disappear. Desminda was nowhere to be found. There was no sign of Shade, and she couldn't see Magnus.

She was, once again, alone.

CHAPTER THIRTY-SEVEN

GREETINGS FROM THE WITCHES

The light disappeared, the clearing falling silent and
still. Harlow's blood roared through her veins. Her
gaze swept the area, seeing nothing but grass and trees, and
that same iridescent shimmer blocking her from the witch
kingdom. Hands slick with sweat, she nudged Luci.

"We need to go."

The mare didn't budge. A few seconds ago, Luci was
frightened as she was, but now the mare was as docile as a
lamb. Had the magic done something to her?

She kept her voice low and urgent. "Luci. We're in
danger. We need to go. Let's find a place to camp and I'll
come back on foot to search for them."

Luci huffed a breath and stamped one of her massive
hooves.

Harlow tugged on the reins. "Luci," she begged.

But the mare wouldn't move. Frustrated, Harlow slid off
the saddle. "If you won't come with me, I'll go by myself."

Luci stared at her with that steady dark gaze and made no

move to follow. With a frustrated exhale of breath, Harlow unstrapped her bag and threw it over a shoulder. When she turned, a woman stood before her.

Harlow squeaked in fear and scrambled back, bumping against Luci.

"Who are you?" she breathed. Her axe was strapped to her belt. She wouldn't have time to draw it before the woman acted.

But to her surprise, the woman made no move, only watched Harlow for a long moment with an unreadable expression. She wore a plain blue dress with an ornamental belt hanging on her hips. Long curly blonde hair flowed to her waist and blew gently around her head. She had bright blue eyes, similar to Harlow's. Fine features and a small nose enhanced pink rosebud lips. High cheekbones and a sharp jawline gave her a slightly fey appearance. She looked human, but there was something decidedly other about her.

"My name is Miriam," the woman said.

It sounded similar to her mother's name, but Harlow held her tongue.

"And you are Harlow. You will come with me."

Harlow's fingers itched toward her axe.

The woman's lips curved into a smile. "You can come willingly or the same way your...comrades did."

Harlow stilled. "What did you do to them?"

"They are safe. For now." Miriam held out a pale hand. "Come."

They'd taken everyone in the blink of an eye. Harlow wasn't foolish enough to think she could escape if the most powerful of her group hadn't. "Where are we going?"

"Inside the castle." She flexed her fingers in impatience. "Do not keep her waiting."

"Her?"

Miriam rolled her eyes. A flash of chartreuse magic beamed from the woman's hands and onto Harlow, cool and tingling against her skin. Nausea flooded her, and she swayed, losing her balance. Luci's warmth against her back disappeared.

Seconds later, everything went dark.

A drumming troupe played a raucous beat within her head. Harlow groaned, pinching her eyes together, and slowly sat up. Her earlier lunch roiled in her stomach, and she let out a deep breath, slowly inhaling and exhaling until the feeling passed.

Squinting against the bright light pouring in, she lifted a hand to shield her eyes only to notice two dainty feet close to her body. She jerked in surprise and scrambled away, lifting her face to the stranger.

Miriam and another woman, this one older, stood before her. Miriam's expression was one of bored complacency, but the older woman stared at her intently. Like Harlow was important and necessary and…

Harlow swallowed and looked back down at their feet, uncomfortable with the woman's scrutiny. A hand came into her field of vision. Not Miriam's. Older, but still smooth. Lined and pale veined, the nails buffed to a shine.

"Rise, child."

Harlow lifted her eyes. The older woman was stunning, out of the blush of youth, past the mother stage, but her face was free of wrinkles except for crinkling around the eyes. Her eyes were bright blue as well, the color of corn-flowers.

Exactly like Harlow's.

Her brows drew together as she studied the woman, ignoring the outstretched hand.

"Your friends are safe. Please. Let me assist you."

Harlow looked between them. Miriam stared down at her, an amused tilt to her lips. The older woman wasn't amused, but her expression had an earnest hope Harlow wasn't comfortable with. What did they want with her?

Why was she alone, and where were the rest of her friends?

And why did it seem like these women knew who she was?

Harlow barely knew who she was anymore, so it didn't seem fair for a total stranger to look at her like they knew everything about her.

She reached for the woman with trembling fingers.

As soon as they touched, warm magic traveled through her hands and seeped beneath Harlow's skin. She tried to jerk away, but the woman held her with a firm grip, assisting her to her feet. When she gained her balance, the woman let go, tears shimmering in her eyes.

Harlow frowned and took a step back. "Who are you?" she asked again.

The woman cleared her throat. "Come. Your friends are in the Throne Room. Everything will be explained there."

Harlow studied the women, trepidation in every bone of her body. Finally, she nodded, and Miriam stepped aside, gesturing to the door Harlow had yet to notice. The older woman swept past, her long skirts trailing behind. She was more finely dressed than Miriam, though she wore no jewelry or ornamentation on her body.

Miriam fell into step beside her. "You have clothes on the bed in one of the guest rooms. Change into those when we are through."

Harlow shot her a look and glanced down at her travel worn leather pants and linen shirt. They'd seen better days, but they were still serviceable. She could use a bath, though. The smell of road dirt and sweat assailed her nose, her body in need of a wash but not yet at the point of offending anyone who ventured too close.

It helped that the Shadow Kingdom stayed cool almost all the time, but the grime under her clothes was starting to grate on her nerves.

"Thank you," was all Harlow said.

Miriam inclined her head, the picture of feminine grace, and walked ahead, hurrying toward the door looming ahead. A group of several guards lined either side of the wall, dressed in bright greens and purple. It would normally look garish, but the purple came from the decorative sashes each guard wore, denoting what Harlow thought might be their rank. Their uniforms were a deep forest green color, punctuated with bright gold buttons and medals of all types. The guards were a mix of male and female and varied heights. Many had similar coloring to Harlow, blonde and pale eyed, though she spotted one or two with dark hair and lighter eyes.

She glanced down at herself again, feeling out of place. Though she resembled some of these people, their differences could not be more marked.

The castle had a different air to it than Thornewood. Fresher in an odd way. Not as oppressive. A smothering sense of danger had always surrounded Harlow every time she went into the other castle. One wrong word and things could have gone poorly. Here, no one had that sense of fear hanging over them, or not that she could sense.

Miriam flicked her fingers. The doors clicked open, revealing a grandiose, colorful hall behind it.

Harlow's eyes widened, and she sucked in a breath of surprise at the casual use of magic. It still surprised her every time someone used their powers in front of others with no fear of persecution.

Footsteps slowing, Harlow gawked at the interior of the room. Towering columns loomed above, intricately carved with leaves and stems, animals and creatures she'd never seen before. Stained glass windows loomed on either side of the walls, casting the floor in a kaleidoscope of vivid colors. A single throne sat at the opposite side of the room, made of polished obsidian, so dark it shimmered a brilliant blue when the light hit it just right.

It was empty. Two guards stood on either side, holding wickedly sharp spears before them.

A sob broke from Harlow when she noticed the five people kneeling in front of the throne.

She rushed forward, but a firm grip held her still. "Wait," Miriam warned. "You will reunite soon enough."

The older woman swept into the room. A shout rang out, and everyone except her comrades sank into a low curtsy. Confused, Harlow looked around, but she couldn't figure out why. Miriam pulled her ahead, fingers curled around Harlow's upper arm.

"Why is everyone bowing?" she whispered.

Miriam snorted and kept dragging her down the white carpeted rug.

It came to her a moment later when the older woman swept past the crowd and stopped before the obsidian throne. She turned, inclined her head, and moved her hands in an upward gesture.

"Rise," she said.

Harlow sucked down a gasp. The queen was the one who helped her up from the ground. Confused, all she could do was watch as the Queen of the Witch Kingdom settled onto her throne, adjusted her skirts, and flicked her fingers at the crowd.

As one, they turned and began to file out of the room, leaving only the queen, Miriam, Harlow, and the rest of her traveling party. Miriam pulled her to the side of the throne, far enough back the others hadn't noticed her presence yet, but close enough to see their faces.

No one looked hurt or injured. Dusty and road weary, yes, but unharmed.

The queen studied each of them, her gaze lingering the longest on Harlow's father.

Harlow's heart beat like a frightened sparrow's. Once again, she stood in a foreign kingdom, subjected to the whims of another royal with an agenda.

The queen smiled.

CHAPTER THIRTY-EIGHT

SPILLING THE TEA

"**R**ise," she said, her voice carrying through the throne room.

Magnus and the others rose, Desminda following last. The queen's eyes flicked to her, studying the princess with narrowed eyes.

"I know all of you except for the golden-eyed one." She tilted her head. "Though you look familiar to me. Something about your face."

Desminda stepped forward and curtsied. "I am Desminda, last princess of Thornewood."

The queen's expression cleared. "Ah. You are the traitor queen's daughter."

Desminda jerked like she'd been struck. "Queen Raima's daughter, Your Majesty." Her voice sounded tight and clipped.

"The same," the queen said, her eyes flashing with anger. "After all, your mother betrayed her people, ripped magic away from the world, and held her crown by fear and force, did she not?"

Desminda said nothing, her slight frame trembling with rage.

"The very same woman who forced the man standing beside you to cast the spell that took away Lunamoor's lifeblood or forfeit his wife and his young daughter."

Magnus went deathly still, tension locking his posture straight.

Desminda blinked, her brow furrowed in confusion.

"Ah," the queen said softly. "You did not know of your mother's threats?"

Desminda hadn't known everything. There was no reason for her to. Her mother had won and kept her queendom through force and intimidation. It didn't matter how she did it, and Harlow knew without question the princess never pushed for any answers.

Why would she? Desminda had everything she ever wanted, and all she had to do was give her hand away in marriage.

The queen flicked her hand in dismissal. "Regardless, Queen Raima didn't account for the extent of Magnus' power. He couldn't save everyone, but he sent a warning to all the kingdoms bordering Thornewood's lands." Her gaze landed on Magnus. "*Secure your lands. Magic will fall.*"

Desminda sucked in a shocked gasp.

"A traitorous message, no doubt?" The queen laughed and pointed a finger at Desminda. "A traitor to you, yes. A *hero* to everyone else." She leaned forward. "We keep our magic because Magnus warned us beforehand. But Raima suspected him and delayed his message to the Kingdoms of Roses and the one of Light. And they've suffered for many years."

Magnus stood there like a statue, the weight of his supposed crimes heavy on his shoulders. But Harlow didn't see him as a criminal. The judgment in Desminda's eyes meant nothing to her. What he had done showed the person Magnus was. He saved who he could at the risk of his own life and those he loved, knowing if magic fell everywhere, their fates wouldn't matter anyway. They would all suffer.

A tear slipped down Magnus' face. Her father's head bowed, and he drew in a shuddering breath. The queen rose, empathy shining in her eyes. She stepped over to Magnus and touched his shoulder, bright wild magic emanating from her fingertips. Shade's expression turned wary, but the queen ignored him.

"You are welcome in my kingdom, Magnus Stonehand. Rest and recuperate here. There is much we need to discuss." Her gaze fell on Harlow. "Many important things."

She turned to Shade and the rest. "Your companions are welcome as well, even the daughter of the traitor queen."

Desminda's eyes tightened at the edges.

"However," the queen continued, "Desminda will be watched at all times. She will have free rein of the grounds, but a guard will accompany her." She smiled. "There is something else we must discuss later in regard to her future," she said to Magnus. "I trust you are here as Nova's diplomat?"

Magnus dipped his head in acknowledgment.

"Good. I've received a most...interesting proposal." The

queen's smile made Harlow's stomach lurch. "It is most advantageous to a *displaced* princess."

Shade's expression darkened.

Evara stood next to him, quiet and watchful, posture perfectly still. Those hazel eyes missed nothing, and when she turned her head and caught Harlow's gaze, the flash of relief in them made her tremble. Harlow looked away, biting down a tentative smile.

Maybe later she would seek the guard out and see if it meant anything.

The queen adjusted her skirts and motioned for Miriam. "Harlow, you as well."

Everyone's attention snapped in her direction. Shade's expression was unreadable, but he gave her a quick, short nod. Magnus squeezed his eyes for a brief moment and exhaled, his relief palpable. He stepped forward. "Your Majesty?"

One of her pale eyebrows rose. "Yes, Mage?"

"Harlow is with us. May we take her to her quarters?"

The queen smiled. "I'm aware of who she travels with. I will return her to the guest quarters soon. In the meantime, one of my most trusted people will escort you to yours."

Magnus opened his mouth to protest but snapped it shut at the queen's withering look.

"You know how to reach me," he said to Harlow.

Miriam took her arm and led her away before she could respond.

They walked in silence for a while, the size of the castle overwhelming Harlow's senses. Ancient tapestries lined the hallways, woven with scenes of epic battles and flying witches, pale hair streaming from their heads as they flew through the air with wild abandon. Magic streamed from their fingers, lighting up the evening sky with glorious color.

Harlow followed, her gaze wide with wonder at all the bright shades. From the outside, the castle had looked foreboding and colorless, a gray collection of towers looming against a colorless sky. But from the inside, a riot of color greeted her eyes. Stained glass windows high above them sent a shower of vivid colors raining down. The colorful tapestries hung against white walls, the bottom fringe brushing against the pale stone floor.

Silver candelabras glowed with multi-colored lights, even though the hall was well lit. But the best thing of all was the bright smell of vanilla and citrus that permeated the entire castle.

The fresh comforting scent of it settled the urgency that had filled her veins since she'd left Thornewood with death on her heels. Harlow inhaled, her shoulders dropping and her chest opening, drawing the first deep breath she'd truly had in weeks.

A dizzying array of cookies and treats sat in a tiered tray on a round table in the middle of the room. Next to it was a steaming teapot, the fresh scent of dark tea scented with orange blossoms wafting through the air.

Harlow's stomach growled, a rumble in the air that had the queen's lips twitching.

"Please," she said graciously, gesturing for Harlow to take a seat. "I know your journey was long. Sit and take your fill."

Miriam handed over a warm and damp lavender-scented cloth, gesturing for Harlow to wipe her hands. Harlow thoroughly cleaned her palms and fingers, wishing she had a dozen more to clean the rest of the grime from her face and neck. With regret, she placed the dirty cloth on a tray. She blinked in surprise when a pale hand shot out to take it, replacing it with another brightly polished silver tray with silverware.

Her fingers itched to pour herself a cup of tea, but the manners Shade had tried so hard to teach her kicked in, so she waited for the queen and Miriam to take their places first. Even then, Harlow still waited for the queen to go first.

Her foster mother had instilled manners in her, but things were different when one had an audience with the queen. There were *rules*.

Most of which she couldn't remember.

Harlow's hands rested at her side, her fingers making a *tippety tappety* noise against her thighs.

The queen goes first.

No. Someone should serve her first. Right?

Yes.

Then Miriam. Harlow still wasn't sure who Miriam was, so she had no idea if the woman was of low enough status to serve herself or high enough to wait for someone to do it for her.

But Harlow was a nobody. She would serve herself.

The queen's soft chuckle jerked her out of her reverie. "We have few airs in the Kingdom of Witches, child. Serve yourself, as both Miriam and I will."

Still Harlow waited until the queen sighed and took the small fork to slide off a small lemon square and two small pink cookies. Miriam did the same, though she chose chocolate sweets. When they finished, Harlow went first for the tea, gesturing toward the queen's cup. She nodded and Harlow poured the queen's first, then Miriam's, before finally pouring her own.

She added a little milk but no sugar, and when she took a small sip, tears formed in Harlow's eyes. She'd never tasted anything quite like it in her life. Similar, but nothing as deep and hearty and soul warming as this brew.

"It was your mother's favorite," the queen said, a thoughtful look on her face.

Harlow stilled. "You knew my mother?"

"Quite well," the queen said.

Curiosity raged within her, the desire to ask a million questions overriding her good manners. The queen smiled over her teacup. "Patience, Harlow. All will be revealed soon." She gestured to Harlow's cup. "We have a plentiful supply of tea here. Any time you wish to have it, all you have to do is ask."

Grateful, Harlow smiled and took another sip. "Why am I here?" she asked when silence fell. "Not *here*, but in here with you?"

Miriam and the queen exchanged a glance. "We were interested in getting to know the lost heir. There's nothing nefarious about it." Miriam looked away, focused on her tea too intently.

The lie sang against Harlow's skin. She would find out what they wanted soon enough.

Until then, she would enjoy the excellent tea.

CHAPTER THIRTY-NINE

BLOOD IS THE ONLY TRUTH

Two guards escorted Harlow to her quarters after the odd teatime was finished. The entire time she sat with Miriam and the queen she'd felt like she was on display, a carriage someone planned to sell, and the potential buyer walked around checking the wheels and hinges to make sure everything was in good working order. Feeling like that wasn't uncommon for Harlow, but this time it was different. A sense of anticipation hovered around the two that made her uncomfortable and set her ill at ease.

Even worse than before when she stood alone in the clearing after watching everyone she cared about disappear in a puff of magic.

The guards stopped in front of a room set off from the rest, located toward the very back of a long hall. A large polished wooden door stood in front of her with an ornate brass handle. She reached out to open it, but one of the guards made a strangled sound and gently extricated her hand.

"No," he said softly. "Allow me. Please."

Harlow pulled her hand away. "Sorry," she whispered.

The guard's brow furrowed, but he shook away her apologies. "No need for that," he said gruffly. The guard pushed open the door and gestured for her to go in.

Harlow hesitated at the opening, gawking at the sheer expanse of the room they'd put her in. A massive balcony appeared ahead of her, open to the elements. The tree-blanketed mountains looked almost fake as she gasped in awe and headed straight for it, passing by a stunning bathing pool, a bookshelf filled to the brim with tomes, and the largest bed she'd ever seen in her life.

She stopped at the edge of the balcony, her eyes unable to process what she was seeing.

"This is stunning," she breathed.

The female guard who'd followed in behind her stopped close. "Those are the Witch Mountains. We share a border with the Kingdom of Beasts, separated by the Lake of Clarity." She shrugged. "It's a point of contention with them, but even the beasts don't venture into the mountains too often." Her eyes sparkled with good humor. "Witches might look human, but we are often more bloodthirsty than the beasts."

The male guard hummed in warning. "She is joking," he said.

The female chuckled and stepped away. Harlow thought she'd very much *not* been joking and made a mental note not to venture into those mountains unless absolutely necessary.

He cleared his throat. "Regardless, the queen has asked for your presence at dinner this evening. Fresh clothing is on the bed, and all you should need for bathing is by the pool. If you need anything, pull the cord by the door and someone will attend you."

He bowed his head, gave his companion a long look, and turned to go.

"Thank you," Harlow said.

The guard stumbled a little before righting himself. "You are welcome, Miss Harlow." He offered a hesitant smile and let himself out, the other guard following behind.

Why was everyone acting so strange around her? She shook her head and sighed, her attention going back to the stunning scenery in front of her.

Thornewood was a beautiful kingdom, but this place had a wildness to it that called to her soul. So much of it seemed uninhabited and unexplored that she longed to venture into the woods and get lost.

Nova swam into her thoughts, the adventures she and Harlow took together making her smile. She missed those carefree days.

Harlow stood there for a long time before she pushed away and turned to the pool. Bathing sounded like a wonderful idea.

She dipped her fingers into the crystal-clear water and gasped at the delicious heat. Nova needed one of these.

Harlow glanced back at the bed to see an outfit laid out with a hairbrush and hair pins next to it. When she saw it was breeches and a white shirt with a matching vest, she let out a deep sigh of relief.

No dresses. Had she somehow stumbled into a perfect kingdom? Snorting at her thoughts, she shucked out of her grimy clothing and slid into the bath, undoing her braid as the heat soaked into her sore muscles.

Her mind raced with hundreds of thoughts, but soon enough the relaxing pool won the battle against her mind, and Harlow leaned back against the stone and closed her eyes, letting all her worries slip away for a brief amount of time.

The bath and fresh clothes made Harlow feel human for the first time in quite a while. She allowed her hair to air dry, but the cool air in the kingdom wasn't warm enough to dry it completely before she had to leave for dinner. Harlow decided on two long braids, tying each at the back of her head. She kept them loose and more relaxed for dinner than battle, and when she finished dressing, she stepped outside to see the same two guards waiting for her.

She smiled. "I hope this is okay?"

The female nodded. "The queen does not put on airs. What she gave you is fine to wear for any event here unless you are instructed otherwise."

The queen had said the same to her, but it was nice to know it really was that way, and it wasn't some strange attempt to put her at ease because they'd separated her from the rest of her party.

"Where are the others?" Harlow asked.

The male gestured for her to walk ahead. "On their way to the dining quarters, I'm sure. Let us go before we are late."

He shut the door behind her, and both fell in step beside Harlow.

The castle was a maze of hallways and warrens and odd little doorways, so many Harlow knew she'd be hopelessly lost if she tried to navigate it herself. At the fifth turn, she'd lost track of where she was.

The halls remained mostly the same. Stained glass, gorgeous tapestries, and artwork scattered around on small tables against the walls. High arched, carved ceilings, and massive windows brought in so much light it lifted Harlow's spirits.

She finally stopped trying to remember how to get back and let the guards guide her where she needed to go. About ten minutes later, they stopped in front of two massive double doors that opened when they approached.

The guards escorted her in and brought her over to her seat. She smiled when she saw Shade and the others sitting on one side of the table. Fully expecting to be seated beside them, she picked up speed only to be firmly guided to the other side and placed firmly next to the queen herself.

She caught Magnus' attention when this happened. His face had turned not angry but contemplative, his eyes narrowing. A moment later, a flash of shock came over his features, disappearing so quickly she thought she'd imagined it.

A sense of unease unfurled in her stomach. Something bigger than her was happening here. Once again, she felt like she was the only one not privy to the secret.

Harlow bowed to the queen and took her seat, careful not to scratch her chair along the stone floor when she pushed it closer to the table. Desminda sat at the end, staring at Harlow with a bone-white face, her pinched expression altering her beauty from shattering to something more normal.

Evara looked amused, but there was something in her

eyes Harlow didn't understand. Shade's expression remained blank, but his dark eyes burned with confusion and fury.

The bard chewed on the side of her lip as if figuring out a particularly perplexing problem.

This dinner hadn't even started, and it was quickly becoming one of the most uncomfortable moments of Harlow's life. Everyone was staring at her, and she wanted to sink into the floor.

"Greetings," the queen started. "Thank you for sharing my table tonight. It is an honor to host Magnus Stonehand and his comrades in my kingdom." Her gaze turned to Harlow. "It is an even greater honor to be reunited with someone I thought lost for a very, very long time."

Magnus' face paled.

Harlow squirmed in her seat. She hadn't seen anyone else but them and the guards. Confused, she turned to look at the door.

No one there, either.

"No," Magnus whispered. His chair scraped back, and he stood, hands hovering over the axe he'd tied to his belt.

Harlow blinked at his reaction. The guards stepped closer.

"Hold," the queen snapped to them. "Sit, Magnus."

Magnus did no such thing.

She exhaled a heavy sigh. "Please. There is a lot you do not know. I am not and have never been your enemy. We have both lost the most important thing in our lives. But you have brought something to me that makes me see that something wonderful has been left behind."

Magnus' bright blue eyes held a suspicious wetness. "Why?" he croaked.

Harlow still didn't understand, but something felt very off. She turned to the queen, watching the woman speak to Magnus. There was a familiarity there, something Harlow had felt the moment she'd stepped into the kingdom. But now sitting here, seeing her in the low light, watching the way the candlelight sparked against her golden hair...

Desminda barked a laugh. "Of course. I should have known." she muttered.

Shade sent her a sharp look, the reproval in his eyes enough to make Desminda snap her mouth shut.

Harlow looked at Miriam and noticed a similar resemblance.

To her.

They all had similar coloring, but so did almost everyone in the witch kingdom. Her pale hair wasn't common in Thornewood, but it also wasn't a precious rarity either.

But her eyes...

The queen turned to her and reached over, clasping her fingers in her own. Harlow sucked in a breath. Royalty rarely touched anyone unless...

"Your mother," the queen began, "was a princess of the Witch Kingdom." Her smile wobbled. "My kingdom."

Magnus sank into his seat, his armor making a hard crack against the wood. He blew out an explosive breath.

Harlow froze. "That would mean—" She swallowed. "You would be—" She couldn't get the words out.

"I am your grandmother. Miriam is your aunt. You are an heir to this throne." The queen smiled softly. "I lost track of you after the Thornewilde raids. Imagine my surprise when word reached me of a golden-haired girl with witch blood racing for the Kingdom of Shadows." Tears shimmered in her bright blue eyes. "I have waited so very long to meet you."

Harlow couldn't speak. Blood roared through her veins. Magnus rose from his seat and came around to Harlow's side of the table. The guards tensed, but the queen held up a hand. "He is her father. Magnus has the same rights in this kingdom as Harlow does."

A tear slipped down Harlow's cheek. Not one of relief. One of fury and loss and hopelessness. "You could have taken me in at any time," she whispered.

Magnus settled beside her, his looming presence a balm to her raw soul.

"You could have come, and I could have known my family. But you abandoned me."

The queen flinched. "No," she whispered. "No. I never would have done that. Harlow, you must understand—"

Harlow scraped her chair back and rose. A second later, Magnus rose beside her. She turned on her heel and walked out of the dining room, her father on her heels.

They must have walked for twenty minutes before Harlow could form words.

"Did you know?" she rasped.

Magnus barked a laugh. "No. Your mother presented herself as a representative from the Kingdom of Witches when I met her. A diplomat in some ways. Marion came under the guise of a teacher." He scrubbed a hand through his golden hair. "But it's evident now she came as a spy."

Harlow glanced up at him. "She was a spy?"

He shrugged. "It's the only thing that makes sense. But why would they send Marion and not someone of lesser blood?"

"Maybe she was the only one with the power to succeed," Harlow ventured.

Magnus glanced at her, a small smile curving his mouth. "She was a powerful earth witch. Marion could manipulate anything living—wood, flora, fauna, rock...a little like my own magic, but where I come in like an earthquake, Marion's magic was like a gentle whisper of wind." He shut his eyes for a moment. "But now I wonder if it was all a lie."

"I am a princess," Harlow whispered, a hysterical laugh escaping her throat.

Magnus shook his head. "I suppose you are. How does it feel?"

"Terrible," Harlow confessed.

Magnus laughed. "Understandable." He ducked into a small alcove, tugging Harlow with him. Magnus opened a couple of doors and peered in before he gestured for her to follow.

The room was small and quiet, holding only a small table with four chairs and a few pictures on the wall. Harlow sank into the chair her father pulled out for her and took the one opposite.

"What would you like to do?" he asked when the silence had gone on too long.

Her head jerked up. "Excuse me?"

"Do you want to leave? We don't need them to win this thing."

Harlow snorted. "I believe you and Shade said the opposite before we left the Shadow Kingdom."

Magnus shrugged. "There are other ways to win the battle. We can get you out of here if you want to go. Leave and pretend we never heard any of this information. I can't guarantee things will go back to normal." He frowned. "You're the lost princess of the Witch Kingdom. Queen Moira will go to the ends of the world to find you again, but there are ways around that too."

Overwhelming emotion surfaced in Harlow. Tears spilled from her eyes. "Why didn't she come for me?" she whispered.

Magnus shook his head. "I don't know Queen Moira well, but Marion—" He laughed. "She always spoke highly of her mother. They remained close." A thought crossed his face, and Magnus paused before he swore. "She lied," he murmured under his breath.

"Well...yes," Harlow murmured.

He shook his head. "No. Queen Raima. She said she had spoken to the witch queen, and she'd approved Marion's indefinite stay in Thornewood. Raima was lying about it, and Moira couldn't pull Marion back without causing an incident or revealing who Marion was to her." He sat back and scrubbed a hand over his chin. "Things make much more sense now." He tilted his head up. "She was trying to get you back to the Witch Kingdom, and when Raima went after her, she changed the plan to keep you safe."

She'd heard the story but had no memory of being with the wolves. The thought of it seemed fantastical, but Shade was the one who took her there, and he rarely lied.

Knowing the risks he'd taken for her still tied her heart up in knots. There'd never be enough thanks for what he'd done for her, just like there'd never be enough for Nova.

The thought sobered her. She sat here with her father bemoaning being a princess when a princess had risked her life multiple times to keep her safe, and the man who cared for her mother had taken her as a newborn to an enemy kingdom to give her the best chance at life.

Harlow groaned. "I am a brat," she said quietly and let out a long exhale. "A massive fool, blind to everything except my pain."

Her father watched her steadily, remaining quiet. Not agreeing, but not disagreeing either.

"Nova, Shade, and you risked everything to keep me safe, and I am wallowing, bemoaning my own fate when I am here because of you all." Harlow rubbed a hand over her face. "I am sorry."

Magnus looked down at the table. "You never have to apologize to me, Harlow. Do not forget you are still young. No matter our youth or even our advanced age, it is human to have those moments of selfishness. You've lost as much as we have. Mistakes were made. Queen Moira is a good queen and was a good mother to Marion. I can only hope she will be a good grandmother, too." He reached out and took her hands. "But I still leave the choice to you. If you wish it, we will leave this place and try another kingdom to ally with."

A throat cleared quietly, and Shade stepped in, followed by Evara. "I've found multiple exits since we've arrived," Evara announced, her hand resting on the handle of her dagger. "Say the word, and we will take one."

Shade snorted and headed over to the table, dragging a chair out for Evara who gave him an odd look before sitting, and then himself. "I think we need to strategize before we burn it all down," Shade said dryly.

"Astrid and Desminda?" Magnus inquired.

Evara leaned back in her chair, a sly smile sliding over her face. "The former princess drowns in jealousy."

Shade gave her a dark look.

Evara winked at him. "The bard and Desminda are still enjoying the six-course dinner with the queen. Astrid is dying to meet with us, but someone had to stay back and babysit."

Magnus shook his head but couldn't help his smile. "You are borderline cruel to her."

Evara shrugged. "She is cruel to most she meets because she is angry. It is a personality flaw."

"It's a flaw of youth," Shade countered.

Evara flicked her gaze to Harlow. "She is at least two years older than the newly discovered princess, isn't she?"

Shade frowned, flicking his fingers in dismissal. "Point made."

Evara wiggled her eyebrows. "Now, *Princess* Harlow, what is your first edict?"

Magnus chuckled. "She is not the first heir to the throne, Evara."

The guard grinned, her hazel eyes sparkling. "Queen Moira did not say as much," she admitted, "but you forget what I am capable of." Her voice dropped to a soft whisper. "Miriam is not fit to rule. The queen has no other heirs."

Harlow blinked. "Surely not," she whispered.

"She is a powerful Seer, prone to fits and long periods of stillness. Moira has begun to live in her visions, sometimes not coming out of them for weeks at a time. Many things can happen in weeks, and a comatose queen would do more harm than good." Evara shrugged. "Regardless, I'm always up for a harrowing escape plan, but they will be watchful now that she's revealed your identity. We barely slipped the guards, so I expect we have only a few more minutes before they find us and escort us back to our rooms."

"We are not prisoners," Magnus said.

"Not you, father of said princess," Evara said. "But we are from another kingdom, and do not have the freedom you do. If we're to escape, we must do it soon. Before they have time to come up with a better plan to keep us here."

Shade watched Harlow.

"No," Harlow said after a moment. "I've been running for a long time. They are my family. My real family." Her voice choked. "It's best if I try to stay in their good graces." She straightened in her seat. "We need this alliance, correct?"

Magnus and Shade exchanged a look. "We do," Shade admitted.

"Then perhaps my new heritage will help." Harlow stood. "It is time to stop running and accept who I am meant to be."

Evara stood as well and to Harlow's utter shock, bowed low. "You will make a fine queen one day, Princess."

Harlow's throat closed. Tears threatened to spill. She took a deep breath. "But if I decide I want to escape?"

Evara rose, her lips curving into a savage smile. "Then

you come find me, and I will sweep you away to worlds unknown." With a wink, Evara slipped back into the hallway.

Shade and Magnus watched her go, before Shade turned to Harlow, giving her a wary look. "Be careful," he warned.

"You said the same thing about Desminda," Harlow said. What she didn't say was Evara never threatened her. She suspected she could approach the guard with a harebrained plan and Evara would go along with it simply for the adventure of it. And she found she liked that about the guard.

More than liked it.

Magnus chuckled. "Evara hides massive power. But behind all that dry wit is a sharp mind and a tender heart. I agree with Shade about taking care with her, but know if you ever earn Evara's heart, daughter, you will never lose it."

"What about..." Harlow paused. "This?" she whispered and waved a helpless hand around.

"The Witch Kingdom has no rules about who one marries. Their power always lies through the female line, though they keep their birthing practices secret. Many queens never marry. It keeps the lines of succession much clearer." Magnus shrugged. "It is too early to discuss such things, but if you give your heart to someone common, Queen Moira will not stand in your way." He laid a hand over his heart. "And neither would I."

Harlow's lifted for the first time that day.

It didn't mean anything would come of it.

But it meant something *could*.

CHAPTER FORTY

Desminda seethed all the way back to her room. A princess. A *princess*! Of all the rotten twists of fate to happen, the once dirty orphan girl she'd come to care about had royal blood after all. Fate laughed in her face. She rubbed her chest absently, that odd spot feeling like it had grown in the hour since dinner.

The guard by her side had said nothing to her the entire walk back. Fine by her. Her blood boiled in her veins, and the urge to scream became difficult to hold back.

Why did everyone have everything, and she'd lost it all?

They stopped at her door a few minutes later, the guard gently touching her elbow with a murmured word. She halted, surprise on her features when she realized they were already back. She'd been so lost in her thoughts she wasn't paying attention to anything.

The guard opened the door and escorted her through the door but made no move to follow her inside. When she was in, he bowed his head and left her alone.

The silence inside her room was deafening.

She bet Harlow had a better room than her.

The cool breeze from the small balcony ruffled her hair. She headed for it, breathing in the cool, crisp air. Even she had to admit, the Kingdom of Witches was beautiful. A sparkling clear lake lay ahead, the edge of a mountain range to the west.

Thornewood was beautiful, too, but there had always been an edge to its beauty. Desminda had never been in danger by virtue of her blood, but even she could feel that deadly sharpness to it.

She took a deep breath in and tried to clear the fog of rage permeating her mind, but all she could think about was Harlow and that announcement from the queen.

Harlow was the lost heir in more ways than one, then. The Heir of Magic and heir to Queen Moira and the witches.

Which meant in addition to the magic she gained from Stonehand, she had another unexplored arsenal flowing through her veins. The power of the witches.

Not much was known about this kingdom. Few were allowed to enter, and even less allowed to explore its secrets. Her mother had always seemed wary of this place. Perhaps she was right to be. On the surface Queen Moira appeared docile and nurturing, but holding onto power in a kingdom of bloodthirsty witches required a stiff spine and remarkable power.

Power that Harlow had earned through her own blood.

Desminda's jaw clenched. She should have seen it the second Harlow was dumped into the throne room. Those blonde curls, the same bright blue eyes, and the power that gently beat against her skin. Desminda had been a fool to overlook it, mistaking it for her own power.

She had no formal training in magic, and it had become an issue. Pushing away from the balcony, Desminda undressed and slid into the small pool at the back of the room. Teeth chattering, she cursed the tepid warmth of the bath and quickly scrubbed while she thought.

Her mother had also held onto power through sheer grit and wiles. Earlier, Desminda had wondered if it was worth it. Freedom might hold more of an allure due to the lack of responsibility, but that kingdom was hers by blood and right. She had a duty to herself and her mother. If Queen Raima saw her now, she would be ashamed of Desminda's behavior, her waffling about what she wanted to do.

There was no choice.

Thornewood would be hers by might, because it belonged to her by right.

In the darkness, a shadow seeped closer to Desminda's heart.

It is yours, a voice whispered through her mind. *Take it. I can help you.*

Desminda stirred in her sleep and rolled to her side. Her eyes opened, and she stood in the same wasteland she'd barely escaped.

A pale-faced male stood far away, dark robes whipping in a wind that did not exist where she stood.

Who are you?

Golden eyes, the thing whispered.

Did it speak to her or itself?

A sense of satisfaction burned in her chest, but the

emotion didn't belong to her. It belonged to the thing living inside of her.

I've sought you for thousands of years.

Desminda frowned. *I do not know you.*

I can help you.

Why would you do that? You tried to kill my— She almost said friends. They weren't her friends, were they? They weren't even allies. Not really.

But they'd saved her life.

They had to. It was their duty.

For every positive thing she thought about the people who'd ushered her out of Thornewood and those who'd kept her safe in the land of shadows, she thought three negatives.

They'd kept her away so long Celestine had established a firmer foothold as queen.

They never deferred to her anymore and treated her like a commoner rather than the queen she was meant to be.

Yessss, the thing hissed. *Show me your darkness.*

Desminda's attention snapped to it.

They are not your friends, the thing said.

Could it read her mind?

They do not respect you. I see how they treat you in your memories.

Desminda's brow furrowed. *You see my memories? How?* she demanded.

I am a part of you, it hissed. *I live inside of you.*

The dark thing inside her chest pulsed with a sickly, ebony light.

Desminda's fingers hovered over it, a sense of horror

roiling through her. Was this why her thoughts had turned so...awful?

Or were those awful, dark thoughts only enhancing her true self? The confusion over it scared her more than anything. If she didn't know, could it be that she'd always been like this and hadn't been pushed far enough for it to manifest? Before this thing had infected her, she'd already been angry and jealous. The thought sobered her.

No, she said.

You do not have a choice, the thing said with glee. *You will soon belong to me.*

I belong to no one, Desminda snapped.

I can help you. You want your kingdom back? I can take it. The false queen Celestine sits on the throne rightfully yours. She gloats over her power, when it rightfully belongs to you.

Sick jealousy flooded Desminda. She tamped it down with great effort. *I will get my kingdom back without you. Celestine is weak. She will crumble underneath our might.*

The thing laughed, a hissing, rasping sound grating against Desminda's nerves. *There is no our. You saved everyone when you stepped into my world and sought to save the girl and her father, and no one thanked you, did they? No one even tried.*

Desminda swallowed. Harlow had tried, hadn't she? Before she said something unforgivable to her. Tears swam in her eyes, and she choked back her regret.

They know you are infected, the thing said. *You know they know. The wary way they look at you...they think of how to dispose of you.*

Fear spiraled in her veins. *Lies*, she growled.

I am not voicing any doubts you haven't already had, it said.

You are not their queen. They've found a new one to follow. The beautiful one with bright golden hair. She is a sunrise, and you are the darkness, queen no more.

Power spiraled around Desminda, building within her blood. She'd wounded it once. Maybe she could do so again.

You will come to me one way or another, it said. *If you do not come to me of your own volition, I will take you eventually.*

Threads of power, the color of a moonless night, tore from the ground, wrapping around her ankles. Sick, corrupted power crawled up her calves and her knees, sinking its tendrils deep beneath her skin.

A scream tore from her throat, her magic sputtering and dying in her palms.

"Desminda!" The shout shattered the eerie silence in the princesses' room.

Shade rushed into the room, Astrid close behind, and found Desminda lying on the bed, her golden eyes wide and open, a strange black thread of glowing darkness outlining her iris. Her mouth was stretched in a grimace of pain and her hands had formed claws, scratching into the linen sheets.

Shade uttered a curse, but Astrid shoved him aside. "Stay away," the bard said. "You cannot risk being infected."

"Be careful, bard. We cannot lose either of you."

Astrid nodded and closed her eyes, bright green magic flowing from her hands. With a deep breath, she laid both her hands on the princess's chest.

A howling, agonized cry tore from Desminda's throat.

She tensed, her small body tight, effort screaming from every muscle.

The bard's eyes glowed a brilliant green before they fluttered shut. Her pale face stilled.

The two were locked into a battle only they could see, Shade standing as a silent witness.

Astrid appeared in the wasteland next to Desminda. "Go!" the princess screamed.

"No." Astrid studied the tendrils creeping up Desminda's arms and legs, the creature standing so far away. The dark spot in her chest pulsed in time with Desminda's heartbeat.

That's how he had found her. Slipping into her dreams must have been easy with the link he'd made between them.

"You need to use your magic," Astrid whispered. "Your power is stronger against him than mine."

"Can't," Desminda whispered. Sweat beaded against her tanned brow, her jaw clenched with effort. The tendrils hadn't moved past her knees, a golden thread of magic holding them at bay. "Blocked."

Astrid's mind spun. Her magic and Desminda's weren't similar in any way. Bards could heal, but it wasn't like Desminda's pure, golden power. That power had the possibility to resurrect if the princess learned to use it correctly, but that was something to explore later.

Now, she had to stop this thing from draining the Thornewood heir. Emerald magic spun from her hand, not into the tendrils wrapped around her, but into Desminda.

She searched for the block against Desminda's magic, scanning inside her body for the pool of magic innate to every mage. Sweeping through her veins, her mind, down through her chest and lungs, Astrid finally found it right in the center of Desminda's heart. It wasn't a pool, not like most had.

It was a bright, shining star, small but mighty, and it was surrounded by a sickening pulse of darkness, the power cut off from the mage. If she could find a weak spot, Desminda could overpower it and free herself.

"Listen to me," she said urgently. "If you feel any weakening, you need to fight. Break free from its hold and send everything you have against it, do you understand?"

Desminda moaned.

"Ready?"

Desminda huffed a pained breath. Astrid had to take the noise as a yes. She sent her magic circling around the creature's power, careful not to touch it. If it was inside Desminda's body and had lodged a piece of itself inside her, it might know what she was trying to do, but it was a risk she had to take.

The magic seemed airtight, immovable, and yet, strangely familiar. Astrid explored, seeing it inside her mind's eye, but she couldn't find a way in. Exhaling, she grimaced.

She'd have to take the fight to it.

Astrid pulled most of her magic from Desminda, leaving a tiny little spark to monitor, then looked across the field at the creature.

Its dark laughed boomed around the wasteland.

Astrid smiled.

A lute appeared in her hands. She strummed her fingers over the strings, sending a pulse of bright music through the stale air.

And then she began to sing.

In the land of Thorns,
A woman finds her wings,
In the land of Beasts,
A woman learns to sing.

Emerald light streamed from Astrid's mouth, the song its own form of bard magic, and sailed toward the creature whose head tilted back with glee, drinking down Desminda's magic. Astrid made note. While magic could wound, it could also eat another's power, no matter if it was anathema to it.

In the land of Light,
A woman finds her hope,
In the land of Shadow,
A woman turns to smoke.

The words didn't matter. It was the intent behind them that powered the spell.

Your magic tastes like wine, Desminda, the creature whispered. Astrid's thin strand of power still inside the princess allowed her to hear their conversation. The bard powered her focus, honing the song as it flew toward the thing, Emerald magic formed into silver tipped arrows, sailing straight for it.

This magic was the bard's deepest secret, the reason they were ousted from Thornewood and why they were welcomed in most kingdoms as spies and courtesans.

In the land of Witches,
A child rises to riches,
A crown on her brow,
A star on the prow,
Brings the ship back home.

The first arrow struck true. Then the second and third.

The creature jerked, an ear-splitting shriek shattering the wasteland's silence.

Desminda took a breath.

"Now," Astrid snapped, that thin thread of her magic shooting through the broken darkness of the circle around the heart of her power and tearing it apart.

The sickly magic snapped and shattered, dissipating into the ether.

Desminda's eyes snapped open.

Power exploded from the young princess, tearing the dark tendrils from her feet and legs, until she stood untethered.

Desminda didn't wait another moment. She threw every ounce of raw power at the creature, and Astrid guided it with her own, until the creature was trapped between the gold of Desminda's healing power and Astrid's nonsensical song.

"We have to go," Astrid whispered.

But the princess was past hearing her. A ragged, furious scream tore from her throat as she pumped her power into the thing.

Its screams turned hoarse and weak, and it fell to its knees.

"Now, Desminda," Astrid warned. "I don't think we can kill it. Its power is everywhere. We can wound it and then regroup. Drop the power and take my hand."

Golden tears spilled down Desminda's throat. She pulsed with power, its glow shimmering around her. "I am weak," she whispered.

Astrid started. "No. No, Desminda. Look at you. You are glowing like a *star*."

Desminda trembled. "I can't make it stop."

Astrid sighed softly and came closer. "Take my hand."

Desminda reached out with trembling fingers.

Astrid wrapped her hand around Desminda's.

And then she opened her eyes back in the princesses' bedroom in the Witch Kingdom.

The door burst open revealing Magnus and Evara. The guard had both daggers drawn, her face a mask of concentration. She dropped them when she saw Astrid and Shade.

"What happened?" Evara barked.

Desminda's hoarse inhale of breath was followed by ragged coughing.

Shade helped her to a sitting position, adjusting the blanket around her for modesty. He spoke in low tones, his words soft and urgent.

Astrid stood, off balance for a moment, before a firm grip helped right her.

Magnus.

She smiled weakly up at him. "Thanks."

He helped her over to a chair, and Astrid sank into it.

"That thing," Desminda breathed. "It's..." She paused, a tear rolling down her face. "It's inside me."

Magnus kneeled next to Desminda's beside. "It's diminished." His eyes snapped to the bard. "What happened?"

Astrid shrugged, the smile not reaching her eyes. "It trapped her power. I helped the princess free it, and Desminda managed to wound it. We have some time before it recovers, I think."

"How much time?" Shade asked.

"I can't say. It draws its power from that wasteland." Astrid shook her head. "I don't know how. The place seems lifeless, but it's not. Killing it will be difficult. Maybe impossible."

Magnus' face went grim. "Nothing is impossible," he said when the silence stretched. "We will find a way."

The doors opened again, revealing three of Queen Moira's guards. They started when they saw all of them together, but instead of reacting, they put their weapons away.

The first one to come in, a tall male with dark hair, spoke. "Queen Moira senses darkness in your princess. She wishes to see you all at first light." His gaze lingered on Desminda before he nodded once and turned on his heel, the other two silent and watchful behind him.

No one spoke until they were sure they were alone.

"This visit could have gone better," Shade said dryly.

Evara's merry laughter burst the tension better than anything else, and soon enough, even Desminda was smiling.

CHAPTER FORTY-ONE

A MEETING AND A FAREWELL OF A SORT

Desminda looked like death warmed over the next morning. Harlow's jaw dropped when she saw the normally serene and beautiful princess, but Desminda looked like she'd gone to war in the last twelve hours. Concern warred with dislike inside of Harlow, but empathy won.

She picked up her teacup and carried it over to Desminda's table, pouring herself a cup from the pitcher in the center. Desminda glanced up, her golden eyes bloodshot, widening in surprise when she noticed who stood there.

"Good morning," Harlow said lightly. "Mind if I sit?"

Desminda shook her head, so Harlow took the chair opposite. "Are you alright?" she asked quietly.

Desminda snorted, a sound so unlike her it made Harlow snicker. "I'm surprised you haven't already heard."

Harlow blinked. "I haven't heard anything at all. In fact, I haven't spoken to a soul since I went back to my room last night." The silence had been glorious. She'd gone straight back to her room and gotten back into the pool where she marinated for so long her skin had turned pruney.

"That thing visited me last night."

"Thing?" Harlow inquired, blowing on her tea to cool it. A tray of golden brown pastries filled with several varieties of fruit lay before them, decorated with glistening sugar crystals. Harlow slid a plate over and snagged one with a shiny red filling.

Desminda's dimple peeked out from her cheek. "The blue one is good, too."

Harlow shrugged. "I'll try that one next."

Desminda huffed a laugh. "You are a princess now," she said lightly. "You can try them all if you like."

Harlow had tried her best to forget last night, but she'd tossed and turned most of the night, wondering how things might change.

It didn't feel good. It felt awful, knowing the things that had to happen to get her to this point in her life.

Her mother, her *real* mother, had been sent on a mission to spy on the Thornewood queen and had died for her efforts. Because of Marion's death, Harlow was swept away to another kingdom, raised by strangers to hide her identity, then taken to Thornewood where the unthinkable had happened.

And now here she was, in the castle where her mother had lived, potential heir to the throne.

Harlow tried to smile, but it slipped from her lips. "Yes. I suppose I am."

"It is difficult to wear a crown," Desminda said softly.

"I don't plan to wear one," Harlow said honestly.

A soft laugh escaped Desminda. "Plans don't matter when you have royal blood. You are subject to the whims of your parents."

Harlow stared at Desminda. "Well," she said lightly, "for the longest time, I had no blood parents. My foster parents only sought survival. We led a simple life, Desminda. Then I came to your kingdom and found out your mother murdered mine and tried to do the same to my father."

Desminda blanched. "I—I'm sorry. I didn't think."

Harlow raised her hand. "I am not like you. No one can steer me to their whims." She sighed and shook her head. "I merely came to see if you were alright. You look exhausted, and I was worried."

Desminda studied her. "The creature has left a piece of itself within me." She rubbed at the diminished spot. "We wounded it but couldn't kill it."

"We will," Harlow said with confidence. "Everything can be killed."

Desminda's smile reached her eyes this time. "Spoken like a true Virago."

Fierce pride soared within Harlow. She nodded to the princess and stood, taking her tea and pastry. They might no longer be friends, or more, but they didn't have to be enemies.

"The queen has asked us to meet with her in half an hour," Desminda said. "I trust you will be there."

Harlow shrugged. "I haven't heard anything about it." She smiled and headed off toward Evara, who stood in the corner eyeing her with bright hazel eyes.

Her heart skipped a beat before thundering in her chest as she got closer. Evara's braid, as usual, was messy. Dark curls floated around her face, strands hanging free from her braid.

"You should let me braid your hair," Harlow said.

Evara's eyes widened before a laugh bubbled from her. "Of all the things you could have said, I wouldn't have expected that."

"It's messy," Harlow blurted.

Evara smiled. "Hair is an inconvenience for me." She shrugged. "There are lots of other things I can do in the time it takes to braid my hair correctly." She winked.

Harlow's cheeks burned. "A tight braid is imperative in battle."

"Ah," she said lightly. "I hear Shade, but I don't see him." She cupped a hand over her brow and squinted her eyes. "Do you see him?"

"It's true!" Harlow protested.

Evara reached over and tweaked Harlow's nose. "I know it is, sunshine, but I don't see a battle here, do you?"

Harlow scrunched her nose. "It's a good habit to get into," she muttered.

Evara laughed and slung an arm over Harlow's shoulders. "Come. Take a walk with me. I have a little while before we meet the queen."

Blood roared through Harlow's ears. "Where?"

Evara reached and tugged one of Harlow's curls, warm fingers brushing against her cheek. "Here. There. Everywhere." She wiggled her brows. "Doesn't matter, does it?"

"No," Harlow said faintly. "I don't suppose it does."

"That's the spirit." She winked and took Harlow's hand.

On their way out, Harlow caught Desminda's eye. The

princess stared at them with an unreadable expression. She looked away, only to catch Evara winking at Desminda and giving her a little finger wave before she led Harlow out of the room.

Harlow hid her smile under her hand.

Evara navigated her toward a solarium tucked into one of the numerous alcoves in the castle. Harlow gasped when she stepped outside, a riot of colors surrounding her from all sides.

"This is the night garden," Evara said. "In another hour or so, all the blooms will close until the suns set."

The smell of sweet citrus and vanilla tantalized her senses, but as she walked further into the solarium, the scent changed to something headier, deeper. Greenery heavy with open blooms wound around small flowering trees. Every inch of space by the walls was occupied by plants of all shapes and sizes. "Stunning," Harlow murmured.

A rustling in the back startled her. Evara, hand on her daggers, peered around the corner, Harlow looking over her shoulder, and relaxed when she spotted a young blonde woman on her knees digging in the dirt.

"Oh!" the witch exclaimed. She slapped her hands together to wipe off the dirt and rose to her feet, shaking grass and leaves from her skirt. "Hi! I'm Hannah."

"Evara." The guard tilted her head. "And Harlow. We're just out here for some peace and quiet."

The witch smiled. "Then I'll leave you be. I'm finished here anyway. This is one of three night gardens. If you want all day blooms, there are four other solariums, one in each wing." Her cheek dimpled prettily. "My favorite is in the south wing. There are many varieties of roses, one bright yellow. Double petaled and smells like vanilla cake."

She lifted her shoulders and smiled before turning away and leaving them alone.

"Is she a flower witch?" Harlow asked.

Evara laughed. "I'm not sure if that's the official name, but I'd assume so. Every witch here has a natural affinity." She gestured toward a small round table with two chairs and sat down close to a vine heavy with bright white trumpet-shaped flowers. "Have you discovered yours?"

Harlow blinked. "Mine?"

"You're a witch, aren't you?" Evara tipped a pink bloom toward her face and inhaled, a dreamy smile crossing her lips.

"Uh. Well, I suppose," Harlow admitted. "I haven't thought about it much."

Evara's gaze turned thoughtful. "I think your affinity is earth like your father, but since you have witch blood, too, I wouldn't be surprised if you have a talent for animals, maybe plants, too. Most witches, no matter their affinity, can grow things."

Harlow thought about it. Was that why Luci seemed so drawn to her? "Maybe. Luci does seem to like me." She remembered Magnus' words about how powerful her mother had been, but it didn't feel right to speak of it yet.

Evara laughed. "Luci is a brute, so I think someone would have to be magical to get in that beast's good graces."

They sat in silence for a while, but it was a good silence, the kind you get when someone you trusted sat beside you. And Evara, even with all her secrets, was the kind of person

Harlow had come to trust, even if she didn't know exactly why.

Evara broke the easy silence. "I need to tell you something."

The safe bubble Harlow was in burst. Apprehension tightened her muscles. "What is it?"

"You and Desminda have history."

Harlow shrugged. "Some. Whatever it was never got off the ground."

Was that relief that flashed in Evara's eyes? "You still care about her?"

Harlow thought about it. "I do, but probably not in the way you're thinking."

Evara's eyes sparkled. "Oh? What way was I thinking about it?"

Harlow became itchy under her shirt. Heat crept up her neck. "She and I are not—We aren't—There never was—"

One of Evara's eyebrows went up before she laughed. "Relax, Harlow. I know what you're saying."

"Thank the gods," Harlow muttered. "What is it then?"

"Offers are coming in."

Harlow shook her head. "I don't understand."

The sound of a throat clearing startled both of them. Evara sent the guard standing a few feet away a dark look. It was the same man who'd escorted Harlow to her room the first time.

He dipped his head. "Excuse me, Princess Harlow. Evara, the queen awaits your presence."

Harlow cringed at the title, even as the guard's eyes lit with amusement.

Evara sighed. "I have to go. I'll meet you in your room when I'm finished."

Harlow nodded, confused about what Evara wanted to tell her. "Is it important?"

"Perhaps not to you," Evara said, "though I thought you might want to know." She touched Harlow's arm. "The timing is certainly...convenient."

With those cryptic words, Evara and the guard left her in the solarium.

Harlow made no move to follow. This place was the first time in the castle she felt like she belonged, and she wanted to stay just a little longer.

A bead of sweat rolled down Desminda's spine. She stood before the throne with Magnus, Shade, Astrid, and Evara standing behind her. The queen studied her, bright eyes giving no hint as to why Desminda was the center of attention this morning.

Evara's gaze burned against her skin. The guard didn't like her, hadn't liked her from the moment she arrived in Thornewood. It upset her at first, but now that she'd caught a few of the looks Evara had sent Harlow's way, Desminda understood it a little better.

Harlow was a lot of things, but no one could accuse her of being ugly.

The new princess wasn't with them today, and Desminda had the uncomfortable feeling she was about to be the recipient of unwelcome news. There was a lot of that going around lately, it seemed.

She wore a dress of soft purple in a supple shimmering fabric this morning, her long, dark hair flowing freely down her back. If her mother saw her now, she would be appalled. Back home, dressing for any meal meant being poked and prodded, tucked and folded, braided and sprayed. Layers upon layers of clothing, adornments and belts, uncomfortable shoes pinching the first three toes, and a corset so tight it shrank her waist by two inches and left her unable to breathe.

This morning, she wore a dress and slippers. The only extras were a thin silver bracelet and a few headpins to hold the top half of her hair out of her face. She felt free. Untethered. Desminda could breathe for the first time since childhood. The feeling was odd but not unwelcome.

If she took her kingdom back, she'd make changes for the better.

Starting with the outlawing of corsets.

"Desminda, I am aware of last night's events," the queen began.

It took everything for Desminda not to shift uncomfortably. The darkness was still there, a tiny spot in her chest, but her anger had greatly diminished since she'd wounded the creature, so she stood stock still, counting on all the training she'd had over the years to keep her face carefully blank.

"Witches are attuned to magic," she continued. "All magic, but especially foreign magic that does not belong in our kingdom." The queen showed no emotion as she spoke, each word spoken like it had been carefully rehearsed before this meeting.

"I was unaware of being under the influence of any kind of entity until it approached me in my dreams," Desminda said.

"Magnus made me aware." Queen Moira flicked her

hand in dismissal. "It still doesn't diminish what you've allowed into my kingdom."

Desminda's lips parted in surprise. "Your Majesty, I didn't allow—"

"We know of your past betrothal to Lucien Talbot."

Desminda nodded. "Yes. Things changed when his sister stole my kingdom," she added dryly.

A soft snort came from behind her. One of Queen Moira's eyebrows went up.

"Be that as it may, there are other...offers."

She couldn't stop the horrified expression forming on her face. Queen Moira's eyes flashed with anger. "These are all good matches. Advantageous matches. And we have Queen Nova's permission to pursue them."

Desminda's heart dropped into her stomach. "You—" she breathed. "You can't do this!"

"You are an enemy princess who stepped into the heart of your enemy's land, a danger to yourself and our rule. This is your best opportunity to re-secure your kingdom. You need allies." This time Queen Moira smiled. "The best way to secure an ally is through marriage."

Her mind spun with the possibilities, all of them terrible. Once magic fell, all Desminda's travel had halted, and she'd never experienced the other kingdoms. Lucien was barely tolerable. She couldn't imagine marrying anyone else other than someone she chose. Desminda liked who she liked. It didn't matter whether they were male or female. But the thought of giving up her autonomy to someone who only cared for her coffers was untenable. Though she had no coffers anymore, so what was the draw? The potential of treasure and the Luna stones?

There was the Kingdom of Light, two princes there. Roses, only Lucien and already a failed betrothal. Crystal with one prince no one knew anything about. The Beast Kingdom—even the thought of that made her shudder. Wolves—too similar to the Beast Kingdom and then Shadow where only Nova remained. No princes and no princesses. Except...there was The Kingdom of Witches where there were no princes.

Only a new princess.

A plan formed, one that would ensure Harlow would hate her for the rest of her life.

But one that might save Desminda's life, as well as her heart.

"Who offered?" Desminda breathed.

Queen Moira smiled again. "A prince from the Beast Kingdom has sent a written offer."

Desminda kept her face uninterested.

"And the prince from the Crystal Kingdom." Queen Moira's eyes flicked behind her. "Both generous offers, but both require you travel to meet them."

"Magic doesn't exist in the Kingdom of Crystal," Desminda said. "If I travel too close to Thornewood, I will be recognized."

"Then travel to the Beast Kingdom first." Queen Moira rose. "You will travel with your party. Harlow will stay here."

"I will stay back, Queen Moira," Evara said, stepping up beside Desminda.

"Shocking," Desminda drawled under her breath.

Evara shot her a frown but remained silent, her head bowed to the queen.

"Good," Queen Moira said. "Harlow needs someone here with her as she adjusts to her new role."

Magnus cleared his throat. "New role, Your Majesty? She is imperative to restoring magic. Harlow is untried and untested in the magical world. There is much to be done."

Queen Moira studied him for a long moment. "I agree. There is much to be done to ready Harlow for her new role. But you forget, she is half witch, mage. No one else is familiar with our magic except for other witches." A faint smile curved her lips. "And only our blood is familiar with our *particular* type of magic."

Magnus' jaw tightened. Queen Moira had a point, but it was obvious he did not want to let Harlow stay in this kingdom.

"You will stay with her," the queen said with finality. "You and Nova's guard." Her gaze flicked to Shade. "You and the bard will travel with Desminda to the Beast Kingdom to see if this match is appropriate." From the look on her face, Queen Moira expected it to be *perfectly* appropriate.

"Of course, Your Majesty," Shade said from behind. "It is an honor to escort the Princess Desminda."

She almost laughed. Shade barely tolerated her most days. It should be an interesting trip.

There wouldn't be a marriage on this journey.

But there could be a marriage *here*.

A sense of deep satisfaction filled her at the thought, and that tiny spot in her chest flickered as if it agreed.

CHAPTER FORTY-THREE

A NIGHTMARE MADE FLESH

"She's up to something," Evara whispered to Shade once they filed out of the throne room. Desminda had left half an hour ago, escorted out by a young female guard to prepare for her trip. The queen asked them to stay behind to talk about logistics.

Shade glanced at her. "Why do you say that?"

"She's entirely too calm about being married off to the first bidder." Evara pressed down the empathy bubbling inside of her for Desminda's plight. No woman should be paraded around like cattle for someone else's viewing pleasure, and that's what was happening to the princess.

"Desminda always knew she'd marry someone from another kingdom."

Evara inclined her head in acknowledgment. "Yes, but that was before her kingdom was stolen from her. She thought she was free."

Shade frowned. "And now an enemy is forcing her into an alliance."

"And has offered nothing in return," Evara remarked.

"What do you think she's planning?" Shade touched her elbow, guiding her into an empty room. When the door clicked shut behind them, Shade sighed and sank into a wooden chair that had seen better days.

"What is the one thing prized from a princess bride?" Evara murmured. "The one thing if taken away that would ruin a marriage before it has even begun?"

Shade studied her. Evara watched as the thoughts flickered over his face.

Men. She rolled her eyes. "Virginity. Every kingdom but ours uses a test to check a bride is...pure before she is wed."

"I haven't seen a single man in this kingdom," Shade mused.

Evara laughed. "Rods aren't the only thing responsible for despoiling virgins, Shade."

The unflappable former Commander of the Guard turned crimson, heat creeping up his necks and onto his cheeks. His lips parted, and he exhaled. "True," he said slowly. "But the purity test would still show she is unspoiled if she were with a woman."

"Not necessarily," she said, but it opened up a world of possibilities. Evara's eyes narrowed, a hundred scenarios unspooling in her mind. One snagged and caught hold. She chewed on the side of her lip. "Unless she were to get caught in the act."

Evara and Shade locked eyes. Her heart thundered in her chest.

"We have to find Harlow," they blurted at the same time.

They passed Magnus on the frantic search to find her. The big mage smiled in greeting, but it fell off his face when he saw their expressions.

"What is it?" he demanded.

Evara took his arm and told him on the way to Harlow's bedroom.

Magnus' expression turned thunderous. "She wouldn't," he seethed.

"I can't say for sure, but if Harlow and Desminda are caught together in a position like that, Desminda won't get what she wants. She'll get a death sentence." The witches had no patience for foolish little girls trying to strongarm them. What she didn't tell the rest of them was it was exactly that kind of idea a spoiled princess like Desminda might have. Evara shook her head in disgust. When she found the princess, she was likely to beat her black and blue for thinking up such an awful, harebrained scheme.

"And Queen Moira will toss the rest of us out on our ears," Shade muttered.

Harlow left her room less than a half hour after she'd come back to wait for Evara. The solarium was such a relaxing place that she'd found it again and asked for tea and cookies to be brought to her. Doing so had sent a squirming sense of discomfort through her, but the guards scrambled to take care of the task.

No one else had entered the place since the guards had brought her tea, and Harlow reveled in the quiet, finally taking the time to sort out the racing thoughts in her mind.

She was a princess.

A princess!

Some girls dreamed of being one. Harlow had only ever wanted a family. She was content with her life, happy with her adventures with Nova, the lessons she'd learned, the quiet nights sitting by the fire when her sister braided her hair.

She had no desire for more, no long-running dreams of riches beyond her wildest imagination, of power and majesty.

To be honest, it all sounded quite terrible.

Though someone bringing her tea was nice.

She smiled as she sipped her tea and nibbled on a rose-flavored cookie.

Queen Moira, her grandmother, had left her alone, possibly sensing rightly Harlow needed some time to process everything. She hadn't seen Miriam since the dinner, but it didn't bother her much. Miriam had been difficult to read from the second she'd met her, and people like that always made Harlow uncomfortable. She liked things straightforward, and that hadn't happened since she'd gone to the castle to seek work.

Everything always felt so underhanded and secret.

She thought she might make a poor princess, indeed.

Sighing, she took the last sip of her tea, brushed her hands off and started to stand, only to hear the solarium door open.

When she turned, she spotted Desminda coming toward her, a wide smile on her beautiful face.

For some odd reason, Harlow felt instantly wary. Desminda never smiled at her like that. She'd smiled before, but it had always been softer, more secretive. Looking back,

Harlow had to admit that neither one of them had made the other happy.

She'd spent the entire time in the castle nervous and being around Desminda had only worsened that feeling.

"Harlow!" Desminda breathed. "I'm so happy I caught you."

Harlow tilted her head to study the princess. Desminda had a frantic air of desperation about her.

"We saw each other not too long ago," Harlow said slowly.

Desminda's eyes flashed. "Yes. Yes, we did. I just—" she cleared her throat. "There's much we've left unsaid."

Harlow didn't think so, but she'd listen if Desminda had come to apologize. If Harlow were honest, the princess wasn't very good at it.

"Alright," Harlow said. She waved a hand at the chair opposite. "There's some tea left. Would you like some?"

Desminda glanced at the tea and shook her head. Instead of sitting, she came close—too close—to Harlow, invading her personal space in a way that sent Harlow's heart beating too fast.

The princess smelled of jasmine and fresh things. Up close, her golden eyes were a kaleidoscope of all the colors of the two suns, and she had a tiny bit of freckling on the bridge of her nose, something Harlow hadn't noticed in the dimmer lights of Thornewood Castle.

Desminda reached out to toy with one of Harlow's curls, her eyes focused on Harlow's lips. "Tell me, have you ever...?" Her voice trailed off, long lashes brushing the upper bridge of her cheekbones.

"Ever what?" Harlow asked, her voice soft. She cleared her throat and thought about stepping away, when even a few months ago she would have given anything for this to happen.

But this was before a dark-haired guard had made her laugh and question things. Nothing had happened between them, but it didn't mean nothing ever would.

"You know what I mean," Desminda whispered, her fingers trailing across Harlow's cheek and down her jaw, brushing across her lips.

Harlow's cheeks burned. "What are you doing?"

Desminda shrugged and leaned in. "I am taking what I should have those months back. Something we both wanted." Her golden eyes burned as she met Harlow's gaze. "Do you deny it? That you want me?"

Harlow stared hard at the princess. What had changed between this morning and now? One thing Harlow prided herself on was learning her lesson the first time, and she'd learned that Desminda did little without a purpose. She was not driven by heated passion or emotion, and a girl like Harlow who could usually give her nothing had moved up in station.

Now there were a lot of things she could give Desminda.

So what did she want?

Rage burned through Evara as she raced through the castle's halls in a frantic search to save both of these girls from their fate. Harlow, from her heart being broken, and Desminda from winding up with her head on the chopping block.

They'd managed to slip the guards discreetly following them a few minutes ago, but it was only a matter of time before someone else found them and questioned where they were going with such urgency.

But it wasn't the only reason she was angry. For the first time in Evara's life, something, no *someone*, had interested her. She'd given up her life to serve Queen Nova and accepted that her place in life was to one day give up her life in service to the kingdom.

She never planned to marry or have children or do anything other ladies of her age might do.

But that was before a grieving girl of sunlight had stumbled into their kingdom and made her laugh at every turn.

Harlow had such innocence, and even though there wasn't much of an age difference between them, Evara hadn't been innocent for many years.

She'd seen too many things and been granted a power so deadly, having a relationship seemed an insurmountable obstacle. After all, why would she give her heart to someone lesser than her, someone who feared the darkness swimming in her veins? She'd tried once and had her heart broken for it, so she'd locked it behind an impenetrable door that had never opened again.

Until now.

It wasn't that Desminda wanted Harlow. If she did and Harlow wanted her too, Evara would step into the shadows and allow it.

But Desminda planned to take what was left of Harlow's innocence through either trickery or manipulation, and that was something Evara could not abide.

Magnus and Shade said little, their steps matching her own urgency. Astrid had gone the opposite way in her search, and whoever found Harlow first had strict instructions to do whatever they had to do to contain the incident. They could only hope none of the witches caught them.

Crimson shadows snapped from Evara's skin. A shocked inhale from behind her made her growl in frustration. She was losing her grip on her magic, and that rarely happened.

Not yet, she told her shadows. *We aren't there yet.*

But they sensed her urgency, her anger, and though they settled a little, they still snapped around her body, ebbing and flowing with her movements.

She would dry Desminda to a husk if she hurt that girl.

And she would gladly pay the price for doing it.

"Taking something seems very much like something you would do," Harlow said lightly.

Desminda flinched as if she'd been struck, her fingers dropping from Harlow's lips. "Why would you say that to me?"

"Only a few days ago we were at each other's throats. Now you come to me with seduction on your mind. Why?"

Desminda shrugged, a coy smile playing on her lips. "The heart isn't rational. The things you've said to me have made me think. Why shouldn't we pursue this now?"

Harlow's lips parted. Ah. "Now that I am of royal blood?"

Desminda smiled. "Yes. There is nothing standing in our way now. Why shouldn't we take what we want?"

She stepped closer, taking hold of Harlow's braid. Desminda tugged the fastener from the bottom and undid the intricate style, the one that had taken her forever to get right.

Annoyance flickered in Harlow, but she didn't move. How far would Desminda take this?

"We could do so much together," Desminda whispered, a snake in Harlow's peaceful garden. "You and I hold so much power. We could make the Lands of Lunamoor quake. Together we could wrest Thornewood from Celestine, free magic, and rule together for as long as we wished."

Harlow sighed. None of that sounded enticing. In fact, it sounded pretty awful. "Desminda, I don't think—"

"Shh," Desminda said, touching a finger to Harlow's lips before dropping back to finish undoing her braid. Her deft fingers slipped through Harlow's hair, combing through it until it became a wild riot of curls around her head.

When Desminda's fingers slid down her neck, past her collarbone, and flicked the first button of her vest open, Harlow gripped her roaming fingers.

"Desminda."

The princess freed herself, flicked the second button, and pushed the edges of Harlow's vest back.

"No," Harlow said.

Desminda huffed a laugh and didn't stop.

"No," Harlow said again.

Anger flickered in Desminda's eyes. "Why? You wanted me before. What's changed?"

A sharp laugh cracked from Harlow's throat. "Everything. But especially me."

The atmosphere between them crackled. Harlow tried to steady her breath, but anger and sorrow warred in her heart. The earth underneath her feet responded to her emotions, and it felt like the plants themselves heard her anguish.

"Because you're a princess now?" Desminda huffed.

Sometimes physical beauty hid internal ugliness. Standing there staring at the girl she might have fallen in love with if things hadn't crumbled, Harlow realized for all Desminda's outer beauty, she possessed a selfish heart. She didn't want Harlow because she cared for her, Desminda wanted her because she was a stepping stone on the path that would attain her goals.

So when Desminda ignored her again and leaned in to kiss her, Harlow responded appropriately.

Evara, Magnus, and Shade skidded to a stop in front of the solarium. The guard's heart pounded in her chest, and she prayed she wasn't too late.

She reached for the door, absently noting it felt warm in her hand.

The moment they stepped inside, Magnus scoffed. "It feels like a steam bath in here. Are you sure she's in here?"

Evara's brow furrowed. The temperature had been a touch humid before, normal when so many plants existed together, but the oppressive heat she felt now wasn't present.

She sent a tendril of magic out, seeping into the ground as it sought out Harlow's unique aura.

"Yes," she said grimly before heading further into the solarium.

"What is it?" Shade asked, hearing the tone of her voice.

"Not sure. Someone has used magic." Evara didn't draw her daggers, but she sent more tendrils out seeking the source of her anger.

When she found it, Evara huffed a surprised laugh and

straightened, steps picking up speed until she saw Harlow and Desminda locked in an epic glaring contest.

Shade and Magnus came up beside her. The mage looked first at Desminda, then to Harlow, fury darkening his face when he caught sight of Harlow's askew vest.

Shade took everything in, scrubbed a hand over his face, and chuckled. "Seems she didn't need us after all."

Desminda hung suspended in the air, arms and legs wrapped with tendrils of thick vines. A fat leaf covered the princess's mouth, preventing her from making noise, and her eyes sparked with anger.

She bucked and squirmed violently, but Harlow's magic held her tightly in place.

The other princess, the one they'd worried so much about, sat at the table munching on a pink cookie. She noticed Evara and gave her a strained smile.

"Turns out you were right about the plants," she said mildly. "I asked them for help and..." She waved a hand at Desminda. "They responded."

"Neat trick," Evara said, smirking up at the restrained almost queen. "That will teach you to keep your hands where they belong, won't it?" she added lightly.

Desminda glared at her, poison in her eyes.

Magnus wasn't as amused as the rest of them. "You thought to secure your place here by sullying Harlow's reputation?" He shook his head. "We will leave after lunch."

Desminda's eyes widened, and she shook her head wildly.

Magnus snorted in disgust. "You wish to act like a beast? Then you shall marry one."

Without another word, he spun on his heel and exited the room, leaving Evara and Shade alone with Harlow and the spoiled princess.

"How do we get her down?" Shade murmured.

Evara shrugged. "Don't rightly know." She looked up at him. "I think she should get herself down, don't you think?"

Desminda gave him a desperate look.

Evara thought Shade might demand her release, but he surprised her. "I believe you're right." He motioned for Harlow to rise before turning to Desminda. "I am ashamed to know you, Desminda."

Her nostrils flared, a tear slipping from one of her golden eyes, but not one of them relented. Harlow gave her a long look before slipping out the door.

Shade followed, eyebrows rising when Evara made no move to go with him. He shook his head and dipped down to whisper in her ear.

"Killing her would complicate things," was all he said.

Evara smiled, a flash of admiration burning inside her for the dark knight her queen had come to love.

She had no plans to kill the princess.

When Shade passed through the door, Evara sent a tendril of power out and locked it behind him.

No, killing her *would* complicate things, but it would also be too easy of a punishment for what the spoiled girl had tried to do.

When she turned to Desminda, fear flashed in the princess's eyes. She watched as Desminda floundered for her magic, but Evara knew it would do nothing.

She was terror made flesh, unmasked as Evara's true and

tremendous power unraveled from her pale skin. Only Nova knew what she was, but Evara had one tender flaw. To save those she cared about, she would unleash the nightmare living underneath her skin

Desminda's low moan of fear made her smile.

"*Hello, princessssss,*" the being made of nightmares whispered from between Evara's lips.

CHAPTER FORTY-FOUR

A LESSON LEARNED TWICE OVER

S hade, Astrid, and Desminda made for a quiet, somber traveling group later that afternoon. Evara, Magnus and Harlow stood at the edge of the Kingdom of Witches to see their companions off.

Harlow was uncharacteristically silent, her usual smattering of questions silenced as Desminda mounted her horse. She watched the pale-faced princess adjust her seating and come into a stiff-backed position. No bruises, no cuts, nothing marred Desminda's skin.

There was no evidence of Evara's ministrations from earlier, nor would anyone find them if they looked, but Desminda had learned her lesson and learned it well.

Unless you are invited to touch, keep your hands to yourself.

And just in case Desminda lost that lesson somewhere along the way, Evara left a little gift inside of Desminda's mind to be opened in case those hands wandered again where they were not wanted.

Remember, Princess, Evara whispered into Desminda's mind, *you can hide, but I will find you. Harlow is not your plaything. Touch her again, and your life will be forfeit.*

Desminda flinched, her lips pressed so hard together they turned white.

Shade gave her an odd look before he turned to look at Evara. There was no disapproval there, but there was an uncomfortable curiosity about what she might have done to Desminda.

Neither of them would tell. Desminda because she pissed herself in fright that morning, and Evara because she never unleashed her secret unless there was no other choice.

Only once in her life had there been no choice, and somehow, in spite of it, she'd wound up in the queen's trusted guard.

Evara smiled at Desminda, wiggling her fingers in a mocking wave.

Perhaps now Desminda would learn what it was to be a true ruler. Evara had shown her what it was to be powerless, helpless, and subjected to cruelty when you could do nothing about it.

If she didn't finally learn the lesson, Evara knew she never would.

Desminda turned away, but not before Evara saw the shimmer of tears in her eyes.

No pity welled inside of Evara.

She tried not to be a monster.

But sometimes she didn't mind it.

Harlow placed a tentative hand on Evara's arm. "Did something happen between you?" she whispered.

"We came to an agreement," was all Evara said. "You will never have to worry about her putting unwelcome hands on you again."

Harlow studied her. "Unwelcome?"

Evara shrugged, her heart tightening at the thought of *anyone* putting their hands on Harlow. "If you welcome her touch, it is different."

Her light eyebrows crinkled, and she gave Evara a curious look. Deciding something, Harlow nodded. "I would not welcome it," was all she said.

Evara ducked her head to hide her smile.

Shade finished adjusting his saddlebag and came over, winking at Evara before he turned to Harlow. He studied her for a long moment before opening his arms.

Without hesitation, she stepped into them. He wrapped his arms around her, and Harlow tucked her head against his chest and closed her eyes. Shade's expression turned stricken for a moment before a flash of grief went through his eyes. He squeezed them shut and bent down to kiss the top of Harlow's head. "You are safe here," he murmured against her hair.

"For now," Harlow agreed, tilting her face up to him. "Be careful," she whispered. "There is still darkness in Desminda. It's barely there, but I sense it lying like a snake in wait."

Shade nodded and exhaled a breath. "Astrid is with me. She is attuned to this creature." A rare smile crossed his face and reached his eyes. "Besides, soon enough, she will be a problem for the beasts."

Harlow snorted. "I feel a little sorry for her."

"Do not," Shade said, his voice hard. "She has made consistently poor choices. All of this is on her own head."

"She will be safe with the beasts," Evara murmured. "They are a strange people, but they have their own sense of honor." She shrugged. "Unless she decides to pull similar shenanigans. Then nothing is guaranteed. Desminda goes as a bride. They will allow some behavior on her part as a gesture to Queen Moira and Nova. But she will be required to conform to their ways soon enough if a match is to work out."

"That's what I'm afraid of," Shade said quietly. "If she pulled this stunt with Harlow to get out of it, what will she do to them?"

Evara shook her head. "Desminda failed to notice Harlow's claws until it was too late. The Beast Kingdom has its claws out all the time. She will be more wary there."

Evara didn't add in the suggestion she'd given Desminda that morning, the only kindness she'd shown her. *You will find an ally in the beasts. They understand bloodthirstiness far better than the rest of us. If you want your kingdom back, they are the key.*

She hadn't lied to her. The kingdom solved problems with bloodshed. If they wanted to expand their lands, marrying Desminda and helping her regain her crown would bolster their kingdom's standing in Lunamoor. It might also put them at odds with the Kingdom of Wolves, the territory between Thornewood and the beasts, but that wasn't Evara's problem.

Shade stepped away and touched Harlow's chin. "Train hard. Learn everything you can. Nova knows where you are and why you're staying. She said to tell you she misses you and she will see you soon." He smiled sadly. "As will I."

Astrid turned to wave, offering them a bright smile. Shade mounted his horse and trotted up to stand next Desminda who barely reacted to his presence.

Queen Moira had not seen them off, sending only two guards out to ensure their safe passage through the border.

It sent a message, but which one no one knew. The queen was no fool and had eyes everywhere. It was possible she'd seen what Desminda had tried to do but elected not to interfere when she realized what Harlow had done to defend herself. Nor had she interfered in the aftermath when she and Evara were alone.

Either way, her absence sent the message that Desminda was longer welcome in the Kingdom of Witches. Not the most auspicious start to gaining allies, but she hadn't kicked Evara out, so that was good for Nova's kingdom, she supposed.

The three riders nudged their mounts and headed toward the border, Desminda stiff-backed and frightened in the middle.

When they passed through the border and disappeared into the mists, Magnus let out a long exhale and said, "Anyone hungry?"

Evara and Harlow both laughed and followed him inside the castle, the two guards trailing behind them.

CHAPTER FORTY-FIVE

CELESTINE'S PLAN

S he called the nightmare during her dreams. Most of the time he showed up instantly as if he waited at the edge of its desolate wasteland to see if she'd changed her mind. His eagerness told her she'd made the right decision. Over several days she'd spoken to the thing, asking many questions, most of which he refused to answer.

She'd spent the last week hunting down a magician from the Light Kingdom, one who had a reputation for his work against dark magic. It took her longer than expected, and she'd found out the mage had gotten wind of her search and tried to flee to the Shadow Kingdom.

Now he languished in a dungeon cell beneath her, working to perfect a formula to oust the darkness at the moment of her choosing. He proved resistant at first until Celestine revealed the special guests she'd invited a few days after she'd captured him.

His daughter was quite lovely. His wife, not so much, but Celestine could tell he loved the woman's homely face and rounded body. She'd put them up in a room at the top of the castle guarded by two of her best. They were allowed to wander the castle grounds, but the market was off limits.

It was the kindest she could bring herself to be.

Every night she visited the Luna stones, but in the last two days, she'd realized whatever this thing was, it was killing them, covering them with its unique poison and draining the magic out through its veins. Perhaps its power was linked to the desolate wasteland it resided in, but Celestine thought it was linked to the stones as well, a parasite perhaps. Maybe a spell the thing had cast.

Either way, it had to stop. Otherwise her goal of gaining her magic back would be moot.

Tonight, the creature did not wait for her.

"Alaxar?" Celestine called. The thing had given her a name, one that came from no kingdoms she was familiar with. No surname, either. Just Alaxar.

I ammmm herrrrre, it said after a few minutes.

Celestine started. She saw no evidence of it, only heard its sibilant voice in her mind. "You are killing the stones."

It said nothing for a long moment. *Allow me entrance and I will free the stones.*

She snorted. *Why would I trust you?*

A show of faith, it said.

The castle swayed on its foundations. Celestine sucked in a gasp of fear and almost left the wasteland, but a second later it stopped and a thin trickle of something she hadn't felt in so long breezed against her body.

Magic.

Her magic.

She shut her eyes and allowed the feeling to wash over her. The scent of roses and green things washed over her. A tear slipped down her face, one of remembrance.

"How long will it last?" she croaked.

It is permanent, the thing said. *A tiny break in the spell. Enough for a spell or two each day if you ration it.*

She had to find a way to contain the break to the castle. "You can shatter the entire thing and choose not to?" Celestine's voice was hard.

No. I cannot. The magic is too strong, the spell too... complicated *for even me. But*, it whispered, *together we can bring magic back into your kingdom.*

"What is wrong with you?" Celestine snapped. "Why are you not here?"

Do not concern yourself with my actions, it hissed. *Let me in, Celestine. Together you and I can break the hold over your people. We can destroy the usurpers and know more power than we've ever seen before.*

"You will leave the stones alone?"

It laughed. She kept her mind carefully blank, suspecting once this thing was inside her it could see her thoughts.

I will not need the stones when I have a vessel.

"I can't claim to understand, but if you agree to break the spell and relinquish me when it is done, I will allow you to inhabit my body."

Agreed, the thing hissed.

And so, the creature whispered how to free it to Celestine in the dark of night. She rose on bare feet, tucked the white silken robe around her slight body, and tiptoed down to the darkest regions of Thornewood castle, stunned when it directed her to a fire darkened door she'd never noticed before.

It whispered the words in Celestine's mind to open it, the foreign magic slippery to hold onto, and it took her three tries to get it right. The door clicked open, sending a wave of malevolent heat against her body.

Heart pounding, Celestine tiptoed inside the darkened chamber. A lamp hissed on, weak firelight casting shadows over carved symbols in the ancient stone floor.

An offering of blood, it hissed.

Grimacing, Celestine obliged, picking up the knife lying on the stone pedestal next to the carving, and sliced into her forearm. She hissed in pain but massaged the blood out.

When the first drop splashed against the floor, the carvings lit up with a sickly crimson light.

More, it whispered, a scrape of claws against Celestine's mind.

Celestine cut herself again, allowing the blood to splash onto the floor.

A gust of wind blew her shift open, exposing her bare legs. Celestine cursed and leaned forward against the gale.

The circle pulsed. Once. Twice.

When it pulsed again, a figure the color of night stood there, robes of darkness flowing in a fetid wind. But someone, no something else stood behind it.

"Celestine," it greeted. The sound was knives against flesh, the terrified screams of children, a nightmare walking.

She took a step back, regret filling her thundering heart. Blood dripped steadily onto the floor. Celestine swayed, dizziness overcoming her.

"I no longer require your services," Alaxar whispered.

"No! We had a bargain!" Celestine screamed. She turned on her heel, slipping in the blood dripping from her wound, and landed hard onto the stone floor.

"My most trusted will use your skin." Alaxar stepped over her and into the doorway, turning to regard her as the other creature came closer. "Farewell, Celestine," it said, disappearing in a gust of rotted corruption.

Celestine screamed, scrambling away from the thing looming above her.

It was male, that much she could tell. Pale skin and strange green eyes.

"You and I will have so much fun," it whispered just as it reached for her with a skeletal hand.

EPILOGUE

A cloud of magic dotted the Thornewood skies in the deepest part of the night, a shadow of corruption sailing through the skies as if it searched for something.

Desminda, it whispered.

Desminda, I will find you.

ABOUT THE AUTHOR

USA Today Bestselling author S.E. Babin is a mom, a wife, and a military veteran. She has a passion for writing books filled with heroines you'd like to sit down and drink too much wine with and heroes who love those kinds of girls.

Sheryl holds a Master of Fine Arts in Popular Fiction and Publishing from Emerson College and spends way too much time hanging out in libraries and bookstores.

ALSO BY S.E. BABIN

Out of Eggnog Aphrodite

Out of Cake Aphrodite

Out of Sanity Aphrodite

Out of Excuses Aphrodite

Out of Patience Aphrodite

Cozy Mysteries

Psychic Cleaner Cozy Mysteries

Murder by the Brush

Maid for Mayhem

Another One Fights the Dust

An Unfolding Crime

The Grim Sweeper

A Draining Murder

Shelf Indulgence

Booked for Homicide

Foreword Fraud

Copycat Killer

Fictional Fatality

Bookmarked for Crime

Magical Soapmaker Mysteries

No Lathering Matter

Lyer, Liar

A Spotless Crime

Paranormal Rom-Coms

The Deadicated Matchmaker

The Nerdy Necromancer

The Jilted Jinn

The Clumsy Clairvoyant

The Vegan Vamp

The Deluded Demi-god